Black Sails 1715

The Age of Treachery and Retribution

A Historical Novel

Copyright © 2016 by Allen Balogh

All rights reserved. No part of this book may be reproduced in any form by any electronic or mechanical means including information storage and retrieval systems – except with the case of quotations embodied in critical articles or reviews – without permission in writing from its author.

Now and then we had a hope that if we lived and were good, God would permit us to be pirates.
—**Mark Twain**

Always be yourself, unless you can be a pirate, then always be pirate.
—**Robert Fenwick**

Dedication

Christopher Allen Balogh

Black Sails 1715 would not be in print if it were not for my son. On Father's Day, 2012, Christopher bought Angus Konstam's book, *Blackbeard*. Inscribed on the inside were the words, "Dad, *you* should be doing this. Just write the story the way you told it to me." Love, Chris."

Christopher has the same sense of adventure; big game fishing off of the east coast of Florida, Islamorada, Belize, and Costa Rica, the playground of the pirates in the early 1700's and a couple of jaunts to Reykjavik, Iceland, just for the "what the heck, why not" moment.

You're the best son a father could have.

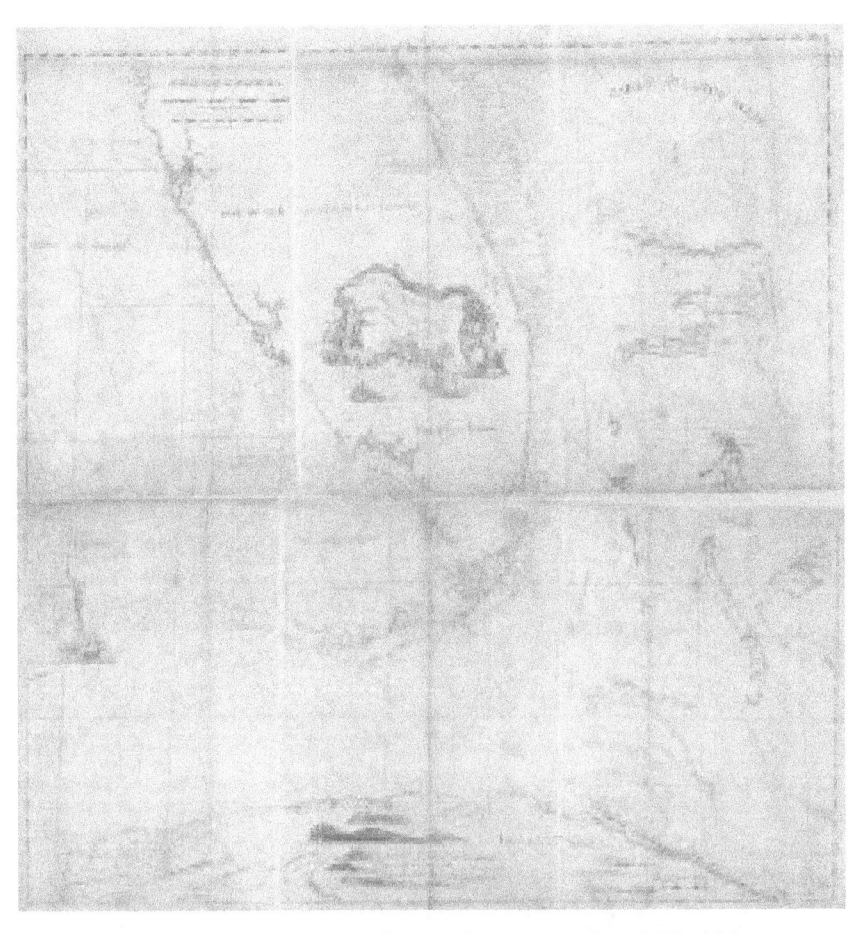

Bernard Romans Map 1774, Library of Congress, (South Florida)
Engraving by Paul Revere

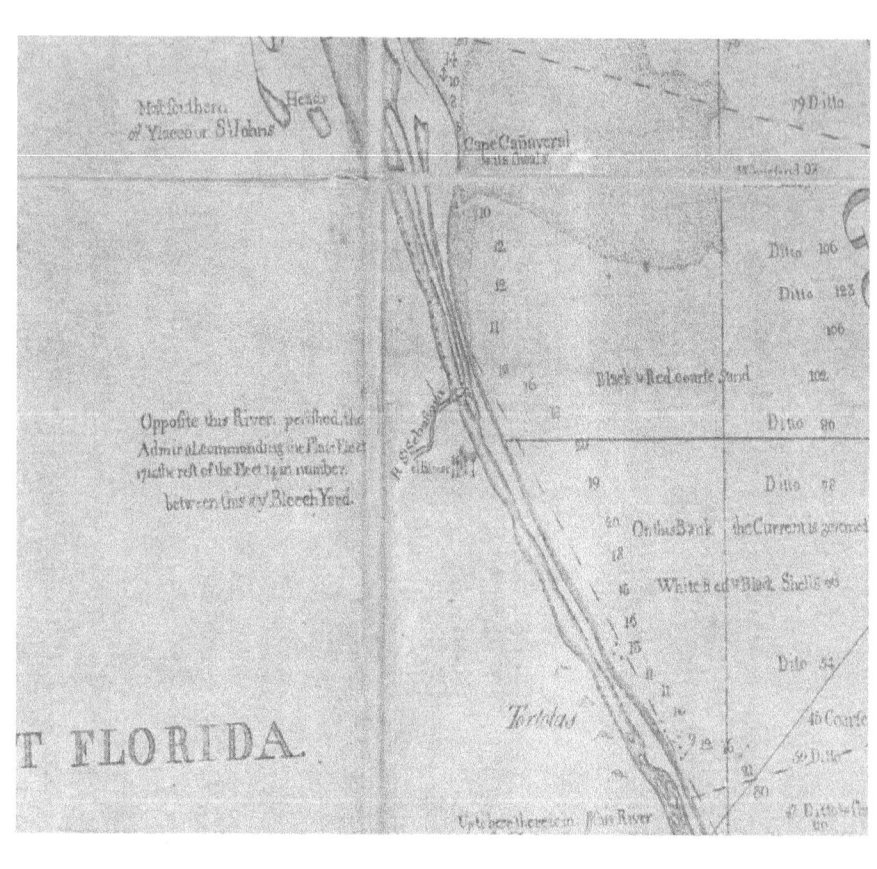

Enlarged Section of Ye Bleech Yards and Sebastian Inlet

CONTENTS

The Golden Age of Piracy and the Origins of the 1715 Fleet

PART ONE	**Edward Thatch —1715 Reflection**	
Chapter 1	The Agony of the Syringe	11
PART TWO	**The Magnificent 1715 Fleet**	
Chapter 2	The Hurricane from Hell	29
Chapter 3	If It Were Not For . . .	38
PART THREE	**1715 Fleet Raid and Double Cross**	
Chapter 4	Insane Vane	43
PART FOUR	**Bellamy and Williams — 1715 Fleet**	
Chapter 5	Prince of Pirates	63
Chapter 6	Maria Hallett	66
Chapter 7	The *Whydah*	74
PART FIVE	**Hornigold and Blackbeard**	
Chapter 8	The Mentor	89
Chapter 9	A Promotion in the Making	97
Chapter 10	The Services of the Devil	109
Chapter 11	Physical Appearance and Intimidation	126
Chapter 12	Home Away from Home	137
Chapter 13	Ignorance Is Bliss	147
Chapter 14	A New Way of Life	154
Chapter 15	Cape Fear	164
Chapter 16	The Hunt Is On	169
Chapter 17	The Last Battle	181

Chapter 18	Black Caesar	189
Chapter 19	The Templar Knights	193
PART SIX	**Governor Woodes Rogers of Nassau**	
Chapter 20	The Mentor Is Overthrown	205
Chapter 21	New Governor of Nassau	210
Chapter 22	The Hunted Becomes the Hunter	227
Chapter 23	Game On	233
Chapter 24	The Whim of a King	246
PART SEVEN	**Jack Rackham and Vane – 1715 Fallout**	
Chapter 25	Rackham and Vane	251
PART EIGHT	**Bonny and Read 1715 Fleet – Full Circle**	
Chapter 26	Female Pirates Dominate the Scene	265
Chapter 27	A Confession Like No Other Before	276
Chapter 28	The Capture of the Mermaids	285
Chapter 29	Trial and Conviction in Spanish Town	290

Epilogue 303

Author's Notes 309

Bibliography 337

About the Author 339

Acknowledgements 341

An Ending Note 343

Introduction

It started in June 1985. Two of my buddies, Del and Ben, and I were in the corporate aviation business, the glittery lifestyle of Learjets, props, and helicopters, flying the rich and famous out of Palm Beach and South Florida. Yet we sought more adventure. The three of us searched an area off the coast of Stuart, Florida, in hopes of finding the southernmost ship of the 1715 Spanish Treasure Fleet. All of us lived on the Treasure Coast; two were born and raised there. We knew that part of the ocean as well as anyone and were acutely aware of the ocean's ecosystem, even in 1985. When you dive into the blue-green waters, you realize the ocean's floor is someplace special.

The Treasure Coast is located on Florida's Atlantic side. It consists of three counties: Indian River, St. Lucie, and Martin. The region's name refers to the Spanish Armada lost in a 1715 hurricane. Salvagers began recovering Spanish treasure off the coast in 1961. The term was coined by John J. Schumann Jr. and Harry J. Schultz of the *Vero Beach Press Journal*. Schumann and Schultz noted that there was no name for the area, which was between the well-known Gold Coast (from Palm Beach to Miami to the south) and the Space Coast (Brevard County to the north). They started referring to the region as the Treasure Coast and the tag quickly caught on.

We discussed the gridding process of one of the possible locations. I bought some replica pieces of eight the previous month at the "Pirates of the Caribbean" attraction at Disney World. To escape a steamy July afternoon, we were snorkeling near a shallow ledge fewer than 300 yards offshore. I knew Ben would double back over my area in our grid. I placed the fake pieces of eight coins under a rock ledge and waited nearby. Arms flailing, Ben surfaced as if a bull shark was on his butt. He was screeching like Long John Silver's parrot: "Pieces of Eight, Pieces of Eight!" Ben knew he found the spot. He inspected each coin only to find that they were new, identical, light in weight, and fake. Furiously, but with a smile on his face, he threw the pieces of eight back in the water. After a light hearted moment, it was time to get serious again and search the rock ledges.

Researching pirate lore and treasure sites is akin to lobster hunting. The prerequisites need to be fulfilled before you dip your toe in the water—researching, gathering the proper equipment, and asking the right questions. Finally, the thrill of the find and the task of extracting the "goodies" from the depths sends an adrenaline rush throughout. The sensation latches on to you like the legs of a crustacean. It won't let go. The lobster submits and the booty is split with your mates. As I researched the history of the 1715 Fleet, I became more enamored with those who actually lived during the time period. Traditional history books disregarded the epic tale of the 1715 Fleet. Little by little, the story disappeared over the course of two and a half centuries, just like its treasure.

The Magnificent 1715 Fleet

In the eighteenth century, the nation-states of Spain, England, France, and Germany had insatiable appetites for New World riches. The New World spanned South America through the Caribbean and into northern Florida. Geographically, it was known as the Spanish Main. The Spanish galleons would meet in Havana, Cuba, before sailing for Europe. The threat of pirate attack was real, so there was safety in numbers. The fleet sailed from Havana through the Bahamian Channel, and eventually along the coast of Florida. As a matter of course, and fortunate for historians, the king and queen's cargo was detailed on the manifests. The gold of the Aztecs, the silver of the Incas, and the gems of the Mayan were in great demand in Europe.

Every year, Spain commissioned two fleets to sail to the New World. One, the Galeones de Tierra Firme or the ships of the Mainland Fleet sailed to Cartagena at New Granada (Columbia, South America) where the galleons took delivery of gold, emeralds, pearls, and silver from Peru's fabled mines in Potosi.

Captain General Don Antonio de Echeverz y Zubiza was the commander of the Tierra Firme fleet. In the winter of 1714, he was delayed in Cartagena, Columbia, waiting for silver and gold being delivered by llamas over the Andes Mountains from Bogota. Captain Echeverz departed Cartagena riding low in the water and sailed heavily back to Cuba. He arrived in Havana in mid-March and waited for Captain Ubilla of the Plate Fleet, who was still in Mexico. The entire combined fleet was called the Plate Fleet, Plate from the Spanish word, Plata, meaning silver. Chests filled with uncut

Columbian emeralds arrived from the Muzo mines. By the time the ships were ready to depart, an overabundance of silver and gold weighed the ship down into the waters of the harbor.

Captain General Echeverz's flagship, *Nuestra Senora de la Carmen* was laden with gold bars, doubloons, silver and seventy-two cannon. His Almirante, *Nuestra Senora del Rosario,* was a massive one hundred fifty-five-foot vessel. It followed close behind for protection and served as a fighting vessel with more than fifty canons. *Nuestra Senora del Rosario* also carried an equal amount of chests of wealth. A third galleon, *Senora de la Concepcion* carried hundreds of chests of coinage as well. *Senora San Miguel, La Holandesa, and La Francesca* brought up the rear of the fleet and served as passenger and supply ships. In most likelihood, the three vessels carried contraband to avoid taxation in Spain.

The other flota, the Plate Fleet carried gold bullions and silver from Veracruz, Mexico. Chinese porcelains and silk from the Kangxi dynasty were added to the manifests. A mule train carried the cargo over the deserts of Mexico to the ships docked at Veracruz. Cochineal red and indigo blue dyes were brought aboard near Acapulco. Captain General Don Juan Esteban de Ubilla was the commander of the Flota de la Plata, or the Plate Fleet.

Captain General Ubilla's galleon, *Nuestra Senora de la Regla,* carried thirteen-hundred chests of nearly three million silver coins and fifty cannon. Gold coins, chests of uncut emeralds, pearls and Chinese porcelain rounded out the cargo. Captain Ubilla's protective Almirante, *Santo Cristo de San Romon y Nuestra Senora del Rosario* carried a thousand chests, each chest containing three thousand coins. A supply ship, *Santissima Trinidad y Nuestra Senora de la Concepcion*, aka *Urca de Lima*, carried eighty-one chests of silver coins and fifty chests of worked silver. A patache, *Nuestra Senora de la Nieves*, carried forty-four thousand pieces of silver. The trailing frigate, Santa Rita y la Animas, also known as, *Mariagalonte* carried supplies and armaments. Her captain was Felix de Acosta Hurtado of Havana. Interestingly, Hurtado sold his personal ship to Captain General Juan Esteban de Ubilla.

Captain General Ubilla was the commander of the Combined Fleet overseeing all eleven ships.

By the summer of 1715, the patience of the King Philip V of Spain had worn thin on the delivery of the treasure. On July 24, 1715, pressure from the king forced the departure from Cuba of two thousand-five hundred passengers and $14 million in gold, silver, gems, and Chinese porcelain.

However, fate had a different destination for these ships, their crew and passengers. Hundreds soon faced death; even innocent grandparents, women, and children were about to sail into a horrific hurricane.

The Pirates of the Golden Age of Piracy

Off the harbors of Nassau and Port Royal were pirates awaiting ships to prey on and catastrophes. Many of the well-known pirates sailed during the Golden Age of Piracy (1715–1725). As imagined, each pirate had their own distinctive personality. In reconstructing each pirate's character, I've tried to present their idiosyncrasies to create the richest and most interesting tales. Most important, I've explored their link to the 1715 Spanish Fleet, which has been unnoticed all these years.

Captain Benjamin Hornigold (c. 1680–1719) was the boss and mentor. He was the master of the seas and taught *Edward "Blackbeard" Thatch* (c. 1680–1718) the importance of intimidation and perception.

Stede Bonnet (1688–1718), known as the "Gentleman's Pirate," enjoyed a lifestyle of wealth and privilege in Bermuda. So what made this guy want to leave it all and join the brotherhood? Stede could no longer tolerate his nagging wife, so he left Bermuda and became a pirate. Blackbeard seized the opportunity to take advantage of a man with no sea experience but a lot of money. He took Bonnet under his wing and let him think that he was a pirate.

Henry Jennings (d. 1745) and *Charles Vane* (c. 1680–1721) partnered on occasion to pillage unsuspecting ships. Jennings was as smart as Vane was vicious. Vane, without provocation, would maim innocent women and children just to see them suffer. A true psychopath, Vane terrorized everything and everyone that he encountered. Even the devil might wince and comment, "What in the hell is wrong with you?" And Jennings became notorious for one single act of piracy. He raided the 1715 Spanish Plate Fleet off the coast of Florida.

Black Sam Bellamy (1689–1717) was known as the Prince of Pirates. Bellamy was well known for his mercy and generosity. He was the captain of the famous ship the *Whydah.* He died at the age of twenty-eight. *Forbes* magazine listed him as the number one top-earning pirate, worth $131 million by today's currency standards. Bellamy was also at the site of the 1715 Spanish Plate Fleet, scouring the area from the Fort Pierce Inlet to the Sebastian Inlet. He later double-crossed Jennings and Vane.

Like Blackbeard, *Calico Jack Rackham* (1682–1720) was a ladies' man but much more flamboyant in dress. Rackham and his crew members were well known as dangerous pirates. Interestingly, Rackham was the quartermaster for Vane. A quartermaster was actually more powerful than a captain in many ways. Essentially, they put the captain in check. The crew, in a vote of no confidence for Vane, ousted the crazy pirate. Calico Jack Rackham became the captain as well as the new leader of New Providence (Nassau). He later became known for having two female pirates on board disguised as sailors.

The disguised sailors were the legendary *Anne Bonny* (c. 1698–1782) and *Mary Read* (c. 1685–1721). Anne and Mary were certainly not damsels in distress. They were first-rate pirates, never shirking duty or battle. No crew member was more able or ready to take on the enemy than these two women. Bonny, who was married, fell for the dashing young man Calico Jack.

The story that follows is an account from the Golden Age of Piracy, including the vanishing of the 1715 Spanish

Armada fleet caught in a violent hurricane off the east coast of Florida.

No GPS, no iPhone, no weather radar service out of Miami, only a compass and a sextant to determine the angle of a glaring sun or twinkling stars and the horizon in front of them. And one must appreciate the tenacity in sailing to a location where X marked the spot. What gutsy, insane men these were just hanging on to the sides of their ships. These remarkable navigators sailed thousands of miles over the open ocean and without falling off the end of the earth. It was flat back then, wasn't it?

I have taken the liberty of creating dialogue, imagining what might have been said and to whom, based on the reports of historical events, the biographies of real characters, and my perspective as a historian of the Golden Age of Piracy.

This is the *only* account that combines historical recordings, inclusive of the 1715 Fleet, and dialogue. In this small circle of marauders, everyone knew each other, whether friend or foe.

Part 1

Edward 'Blackbeard' Thatch

1715 Reflection

ALLEN BALOGH

Chapter One
The Agony of the Syringe

The ship's physician inserted a mercury-loaded syringe into the opening of Israel Hands's penis. All the shipmates winced in fear, and their legs quivered. It took three men to hold Hands down as the mercury concoction overflowed onto the physician's fingers. Yet Hands begged for more. Other crew members stood in line, waiting their turn at the bowsprit.

"Captain Thatch, we be needin' to plunder Charles Town for medicine!" screeched Hands.

"Soon, Hands," reassured Thatch. His booming voice echoed from the hold of the ship. Minutes later, Thatch found himself face-to-face with a distraught Hands.

"All of ye men are in pain and misery, Captain." Hands brushed back his shoulder-length hair, bleached from all the years under the sun. "We can't take the leaky, painful drip anymore. We have to do it now."

Syphilis stung nearly the entire crew of the *Queen Anne's Revenge*. The only cure was a syringe into the privateer's privates.

"Me mates have wart sores and rashes over their bodies, and they piss out yellow puss," complained Hands. His gunmetal eyes were bloodshot and seeping.

Thatch shook his head in disgust. "This drip is like the curse o' Egypt on me."

"We have men going blind wi' bone rot, sir. Some have lost senses," bellowed Hands. "Even the cook has rashes on his feet and palms." Hands scratched his forearms until his long, dirty fingernails drew blood from his leathery skin. "I heard one of me gunners pleading with the Lord to have mercy on him."

"This needs to stop now, or we won't have a working ship," said Thatch. "Too many whores, too many men. Must have been in Nassau or travelin' through Port Royal."

"That fookin' wench—she's a bloodthirsty she-devil," bellowed Hands. "She took all me money and a lot from me crew." Hands stood in front of Thatch, looked up, and said, "We ported too long. I should have blasted her to hell."

Thatch was an imposing man with deep-set eyes, unruly black hair, and a long black beard. His mere presence commanded fear and respect. Unlike most, he was an educated man who spoke with authority.

"Who else of importance has this mange?" asked Thatch.

"Nearly all the crew has it, sir. Men have fever and fatigue. It's a filthy disease, Captain. I've not seen anything like it; the ship has ye stench of death."

"I think I got it me self, Hands. Stinging pain whenever I piss. Startin' to feel like fire comin' out me hole."

Hands grabbed an empty cup. "I don't drink anything, so I don't piss as often. It's the scourge from hell, I tell ye." Hands tripped over a wooden crate. A battle injury to his right leg, earned during his days as a gunner, caused him to walk with slight gait. "Damn it to hell," he yelled.

"We're only two nights out of Charles Town harbor. Order the men to hoist the mains. Tell Caesar we need all the speed the ships can muster," Thatch commanded. Hands and Caesar were Thatch's most experienced and trusted crew members.

Caesar found Thatch in the ammunition room and discussed the fastest way to Charles Town. "Captain, the sun has set. Maybe we should anchor for the night and dead reckon to the mainland in the morning."

"Stay the course, Caesar. Trust the moon and stars to navigate; they don't lie."

In the last week of May 1718, Thatch approached the mainland of the Americas and sailed the South Carolina coastline. It was one of the most prosperous colonies in the Americas. Charles Town had a vibrant economy, founded on huge profits from the triangle trade: slave shipping from Africa to the West Indies, then to the Americas and back to England.

Thatch continued to think about his missed opportunity of pillaging the 1715 Spanish Treasure Fleet, which had disappeared off the east coast of Florida. Eleven Spanish galleons vanished in a hurricane carrying a fortune in gold and silver earmarked for King Philip V. The fleet collected treasure from Cartagena, Vera Cruz, and Portobelo. Thatch was simply too late to pillage millions in emeralds, gold, and silver from the Spanish Treasure Fleet. His colleagues had already picked the sight clean. Besides, Thatch had a much bigger task in front of him.

Edward Thatch reached Charles Town, South Carolina, in the early morning hours, just as the light fog started to lift off the water. The massive *Queen Anne's Revenge* and the ancillary ships sat outside the harbor to make their presence known. The flagship was more than one hundred feet long and weighed more than three hundred tons. The anchor alone weighed 3,100 pounds. She was the largest vessel to sail the Spanish Main.

"Caesar, prepare to drop the anchor and pass the orders to the other ships," Thatch yelled.

"Ready to drop anchor, sir. Say when."

Thatch picked the most strategic spot in the harbor to block incoming and outgoing vessels at the center of the inlet. "Caesar, drop the anchor now." The chains on the anchor clicked one by one until the anchor hit the ocean's floor.

As the sun rose, an orange hue glowed behind the ships. Thatch walked to the upper deck. *I can't believe this. Look at all these ships, eight in number, easy taking. Forgo the medicine? Lucifer is forcing me to make a choice.*

Thatch handed a spyglass to Caesar. "Look at this: the ships are just sittin' inside the harbor like ducks. There are no naval vessels, only merchant ships."

Thatch squinted to see the white and pink Colonial-style houses tucked in behind the docks that lined the waterfront of Charles Town harbor. Each house had a symmetrical, high-pitched roof with a molding of brick headers placed above the windows. The wealthy middle-class dwellings stood in stark contrast to Nassau harbor, with its shanties, taverns, gaming houses, and brothels.

"Aye Captain, 'tis beautiful. What a sight, and we can pillage at will. But we need medicine now." Caesar's mouth ran dry from dehydration. "We can't take this pain. Give orders for the ship's physician to go into town. He's a smart man, and we can trust him to do it. We can plunder whenever."

"Caesar, we're going to terrorize this city like none other before. Prepare the ships as soon as possible. I cannot pass this up. One ship would be sufficient for me, but eight?"

"What are you thinking?"

"I want everyone in Charles Town to know that we're here first. Plunder the ships, then retrieve the medicine. The men need help soon. But there's too much on these ships to ignore. We'll stay here for a week if need be."

Thatch blockaded the entire harbor. He had a force of four vessels in excess of sixty cannon and more than four hundred men sitting a mile off shore. Thatch's ships sat quietly in calm waters. The complacent citizens of Charles Town had just awakened to the greatest terror of their lives, without any indication that this morning could be their last.

The three other vessels Thatch commanded in the waters that day had experienced crews and captains, with the exception of Stede Bonnet, captain of the *Revenge*. Thatch could no longer afford the inexperience of Bonnet: it put the plunder in jeopardy. As a result, Thatch gave command of the *Revenge,* to Lieutenant Richard Richards. Israel Hands, the sailing master of the *Queen Anne's Revenge*, was placed in command of the ship *Adventure.*

Hands and Richards rowed in a dinghy, approximately a hundred yards beyond their ship, to discuss their strategy with Thatch.

"Hands, tell your crew to board any incoming or outgoing ship at will—private or merchant, it doesn't matter," said Thatch.

"I can't wait." Hands grinned and grabbed his crotch. "Maybe I can pass me disease into one of those fair maidens."

"Yor a reckless man, Hands. Not plannin' on makin' yourself clean first for that lil lassie?" Thatch laughed.

"Nope, she gets what I got," replied Hands.

Thatch pulled out his spyglass and looked toward shore. He saw a ship about to depart through the light fog. The crew pulled up anchor and adjusted the rigging. *This captain must be a fool. He thinks we are waiting for him to give right o' way.*

That fool was Captain Robert Clark of the *Crowley*, who would soon become the first victim to fall prey to Thatch and his crew. The *Crowley* was heading to London with wealthy, elite citizens of Charles Town.

"Caesar, after we board their ship, look for men with coats and capes. Their women wear feathery hats and elegant dresses showing a crackin' pair of bubbies."

"Take them as prisoners?" asked Caesar.

"Take them prisoners, especially important ones. I want the politicians first and then the landowners. Tie them to the ship for all to see; hang 'em from the yardarm if need be. Make it painful," Thatch said.

Caesar obeyed his captain. Confused and frightened, the well-to-do of the *Crowley* were hurried at gunpoint onto the *Queen Anne's Revenge*.

Caesar took two of the oldest passengers and hung them upside down by their ankles. He swung the salt-worn, aged yardarm to starboard, dangling the elder gents over the water. The timbers ran horizontally across the ship for the sails to set on. Now it doubled as a torture device.

One of the old men screamed as he was tied. "Please don't!" His skin ripped from the rope, exposing the shinbone.

"When the sun is on the other side of the yardarm, the sharks will smell your soul." Caesar replied. The remaining pirates boarded the *Crowley*. Nearly £1,500 in gold and silver was taken from the crew and passengers, depleting the lifelong savings of those on board.

"Take all the men, women, and children and put 'em in the dark," Thatch ordered.

In the chaos that followed, eighty hostages were thrown into the hold. The gunners pushed and kicked the women down the wooden steps into the hellhole. It was mass hysteria; children and women screamed and cried. Mothers trembled, dropped to their knees, and pleaded that the pirates not do harm to their children. The hold was dark, airless, and scary.

Thatch walked by a gentleman dressed like an English Duke. "Caesar, take this chap to the captain's quarters."

Caesar, a large, muscular man of African descent, picked up the elegantly dressed Charlestonian by the back of his collar and threw him into the captain's quarters with Thatch.

"What's the name?" Thatch asked.

"My name is Samuel Wragg." His Queen's English accent was a giveaway to Thatch that an educated, wealthy man was laying on the floor. "Why do you treat me like a commoner?"

"Sit across from me. I want to look you in the eye."

Mr. Wragg picked himself off the stained wooden floor and sat in front of Thatch. "Why are you wearing such clothing and wig?"

"I'm a member of the Council of the Province of Carolina."

Thatch leaned back in his chair and bit the inside of his lip. *A member of the council under my control. These people are more valuable to me than the cargo.*

"Mr. Wragg, yours was the first ship out of the harbor. Lucky for me, many were paying guests to London. But I need medicine, and I need it now. If you help, then I will release you unharmed."

Wragg, unaware of who was sitting across from him, stated, "And what if I rebuke your request?"

"Are you on board with any family?" asked Thatch.

"Why yes, my wife and four-year-old son are traveling with me for an extended trip to visit our relatives in London. Why do you ask?"

"If you disapprove of my request, I shall start with them." Thatch pulled a dagger from his black belt and picked his fingernails. He glared at Wragg.

"Are your intentions to hurt us?"

"Your namesake and then your wife; what my crew will do to your wife and son will make any husband and father agree to my terms. You have seen my handiwork, haven't you?" Thatch pointed outside the window to the two old men hanging upside down. "Ye be hung upside down by your bollocks, not ye' ankles."

Samuel Wragg carried political clout. He was wealthy and owned twenty-four thousand acres of land in the Carolinas. The power of Charles Town listened when he spoke.

Wragg leaned forward and stated, "Well, then, I will act as a responsible father and husband. I will go myself and speak to the council on your behalf to find your medicine. And to prove my good faith, I will leave my four-year-old son with you," said Mr. Wragg.

"No, I will not give freedom to such a valuable citizen like you. A man like yourself could possibly ruin my schemes, even if you have so much at stake. I'd rather keep you in my sight. Pick someone else aboard this ship with equal status—one with a funny wig like yourself, one that the council will listen to.

"I know of—"

Thatch interrupted, "Someone who is scared to die. Someone who will be looking over his shoulder for the rest of his days if he doesn't obey my wishes."

"I know a man that you speak of. He is alone on this trip. Mr. Marks."

"Mr. Wragg, two of my crew will go with Mr. Marks," said Thatch. "I don't trust a man who gives up his own son as ransom. Shameful, mate." *How does a father give up his only child so quickly?*

Thatch pushed aside a map on top of his desk and reached into the drawer. He pulled out a quill pen and paper. He wrote a ransom note to the governor and the council. It read:

Council, my only demand is a chest of medicine and the safe return of my men. The chest must have the latest medicinal purposes for ones inflicted by disease. My men don't think before they act. If these demands are not met, I will send up the heads of the council to the governor and make a fiery blaze of your ships.

"Lieutenant Richards, disembark your ship," hollered Thatch across the bow. "I want you and your first mate, Hayes, to go into the city with Marks."

Marks, a meek, introverted Englishman, inched his way forward to hear Thatch.

"Marks, listen well. Tell the council that the first person I behead is one of their own, Samuel Wragg. The ransom is the medicines we covet from this harbor. Then we will leave. You have two days to fulfill our demands. If you do not return by then, heads will fall."

Thatch looked into the eyes of Samuel Wragg. "You will stay with me to help make the nooses; that way you know how to tie your own in case Mr. Marks fails. Tell me, the other ships, where are they headed?"

"Most are merchant ships sailing to either London or New England. Several have passengers on board besides cargo."

"Any gold or silver? If so, which ones?"

"None. The ships are not part of any treasure fleets."

"Mr. Wragg, you are most helpful. Or you are most devious and ill to lie to such a man as myself. For the sake of you and your family, I hope it's the former."

The next day, the sun rose, and the pirates continued to board and pillage other vessels that entered Charles Town Harbor. South Carolina Governor Robert Johnson was furious. He repeatedly pounded the oak table with his fist.

"We are unable to mount any offense," yelled Johnson to his council. "We fought a long-running and expensive war with the Yamasee Indians in the backcountry. Now our government treasury is bankrupt. And the residents are in despair."

A loud, rapid knock on the closed doors of the council room startled the governor. "Excuse me . . . me, Governor, for . . . for imposing," stuttered Marks respectfully. "I have dire news that you and the council need to hear now . . . now. It's about the pirates at the har . . . harbor."

"It better be good," stated Johnson. "You're interrupting us at the wrong time."

"I have information for all to . . . to hear," stated Marks. "It will only take a min . . . minute."

Mr. Marks met with the governor and city council. He explained what occurred on the *Crowley*. The governor was now even more fearful for the residents of Charles Town. However, fear soon turned to terror.

"Mr. Marks, please take your time with your speech," stated Johnson empathetically. "Tell us what you have seen."

Marks hesitated and took a deep breath. "Governor and council, while I was rowing with the pirate they call Lieutenant Richards, he told me the captain was Bla . . . Blackbeard. I do not know for sure. He referred to himself as Tha . . . Thatch. But by the looks of him, I would not oppose the idea of him being Bla . . .Blackbeard."

"Good Lord." Johnson held his head with both hands." I don't know what's crazier: what ye said or the fact that ye said it. God save the Queen."

"A very tall man, Governor, his black beard was long and scraggly, started at his eyes and ended at his chest."

"Blackbeard? Blackbeard wants to lay siege to our city and is in position to demand a huge sum, yet he demands medical supplies from Charles Town," said Johnson quizzically. "That doesn't make sense. He wants medicine and not money? That cannot be Blackbeard."

"I think most of his crew has the French disease. They have other diseases as we . . . well. Yellow fever, scurvy, and the bloody flux are common. I saw a couple scoundrels piss. . . . piss puss and vomit green. It's all quite unimaginable," Marks replied.

"Then tell Blackbeard none of his crew can come into our city. The dreaded diseases will spread here, and we'll have no medicine. Damn these pirates!" exclaimed Governor Johnson.

"I think we have to give in to Bla . . . Blackbeard's demands. He has many hostages including women, chi . . . children, and Mr. Samuel Wragg. We must err with cau . .

.caution, otherwise their fates and ours may be written on our tombstones earlier th . . . than expected," rebutted Marks.

"Tell Blackbeard no deal. The answer is unequivocally no. I'll not give in to these bandits. Blackbeard should be hung at Charles Town harbor not aided," said Governor Johnson. "The governor of Virginia, Spotswood, wants his head. Let Spotswood deal with him and his likes."

"I plead with the council. Please re . . . reconsider. I've been on the ship. The pirates are not like you and me . . . me. Some are sodomites. Others look like savage animals with froth coming ou . . . out of their mouths. They hanged two old men upside down on the yardarm. Bla . . . Blackbeard promised to kill everyone in Charles Town. I believe him."

"And what guarantees do we have that Blackbeard will ever leave?" asked Johnson.

"None, but like you said, Governor, he only wants me . . . medicine. I have the list. Let me leave and get it. I beg of you."

"What's on the list, Mr. Marks?"

"I spoke to their apothecary. He gave me a list of needs: sulfur, mercury, charcoal, acids, and salts, but . . . but mostly mercury. Also leeches. Maybe one of our doctors will have a nest full."

While Marks pleaded the case, Lt. Richards and Hayes walked in and out of shops and taverns, getting drunk. The residents were full of rage having to watch these robbers and murderers walk freely throughout their town.

The governor and the council heatedly discussed the options. After an hour of debating, they gave in to Blackbeard's demands.

"Do it quickly, Mr. Marks. Find the medicine. Get these disgusting men out of our harbor," said Governor Johnson.

Back on board the *Crowley*, the deadline for Thatch's demands passed. He walked over to Samuel Wragg. "Wragg, I am not a man of patience nor am I to be fooled with. You will be the first to be hanged."

All hell broke loose aboard the ship. The hostages were frantic, and many crossed themselves in the name of Jesus, knowing they were about to die. The devil incarnate was about to wreak havoc on the innocent.

"Caesar, round up the passengers and take them to the plank in full view. Take the old men down and let's get the next round ready. Prepare them for hanging," commanded Thatch.

Cacsar pulled out his cutlass and waved it about the heads of the hostages. "Tis my pleasure, Captain," stated Caesar as he stared into the crowd.

A younger Charlestonian dove off the ship in an attempt to swim back to shore. Caesar pulled out a pistol from his waist and fired, a puff of gunpowder smoke emerging from the flintlock. A lead ball struck the back of the head of the young man, putting him to his death. Wragg looked on in horror as the body descended into the harbor, a slick of blood drifting out to sea.

"Please, Captain, one more day. I plead on behalf of the women and children," begged Mr. Wragg. "Something had to have happened to Marks. Give him one more day."

Thatch walked away in disgust and into his quarters. Families held one another and prayed. Tears ran down their cheeks. The inevitable was about to happen.

Caesar called out, "Captain, do you see what I see?"

Thatch reached for his spyglass. He saw a small dinghy approaching. It was Marks, Lt. Richards, and Hayes. Thatch's face became red with rage. Mr. Marks climbed out of the dinghy, up the rope, and into the ship.

"Where have you been?" demanded Thatch. "It's outrageous. It took three days to row two miles and back." Thatch removed his sword from his waist. "I best be hearin' a reason."

"That squall of a morning storm cap . . . capsized the dinghy." Mr. Marks turned his hands upside down. "We . . . we got help from some fishermen, but it put us be behind. Ask Lt. Richards, we . . . we were in the water all morning."

Thatch's eyebrows creased. "Tell me about the governor and the council. And slow down when you speak, mate," shouted Thatch. "I will do you no harm as long as the truth spills from your tongue."

"I received permission fr . . .from the council and rounded up the medicine for you. But then I could no longer find your crew. I walked all over town and found them drunk at a tavern. It was your own men that caused the de . . .delay."

Lt. Richards and Hayes climbed aboard the ship with a large chest of medicine. "Get the ship's surgeon. I want to make sure this is adequate," Thatch told Caesar.

The surgeon hurried to the front of the ship. One by one, he surveyed the contents of the chest. The medicine was all there. "Captain, may I take the chest back to my quarters?" he asked.

"Of course." Thatch commanded two crew members to carry the chest to the surgeon's quarters.

In the privacy of his quarters, the surgeon pulled out a syringe and a vial of mercury. He placed a piece of wood between his teeth and injected himself. "Oh my God," screamed the surgeon. "Help me Lord." Even the surgeon had a night with Venus and then succumbed to a month with Mercury.

All of the passengers on board awaited their fate. Thatch held a conference with his own council of advisors. He made most important decisions by a vote. Thatch approached Mr. Wragg and waved his cutlass in front of the older man's face. Mr. Wragg stood perfectly still and silent.

"Samuel Wragg, let the governor and the council know that I am good for my word. Tell all of your friends that they will be released and free to go. Fair winds on your voyage to London. And watch out for Vane. He is a vicious pirate."

It was time for Captain Thatch and the *Queen Anne's Revenge* to leave the harbor. After six days, on June 3, 1718, all of the prisoners were released. In one last gesture of intimidation, Thatch removed the wig of the wealthy Samuel Wragg and threw it overboard. "See, Mr. Wragg, you're a man, just like me," the pirate said with a cackle.

The remaining men on board were forced to remove their clothes and swim ashore, humiliated but alive. Small cap waves and light rain pelted the men's faces. With a broad grin,

Thatch sailed out of the Charles Town Harbor toward Beaufort Inlet, North Carolina.

This day reminded Thatch of one of his first lessons from his mentor, Benjamin Hornigold. Men were vulnerable to fear.

As Thatch sailed out of the harbor, he thought about the big haul that he missed off the coast of Florida. *My goodness, if it were not working in Jamaica, I could have plundered the Spanish Fleet out of Cuba. I missed out on millions because of ill timing. Then, again, I would not have the most powerful ship in the world, Queen Anne's Revenge.*

Part 2

The Magnificent 1715 Fleet

Don Juan Esteban de Ubilla

and

Don Antonio de Echerverz

ALLEN BALOGH

Chapter Two
The Hurricane From Hell

Captain General Don Juan Esteban de Ubilla and Captain General Don Antonio de Echeverz had a contemptuous relationship. Each were in command of different fleets; Ubilla of the Plate Fleet, and Echeverz of the Tierra Firme Fleet.

"Meet me at the dock at sunrise,' ordered Ubilla. "We need to discuss the details before setting sails into the Florida Straits." Ubilla pulled off his white gloves and carefully folded them before tucking them into his sash.

There was awkward silence. Echeverz felt his spine straighten as he gazed at Ubilla. He remembered how his father used the same tone to get his point across. Unconsciously, he placed his hand on his cutlass. "I'm tired of waiting, day after day, month after month. Damn it, Ubilla. I should have left without you."

Ubilla stared at him and raised both arms in the air. "Why do you insist on sailing back to Spain without the protection of the flota's warships," asked Ubilla.

"I'm not. It's delay after delay," exclaimed Echeverz."It's always something, never enough men to load the cargo and you were behind schedule sailing from Mexico."

Ubilla's eyes glittered at the reprimand. "The constant delays are not of my being," Ubilla screamed back. "It's out of my control. How can you depend on Indians to mine and their mules to transport with any degree of timeliness. It takes months, you know that."

"I'm tired of you," shouted Echeverz. He stepped closer to Ubilla. His hand gripped the cutlass handle as he struggled to control himself. "Good God, do something."

Ubilla was nose to nose with Echeverz. "You, sir, are *not* in charge, I am. Please stop with your unceasing complaining."

Echeverz stared back into the deep black eyes of Ubilla, inhaled deeply, and stated, "You are indeed in charge ... for now. The king will hear about this, I promise."

At the entrance to the harbor in Havana was the ship, *Le Griffon*. She was a French Royal Navy frigate, 132 feet long and a beam of 35 feet. She was built in Lorient, France by shipwright Pierre Coulomb. She was attached to the port of Brest, in Brittany. She returned to Brest after the hurricane. The French warship was under the command of Captain Antoine d'Aire. The five-hundred-ton, forty-eight-gun frigate was formidable, serving 40 years of service at sea. Antoine d'Aire was on a special assignment from the king of Spain to collect forty-nine thousand pieces of eight from the Governor of Veracruz for the usage of two ships, the *Apollon* and the *Triton*.

Ubilla stood at his ship's rail overlooking the movement of *Le Griffon's* crew.

"Echeverz, I don't like that d'Aire is leaving ahead of us."

"I agree."

"Finally, we have something to agree on," Ubilla smiled. "Let's approach him and see what he's up to. Gather up the finest, and we will force him to reconsider."

"Why me?" questioned Echeverz. "Why not you?"

"We'll both do it. And bring Jacques, the French interpreter."

Ubilla and Echreverz walked to the portside of *Le Grifon*. Several heavily armed soldiers lined up behind them. Ubilla paused to admire the quality of the French built frigate. *Le Grifon* was light and built for durability essential for long periods of time at sea.

Ubilla studied the armaments. "The lower deck carries 12 pounders and the upper deck carries 6 pounders. The balance and mounting of the cannon is superb."

"I see why the British Navy copied the design from the French," Echeverz said.

Jacques walked in between Echererz and Ubilla. "Captain, cautious with this snail-snapper." whispered Jacques. "I've heard that d'Arie is a friend of Lord Hamilton of Jamaica. He is paid for information."

"Just interpret very carefully for us," Ubilla replied.

Antoine d"Aire appeared at the rail and arrogantly nodded at the Spanish commanders. He wore an elegant full length blue dress coat with rolled up gold sleeves and epaulets. He stood erect with his chest outward.

Jacques politely addressed d'Aire as he formed Ubilla's questions.

"Captain Antoine d'Aire, I am Captain General Ubilla of the Spanish Armada. You will be leaving with us, not by yourself!"

"You are not my captain," replied d'Aire. "Nor do we sail under the same flag. I'll leave when I please."

"With all due respect, Captain d'Aire, you cannot leave alone. You will be sailing back to Spain with us." Ubilla reached for his cutlass. "We need to keep our movements secret."

"And what if I choose not to obey your wishes," asked d'Aire.

"If you leave alone pirates may capture your ship. I cannot trust that you will tell them of our whereabouts."

Echeverz added, "Do you see the soldiers behind us?"

Antoine d'Aire had no alternative.

Time and again, pressure was exerted on Ubilla to leave as soon as possible. He had no choice. King Philip V was desperately in need of an influx of cash, not to mention the lavish dowry for his unyielding new wife. Reluctantly, General Don Juan Esteban de Ubilla gave orders to sail in hopes of not encountering severe weather. On July 24, 1715, the Spanish Treasure Fleet left Cuba, as the Combined Armada of 1715.

"Echeverz, put d'Aire out front as the lead ship in front of me," ordered Ubilla. "I want to keep a sharp eye on him. I may need to throw a volley of cannon at him if he decides to be wayward."

Ubilla and Echeverz's galleons were massive as they left Havana Harbor. Six treasure galleons made up the body of the fleet riding low in the water from the weight of the gold and silver. Two more fighting galleons brought up the rear. Dozens of heavy bronze cannon were concealed behind their gun ports to protect the $14 million in gold and silver. The nation-states of, King Philip V, and his new bride-to-be were going to be ecstatic with the arrival of the fleet.

Captain Sebastin Mendez of *La Holandesa* brought up the rear of the fleet and had the best vantage point. If only a diary would have been kept, it may have rendered the historic event of its time.

"Wednesday, July 24, 1715: Ubilla gave orders to fire a signal boom from his flagship, Nuestra Senora de la Regla. A thunder of cannon fire shook the docks and rippled the glassy bay as the other ten vessels answered Ubilla's call. Boom! Boom! Boom! The ships were surrounded by plumbs of white smoke as the cannon recoiled and shook the ships. The crew manned their stations as the enormous anchors were slowly pulled on board. Cheers erupted on the ships as well as from those who watched from the Havana Harbor docks. The breeze filled the mains and the mizzens as the crew adjusted the canvas sails. Spanish pride was to witness these handsome vessels as they paraded out of the harbor and rolled serenely into the Florida Straits under cloudless sky. The combined fleet of Gen. Don Juan Esteban de Ubilla and Gen. Don Antonio de Echeverz was finally underway.

The ships sailed into the Florida Straits riding *un rio en el mar*, "a river in the ocean." The swift current of the Gulfstream greatly enhanced their speed through the Florida Keys.

Monday, July 29, 1715: Echeverz and Ubilla looked distrustfully at the sky. A slight haze on the horizon, thickened, and began to blot out the sun. Ubilla looked behind him and saw the heavy galleons roll in the long swells of the ocean. Both captains knew a storm was brewing, an uneasiness grew among the passengers as they began to congregate at the stern. With each rise and swell, the navigators became concerned as the bottom of their galleons would glance off of a coral ledge.

As *Le Griffon* and the eleven Spanish ships sailed into the Matecumbes of the Florida Keys, Ubilla slowed repeatedly to wait for Echeverz in his heavily-laden cargo ships. Ubilla's patience wore thin as the ships approached the coast of Florida. However, he had an obligation to stay behind to keep the entire fleet together. The ongoing delays put them behind by at least another day. Ubilla ordered cannon shots to gain the attention of the fleet. He signaled with flags instructing the following ships to tack into the wind and sail to the deeper waters of the Atlantic to avoid the outer reefs of Florida.

Tuesday, July 30, 1715: One week out of Havana, Cuba, and the long journey back to Spain had barely begun. By noon, the wind dies, an eerie stillness plagues the air. Wisps of haze have returned into curtains of low-hanging clouds. The visibility was reduced to zero. The ships roll even more heavily as the hardiest of passengers seek shelter into the hold. Murky green waters break over the bow. The winds begin again, blowing hard from the southeast. The crewmen began to tie down the halyards. The wind shrieks through like a thousand banshees through the rigging, so that crew and passengers alike cover their ears. Stinging rain whips from the breaking waves. The afternoon grew darker and darker, and the great stern lanterns were lit. The yellow glows began to fade as each ship followed the other. In a single night, eleven ships laden with precious cargo began to slam against the outer reefs of the coast of Florida.

July 31, 1715, 2:00 am: The hurricane strikes with all of its fury as the winds shift to ENE. Ubilla and Echeverz shout commands but no one hears them. The last remaining sails were taken down, some captains tried to anchor as others took cover. The anchors fail to hold and the ships hulls were shredded on the jagged reefs. On deck no man can breathe the suffocating mixture of wind and water. In the blackness of night and storm, water poured into the holds. The priests on board gave last rights and the passengers offered confessions. For those washed overboard there is little hope. The seas picked up the massive galleons and flung them time and again against the first reef, then the second reef. Another round of waves turned the galleons on their sides or upside down as they tumbled towards the shore.

Soon it was over. Captain Ubilla and Captain Echeverz drowned in the swells of waves. Ubilla's 471 ton flagship, *Nuestra Senora de la Regla* had the bottom torn off at the reef and sank in thirty-feet of water. One of the rear galleons vanished under a wave, while another, the 450 ton *Santo Cristo de San Ramon*, capsized in the surf a few miles south of the *Regla* and disintegrated. Santo Cristo de San Ramon, the protective Almirante of the fleet, came to rest in twelve feet of water, seven hundred feet off shore.

Imagine galleons climbing waves that were forty or fifty feet tall, the crewmen scaling the rigging to avoid giant combers, others clinging onto the masts. The sails shredding as winds reached more than a hundred miles an hour, bits of heavy rigging crashing onto the decks, trapping crew and passengers alike. The hatches were opening with canon rolling out onto the decks crushing the passengers with some falling into the foamy ocean. People and cargo thrown out of the galleons like toys, vanquished completely beneath the waves.

Don Antonio de Chevas was the senior freight captain and chaplain of the Fleet. His body was thrown on shore by a powerful wave at Wabasso, where he lay weeping uncontrollably.

"Oh Lord, oh Lord. What has forsaken us," he muttered.

Chevas was cold. He lay face down in wet sand, his face cut from debris in the ocean. He wiped away the burning salt water from his eyes. His gold crucifix was tangled around his neck.

"Lord, so many bodies lay lifeless." Chevas took a deep breath. "As far as the eye can see, we need your help and blessings."

All the destroyed ships were miles apart from each other and the bodies of hundreds of passengers littered the beaches along with the wreckage. Fewer than half of the 2,500 men, women, and children made it to the beaches alive. They crawled in terror through stinging rain and darkness to shelter themselves amid the sand dunes.

Chevas crossed himself in the name of the Lord. "Please help us. Help the children first." The stinging rain began to subside. Chevez could see the remains of *Santo Cristo de San Romon* close to shore. The galleon was shredded to bits. The captain, D. Juan de Equilaz and Captain Ubilla's son were tossed around in the waves, face down. The precious cargo was sinking rapidly beside them.

"Oh Lord, give me the strength to help."

A body laying next to Chevaz started to move. It was an elderly Spanish grandmother weeping as she clutched her dead granddaughter. Chevaz held the infant's head against his chest and gave the last rites to the little girl. In a final gesture, he brushed away her black wet hair, and with his thumb, made the sign of the cross on her forehead.

Chevaz stood and walked aimlessly along the beach to find any possible survivors. One after another, Chevaz gathered those who could help each other. Most suffered cuts on their arms, legs and face, others with broken legs and dislocated shoulders.

The survivors set up camp in the palmetto bushes behind the dune lines. There was no food, water or medical supplies. Then more threats came upon them unexpectedly; disease-carrying mosquitos, snakes, and the primitive Indians. Some of the Ais Indians helped the survivors while others proved to be cannibals.

Chevaz fell to his knees and sobbed. "Why Lord, why? Haven't we suffered enough? Why do you forsake us at our most urgent hour of need?"

The sun finally peaked through the disappearing, black menacing clouds. The rays glistened off the choppy waters exposing the massive carnage and wreckage. More than a thousand souls perished by sunrise. And more than $14 million in silver and gold had scattered over the reefs, and vanished into the depths of the Atlantic Ocean, including some seven million pieces of eight.

Captain Antoine d'Aire of *Le Griffon* had refused the orders of Captain General Ubilla. At the first signs of heavy wind, he had abandoned the Spanish Fleet and skillfully tacked in a different heading to the northeast. D'Aire made it back to Brest, France, on August 31 safely, unscathed, and unaware of the fate of the others.

Chapter Three
If it were not for . . .

The Spanish Crown was in desperate need of New World gold and silver to finance the War of Spanish Succession (Queen Anne's War). When a childless King Charles II of Spain died in 1700, there was a dispute over his successor and control of the vast Spanish empire. The last will and testament of King Charles II designated French, Prince Philp of Anjou as his successor. Philip's grandfather, King Louis XIV of France eagerly accepted his grandson's fortune and announced Philip as the King of Spain. France and Spain united would make France *the* world power. Opposing nation-states prepared for war fearing that the balance of power in Europe would be toppled. It embroiled half of Europe until the signing of separate peace treaties in Treaty of Utrecht in 1713. The war continually delayed the sailing of the Plate Fleet for more than two years.

To make things worse, there was angst between the captain generals of the fleet, Ubilla and Echeverz. Personalities clashed: neither of the captain generals cared for each other by the summer of 1715. The stress escalated between the two—personally, economically, and politically. Constant delays were at the forefront of their arguments. Echerverz arrived in Havana in mid-March and waited for Ubilla who was still in Mexico. A mountain of cargo, amassed from prior months, sat at the docks at the fortified harbor of Havana. Ubilla accused Echeverz of being lazy and incompetent in not loading precious cargo in a timely manner. Stress, tension, and temperaments mounted rapidly.

Then there was the weather factor, something neither captain could control. Captain General Ubilla was especially concerned about his fleet escaping out of the tropics before the hurricane season.

The final plight placed the fleet's departure in severe jeopardy. King Philip V had ascended to the Spanish throne under great controversy in the year 1700. After a year of reign, Phillip V married a thirteen-year old, Princess Maria Luisa Gabriella of Savoy. She was chosen by his grandfather. Eleven years later, in 1714, Queen Maria Luisa died at the age of twenty six.

With the Queen of Spain's death, King Phillip V decided to marry Elizabeth Farnese, the Duchess of Parma. The duchess agreed to the marriage. However, she would not consummate the union until she received a dowry, in jewels of her choosing; a heart delicately crafted of 130 pearls, a seventy-four karat emerald ring, a pair of earrings- each complemented with a fourteen-karat pearl, and a rosary of pure coral.

Phillip ordered the elaborate jewels be brought to him by the 1715 Fleet. Left unrecorded on the manifests. Captain General Ubilla's galleon, *Nuestra Senora de la Regla* is the ship believed to have carried the jewels. Unrecorded on the manifests, they were simply listed simply as "62 chests of gifts."

Today, this dowry, over one thousand passengers, and the Fleet now lay at the bottom of the ocean.

If it were not for these circumstances, the 1715 Spanish Armada would have escaped the wrath of the hurricane. Unfortunately, more problems were on the horizon for the Spanish army.

ALLEN BALOGH

Part 3

Charles Vane and Henry Jennings

1715 Fleet Raid

Double Cross

ALLEN BALOGH

Chapter Four
Insane Vane

At front and center of "The Golden Age of Piracy" were Henry Jennings, Charles Vane and Sam Bellamy. Like most pirates, all three men started as a privateer during the War of the Spanish Succession. However, they had a hard time adjusting to the peace that followed the Treaty of Utrecht of 1713. Jennings and the other privateers found themselves jobless, as the treaty made allies of nations that were once enemies.

Henry Jennings, Charles Vane and Sam Bellamy were the pirate reincarnation of the infamous Roman First Triumvirate. None of them would hesitate to increase their own reputation at his colleague's expense.

A ruthless, educated, merchant seaman, Jennings operated from Jamaica under the unscrupulous English Governor, Lord Archibald Hamilton. He and Charles Vane had an unwritten agreement to split profits with him from their plunders of Spanish and French merchant ships in exchange for protection from each other.

Surprisingly, Jennings was famous for one plunder, the 1715 Spanish Fleet that sunk off the coast of Florida after a devastating hurricane. Like a shot out of a canon, word spread throughout the Caribbean islands and the Americas that silver and gold lay on the seafloor. Eleven Spanish ships with an estimated $15,000,000 in gold and silver had sunk in shallow waters off the coastline. Tons of silver, gold and emeralds washed up on desolate beaches.

"We need to scramble as soon as possible," Jennings told Vane. "I already have the dispensation from Governor

Hamilton. He's already counting his share. " Jennings pushed his rough-hewn tavern chair back and leaned forward, muscled forearms tense on the table.

"Spain's ill fate is our good fortune,"

Vane exploded, "I be needin' me own ship, damn it!"

"You have no backing, Vane, from anyone; no crew, no financing, no ship."

Vane kicked his chair and sauntered to the tavern door. He squinted into the bright sunlight and ran his fingers through his hair. "Any captain with a sturdy ship and an ample crew will depart readily for the sunken Spanish Treasure Fleet."

"We need to leave now." Vane and Jennings walked outside the tavern and peered over Port Royal harbor. The crystal clear, blue waters were filled with merchant ships. "We need to move, now. Prepare the ships and crew."

Charles Vane, a hot-tempered and violent pirate, was practically frothing at the mouth, anticipating his newfound fortune. "Ye be ready, Jennings, by the time the cock crows."

"So there's no mistake, Vane, you will be serving under me. Do you understand?"

Vane looked Jennings in the eye, hesitated, and reluctantly agreed to obey. "Someday I'll have me own ships, Jennings." He gripped his tankard as he threw a shot rum back, his fierce eyes never leaving Jennings face.

Jennings didn't falter. "That may be true, but no one will work for you. Now, get the provisions together and do your job."

Henry Jennings acquired five vessels, two ships and three sloops, twenty-one divers, and a couple hundred pirates. On December 27, 1715, Jennings and Vane arrived off the east coast of Florida in an eighty-ton sloop, *Barsheba.,* They found the poorly-defended Spanish camp, right where it was reported to be, at Palma de Ayes.

A young, rising star, Sam Bellamy and his wealthy friend, Paulsgrave Williams, set sail for Florida as well. *The Boston New-Letter* carried an extensive article about the 1715 Spanish Fleet disappearing in a hurricane. Sam Bellamy, a poor sailor, and Paulsgrave Williams, with a lengthy heritage of wealth, left the Cape Cod area for the east coast of Florida.

Bellamy and Williams arriving a couple weeks after Jennings and Vane. They stayed safely offshore south of the Sebastian Inlet. Bellamy pulled his spyglass from his left hip and looked toward shore. "We're too late." Bellamy pulled back his black hair with both hands. "There are only a few slave-divers. I thinks the site has been cleansed by the Spanish salvers and these other rogues. Now what?"

Williams squinted into his spyglass as the glaring sun blurred his vision. "Let's stay 'while and watch," replied Williams. "I see a good amount of movement." About a mile offshore, Jennings's ships encircled three longboats. His oarsmen were signaling hand gestures.

"This should be interesting," said Bellamy. "Somethin's bout to happen."

Williams seemed like an unlikely candidate for piracy, with his tanned skin in stark contrast to his powered blonde gentleman's wig. He adjusted his wig and leaned eagerly against the taffrail.

Bellamy's eyes squinted again. "It's a gang of ruffians. I'm guessing pirates from the Caribbean."

"O' me Lord, this is gonna be good," smiled Williams.

Admiral Don Francisco Salmon of the Spanish Navy was in charge of salvaging the remains of the eleven wrecks. He was one of the lone survivors with the authority to make decisions crucial to the King and Queen of Spain. Salmon fought his way to shore during the hurricane. He sustained bruises to his arms and legs, and his face had several abrasions. Exhausted, he could barely stand upright on the water's edge.

"We're fortunate to be alive," said Salmon to his sergeant. "I tried to swim to the shore but the waves kept coming over me in the midst of the night, again and again. The salt water burned my nose, throat, and near choked me to death."

"Indeed, Admiral. The Commanders Ubilla and Echeverz weren't as fortunate. The surviving men say both drowned as soon as the hurricane hit. The wind and currents ripped apart their ships as they hit the first reef."

Admiral Salmon silently bowed his head and crossed himself, offering up prayers of gratitude as well as prayers for the souls of his lost compatriots. He raised his eyes to meet those of his sergeant. "Two men of great experience, faulted by pressure placed on them by the Crown. All of us knew it was too late in the summer to depart Cuba, a foolish, foolish mistake. It cost us all, dearly."

The sergeant glanced at the ground and coughed from the salt water, before continuing. "Sir, I've been helping the divers and slaves retrieve as much silver and gold as possible. But they are getting sick and vomiting green."

Salmon nodded. "They may be going too deep, too quickly. Tell them to stop using the heavy rocks to sink to the bottom. Have them descend with their heads inside the bells and descend. Teach them to breathe the air inside the bell, then scoop up the coins."

"Admiral, one more thing, we're running out of building supplies for the guard house. We stockpiled palm fronds and timber from the wrecks on the dunes. But we need more."

"I saw that. Make sure the recovered silver and gold cannot be seen from the horizon. There are more sloops arriving every day."

"Admiral, we have sixty soldiers to protect the guard house."

Salmon's tired eyes scanned the several foreign ships on the horizon. He sighed. "We can only do the best we can do with what we have."

In the wee hours of December 28, Jennings lost no time preparing his men to ambush the Spanish salvage camp at the Palma de Ayes.

"Vane, have the men shutter the lanterns and prepare the skiffs to row onshore."

"How many men and boats do you want?"

"Three boats, with a hundred fifty men, put them into groups of fifty. Have them row quietly south of their salvage camp. Not a sound, mind you."

Panic struck as the Spanish troops in the encampment awoke to an invasion of misfits. The pirates swarmed over the beach like ants over bags of sugar, while the Spanish soldiers ran up the dunes and formed ranks to protect the silver, gold, and emerald jewelry. Unfortunately for the Spanish, it was a futile effort.

The most terrifying spectacle to greet the eyes of the frightened Spaniards was that of Charles Vane. Greasy hair flowing, insane eyes glowering, he led one group of fifty men up the dune line. With weapons in both hands, he discharged his pistols as soon as his feet touched the shore. He reached for additional loaded pistols in his bandoleer and reloaded as fast as he could, creating as much chaos as possible in a short amount of time.

"Kill them all," Vane ordered his contingent of men. "Take no prisoners."

Leading another group of men, Jennings, by happenstance, turned and saw the unrestrained viciousness of Vane's attack.

"You crazed bastard, Vane. Stop the maiming!" yelled Jennings.

Vane, in his madness, ignored Jennings and continued to revel in maiming the Spaniards.

Jennings ran down the beach and knocked Vane down from behind. Vane's face was pushed into the sand by the black boot of Jennings.

"Stop or I strike you dead."

"Jennings, you will regret this." Vane was panting in delirium. "Leave me up." Jennings slowly removed his boot from the neck of Vane.

Admiral Salmon was outnumbered, one hundred fifty pirates versus sixty Spanish soldiers. He stood atop the dune line and waved a white flag.

"I haven't even fired a shot at ye," yelled Jennings. "Are you surrendering?"

Salmon walked down the white, sandy dune and approached in Jennings in a defeated manner. "No, I am not.

But, I ask that you leave immediately." Sweat poured down the bruised face of Salmon. "We have no cause to kill."

"Sir, if you have not noticed, I'm the one in control here."

Salmon placed two fingers on a gold crucifix with emeralds hanging around his sunburned neck. "The wrecks belong to His Catholic Majesty, King Phillip V. I will give you and your men 25,000 pesos if you leave now."

Jennings looked out the side of his eye. Vane continued to cut and maim Spanish soldiers as they climbed the dune to escape. He saws a wounded soldier fall to his knees. Vane removed his sword and pierced the soft spot of the stomach, coming out the other side.

"Order him to stop, Captain," asked Salmon. "This is as inhumane as I've ever seen."

Vane pulled the sword from the body and watched the blood drip off the edge. With all his strength, Vane brought down his sword, splitting the man's skull to his chin. The brutal finality was more terrifying than the hordes of soldiers falling in their own footsteps to escape. Gargling shrieks of pain receded as the soldier fell head first into the sand.

"Vane, you crazed bastard," screamed Jennings. "Stop the maiming, damn it."

Dropping the sword, Vane turned around with a pistol in each hand. He pointed one at Jennings and the other at Salmon. His smiled, exposing his rotten teeth. His sharp eyes glinted with malice and darted from one side to the other, settling on Jennings.

He stopped and his eyes squinted harder at Jennings. Time slowed for three heartbeats. He glared contemptuously before dropping his weapons to his side.

Satisfied for the moment, Jennings turned his attention back to the Spanish Admiral. "Salmon, I spare you the lives that you cherish," said Jennings. "However, do not attempt to stop us from loading the silver and gold onto our ships."

"Again, Captain, this does not belong to me or you. I must do what I must."

"And I must do what I must." Jennings pointed to Vane. "The consequences will be dire and tortuous, I assure you."

Salmon looked toward Vane to see the twitch of a smile in the corners of the pirate's thin lips. The Admiral faced a pack of madmen and its leaders, one who could barely be constrained. Despite the fury and confusion running through his veins, Salmon realized his efforts and salvage camp were doomed.

"Well, Admiral, what is your decision?" asked Jennings.

The woeful look on Admiral Don Francisco Salmon's face left little room for doubt. He turned his back to the shoreline and stared at a storm brewing on the horizon.

"Men, raid the camp now," ordered Jennings. "I want nothing left behind."

Over the next several days, Jennings, Vane, and their crew relieved the Spanish of as much silver and gold as *Barsheba* could possibly carry.

Jennings scanned the sea, more ships were arriving and anchoring off Sebastian Inlet.

"The word must be out, it's time to leave, Vane." Jennings wiped his parched lips with his sleeve. "Time for some Jamaican rum."

"Aye, it's been glorious. I be needin' to do this more often."

"Prepare *Barsheba,* Vane. Let's head south. Lord Hamilton will be elated."

Grinning and slobbering, Vane looked out to sea, then back to Jennings. His fingers stroked the hilt of his dagger, tucked comfortably into his belt.

"Tis beyond me wildest dreams, Captain," Vane's grin widened even more. Maiming Spaniards, and pillaging gold, a joyous time."

Jennings arched brows climbed a little higher up his forehead. "So you're happy, Vane, are ya?"

The insane Vane hopped up and down uncontrollably and snorted, "Very happy, Captain."

"Hoist the mains," commanded Jennings to the sailing master. "Let's go home."

Jennings and Vane set sail for Port Royal. It was a very cold evening in January, 1716. The northeast winds caused the wind to whip off the coastline. Crewmembers wore jackets made of worn sails to harvest the warmth of the setting sun.

"Men, hunker down." Jennings dipped a large vat into an oak barrel and filled it to the rim with rum. "Enjoy the spirits, mates, it'l keep ya warm."

Unknowingly, Jennings and Vane just missed the big haul. Before their raid, General Hoyo Solozano recovered and stowed at least four million pesos from the sunken Spanish Treasure Fleet. Solozano sailed back to Havana, Cuba, under protection of the Spanish navy.

On board *Barsheba* was 350,000 pesos, worth £ 87,000. Overweight from the treasure, *Barsheba* lumbered along the coastline of Florida towards Jamaica.

Bellamy and Williams watched with envy. "I guess they can't take any more, filled to max of the ship's capacity," stated Bellamy. "Why can't that be us?"

Bellamy and Williams anchored off shore for another day. "Look, on the horizon, it's the Spanish navy," said Bellamy. "I think it's our turn to set sail." Within the hour, Captain Escobar pulled aside Bellamy and Williams.

"You scavengers need to be leaving this area, now." Escobar stood at the bowsprit. "Do you understand?" The Spanish reinforcements were not to be engaged with.

"Sir, we'r plannin on leaving tonight. Many men have drowned here trying to recover chests of coins," said Bellamy. On January 22, 1716, Bellamy and Williams decided it was time to move on. Even Blackbeard arrived too late. He could only sail off shore to watch the final salvage. A remarkable amount of the Crown's silver and gold had been recovered by the Spanish soldiers and shipped back to Havana. The remaining gold and silver lay on the bottom of the ocean unable to be retrieved. With little left to hope for, Blackbeard shifted his focus and continued onward to Charles Town, South Carolina.

With only five thousand pieces of eight, Bellamy and Williams departed Palma de Ayes.

"I can't go back to New England yet," said Bellamy. "I need more wealth to prove my worth."

"To who?" Williams asked.

"To the parents of Marie, they consider me not worthy of their daughter."

"You mean they aren't sufficiently enamored with your charm and rugged good looks?" Williams laughed. Seeing Bellamy's long face, he adopted a more helpful demeanor.

"Let's continue along the coast and see what fortune may bring us. You may yet win enough to buy your future in-laws."

Bellamy guffawed, then looked thoughtful. "Maybe we can catch up to those five vessels. See what they're up to."

Williams and Bellamy sailed their vessel into the Florida Keys. They carefully trailed Jennings and Vane, staying always on the edge of the horizon. As they sailed, a plan grew in Bellamy's cunning mind.

Maybe we can catch those pirates off guard, wait for a squall or storm, then attack the smaller sloop.

Just west of Cuba, Jennings spotted Bellamy and Williams following close behind.

"Vane, pull your spyglass out. Do you recognize those blokes?"

"It's the same sloop from the Palma de Ayes."

"We can't fire on them, too far away."

Tired of the cat and mouse game, and wondering just who these audacious mariners were, Jennings ordered *Barsheba* about and began to bear down on Bellamy and Williams.

Seeing the turn through his spyglass, Bellamy knew immediately that Jennings had taken the bait. "Men, take our bags of pesos and place them in the two periaguas." He turned to Williams. "We can easily outrun Jennings with less weight."

Barsheba gave chase, but could not catch up. Bellamy's two peso-laden canoes rowed safely inside the reefs protecting Cuba's northern shore. The sheltered bay of Bahia Honda was shallow and narrow, impossible for large ships to venture in at low tide.

Jennings eyebrows arched as he saw the periaguas disappeared around the small headland and into the bay. "Drop anchor at the harbor," he ordered. "We'll block their exit from the narrow entrance. They can't stay there the rest of their lives."

Vane peered over the rail toward the Bellamy now receding toward the horizon. "Who are these fools that trailed us," wondered Vane aloud.

"I don't know, but we are about to find out. I'm sure that I saw them off the coast of Palma de Ayes."

While in shore, Bellamy and Williams pulled aside a French sloop at the dock. They immediately befriended the Captain, d'Escoubet, of a shallow-draft French sloop, the *St. Marie*.

"Bon jour, Captain. I'm Sam Bellamy. This is my good friend, Paulsgrave Williams. We are merchantmen from the Lesser Antilles."

"It is my pleasure," said d'Escoubet in a strained English dialect. "What brings you into the harbor?"

"We're in search of trading partners. I'm sure we can do business by exchanging your fine wines for our salted boar."

"Possibly," said d'Escoubet. "What else do you have to offer?

"Captain, our ships are sitting off the harbor." said Williams easily. "We hold rum, salted boar, tobacco and sugar."

D'Escoubet appraised Williams, taking in his powdered wig, his well-made waistcoat, and the fine silver rings he wore. His boldface lie was appealing to the French captain. In d'Escoubet's eyes, the ships anchored outside the harbor was proof of their wealth of supplies. And he understood that the larger ships could not make it into the narrow, shallow harbor.

"We would like to do more business with the French but the war prevents us from doing that in the open," added Bellamy. His smile with a hint of wistfulness was charming.

"I'm interested in trading. We can talk and trade wine for rum for the time being," d'Escoubet smiled back.

"A splendid idea. Let me talk to the Captain of the larger ship. He is a fine chap of honesty and integrity."

D'Escoubet's smile widened. "Bellamy, tell your mates outside the harbor that I never shirk from an English flag."

Not a problem, I assure you. We are here to trade, not conquer."

Aboard *Barsheba,* Jennings became curious as he peered over the bow to watch. He pulled out his spyglass to get a closer look. Bellamy and Williams were climbing over the portside of *St. Marie* and into their periagues. Was there an argument? Why did the meeting come to an abrupt halt? And where are those two heading now?

Jennings stared in wonder to see Bellamy and Williams rowing frantically toward *Barsheba.* By the time the two men requested permission to board, Jennings was bursting with curiosity. Bellamy and Williams scampered up the side and onto the deck of *Barsheba.* For the first time, Jennings and Vane, Bellamy and Williams, laid eyes on each other.

"Captain, let me introduce myself. I'm Sam Bellamy, an Englishman from Cape Cod. The crew inside the harbor are French. They are hiding silver and gold in chests."

"What do you propose?"

Williams answered. "We need to ban together. It needs to be done in numbers, all of us together. Besides, they're French, the Crown would expect nothing less from us."

Jennings strode across his deck and gazed toward the mouth of the harbor before turning to face Bellamy and Williams once again. His eyes swept the deck and took in Vane, leaning against the bulkhead, touching his dagger.

"Let's set out some terms and conditions," said Jennings.

"We don't need such, we simply divide the plunder among us."

Business concluded with the shaking of hands, Vane stood atop the bow to announce their intentions of boarding the French ship, *St. Marie*. "Men, we have it on good word from these two Englishman that chests of silver and gold are on board. We will unite together and split the takings with them."

"All for one and one for all," cheered the crew onboard *Barsheba*.

On April 4, 1716, Jennings, Vane, and his crew sailed carefully into the harbor on *Barsheba*. at high tide.

As the joint forces boarded *St. Marie,* d'Escoubet, realized that he was outnumbered and vulnerable. He surrendered without fight. Initially, the crews were gentlemanly to one another, until Charles Vane pulled out a sword and pistol from his bandoleer of weapons. He screamed in terror as if he were the one being attacked.

"Every French man, if you even move, I will take an eye out wi' the tip of me sword." None of the French crew understood Vane, and looked at each other in confusion. "Stop in ye tracks, or I sliver each and every one of ya."

A French officer, young and inexperienced enough to have never met the likes of Vane, turned toward his comrades with a laugh, ready to make either a comment or a disparaging remark. He did neither. Vane at once stepped toward the officer, pointed his pistol at the man's smiling face before turning the weapon and clubbing the man with it. He pounded the officer until he was sprawled prone on the deck.

Under the direction of Bellamy, the French crew was interrogated, tormented and terrorized until the location of the gold and silver was given up.

"Paulsgrave, watch out for the chap, Vane," said Bellamy when he had a chance to speak without being overheard. "Did you see how he acted in attacking the French lad?"

Paulsgrave nodded. "I saw, he was smiling as he beat the youg'n til he bled, maybe 14 or 15 years old. "He's crazy, for sure. Keep your eye on him. I don't trust him unless I had some eyes out me back."

As the day wore on, Bellamy and Williams grew increasingly wary of Vane's ill-temperament and did not care to be associated with his undue cruelty. Bellamy's philosophy was fight smart, harm few, and score big.

Jennings, Vane, and their crew scurried to transfer the silver, gold and cargo from *St. Marie* onto the *Barsheba* while d'Escoubet looked on. Occasionally his eye would meet those of one of his crew, laden with gold being transferred onto the English vessel. At those moments, under the accusatory stares, his head hung low, ashamed for not defending his ship or men.

While Jennings issued orders to his crew on St. Marie, Vane held guard over d'Escoubet's crew. A hood wink of master proportions, like none seen before, was taking place in front of their very eyes.

While Jennings, Vane, and crew were on the *St. Marie,* Bellamy and Williams threw sacks and chests of coins from *Barsheba* into the two periagues.

However, the gold and silver was not from the *St. Marie* but was instead the 350,000 pesos from the 1715 Spanish Fleet, that had been stowed on the *Barsheba.*

Black Sam Bellamy and Paulsgrave Williams double crossed Jennings and Vane just as they duped the French Captain, d'Escoubet, a double cross.

As the periagues left Bahia Honda, Jennings and Vane pursued, but could not catch up with them. Within the hour, lo and behold, was the great sloop *Marianne,* sitting off the Florida Straits. The captain was Jennings' nemesis, the great Benjamin Hornigold, flying the black flag. Two types of terror struck pirates, the terror of being hung at the gallows and the Jolly Roger.

Jennings and Vane recognized Hornigold's blue and gold ship immediately. The black flag was their warning. They gave up the pursuit of Bellamy and Williams, swung around, and headed back to the Bahia Honda harbor in Cuba.

Jennings and his crew were distraught and outraged. Not only did Bellamy and Williams outsmart them, but 350,000 pieces of eight from the 1715 Spanish Treasure Fleet were stolen from underneath their noses.

While en route from Bahia Honda to Jamaica, Jennings got lucky. He encountered another Spanish ship and captured 60,000 pesos from the 1715 Fleet. He did not go back to Jamaica empty handed after all.

Jennings thought he'd return to Jamaica to a hero's welcome with the 1715 Treasure Fleet's silver and gold. But it was gone and in the hands of Sam Bellamy. When Jennings arrived in Jamaica, he was warned by friends that he was more likely to be hanged. Without any plunder to give to Lord Hamilton, Jennings was declared a pirate by the very governor who had commissioned him & originally condoned his actions, after taking a cut for himself. He gave official orders to the privateers to "execute all manner of acts of hostility" against pirates. Privately, he directed them to go straight to the Spanish wrecks off the coast of Florida and to bring back whatever treasure they could.

Jennings was forced to flee from Jamaica and eventually established a new base of operations in New Providence in the Bahamas. He and his crew decided to make their new base in small shanty town called, Nassau.

When Jennings arrived in Nassau, it was a pirate hot spot of sorts, though not quite a booming metropolis, but perfect for him and his men. Pirates had been using Nassau as a stopover. The town grew into a city and true pirate haven by 1716.

Jennings was the unofficial mayor, who took tribute from those looking to be lost in exchange for safe harbor. Nassau became the new Port Royal.

In early 1718, Woodes Roger was appointed Governor of the Bahamas and vowed an end to piracy in his waters. Rogers gave the pirates an ultimatum: accept a King's pardon and cease all acts of piracy or be hunted down and hanged. Jennings accepted the King's pardon and left piracy forever. Jennings, wisely, took the offer

However, many of Jennings men later shed their semi respectable cloak of 'privateer' and became out and out pirates and died on the gallows. Charles Vane was the new leader of Jennings's crew.

Part 4

Black Sam Bellamy

and

Paulsgrave Williams

ALLEN BALOGH

Chapter Five
The Prince of Pirates

Hornigold offered shelter to the two upstart pirates, Samuel Bellamy and Paulsgrave Williams. The two young, fearless New Englanders had just stolen treasure from the notorious pirates Henry Jennings and Charles Vane. How bold and crazy was that? Jennings and Vane had to account for the 1715 Fleet treasure disappearing to Lord Archibald Hamilton of Jamaica . . . not good.

April brought wonderful weather to the Caribbean; cool temperatures, plenty of sunshine, and slow rolling seas. The two piraguas pulled aside *Marianne*. Hornigold held his hand out to pull Bellamy and Williams on board as the two climbed the line onto the main deck of the ship. Bellamy turned around and laughed as he saw Jennings and Vane in *Barsheba* in the distance, sailing back to Cuba.

Hornigold placed both hands on his hips and smiled. "My name is Captain Benjamin Hornigold."

"We have heard of you. I am Sam Bellamy and this is my friend, Paulsgrave Williams."

"Sam, my humble respects to you," said Hornigold. He removed his tricorn hat and bowed. "I am much impressed. I have never seen such a daring scheme."

"My friend and I planned the plunder a couple of weeks ago," bragged Bellamy.

"Where did you first see Jennings and Vane?"

"We followed them from Florida, Captain. They were plundering the Spanish Treasure Fleet wrecks. We had to wait for the right time."

"What provided you with such fortune to fool Jennings and Vane?

"Patience, Sir."

"That was no easy task," smiled Hornigold.

"The French captain, d'Escoubet at Bahia Honda, provided a valuable diversion with his small chest of treasure." Bellamy leaned on Williams's shoulder. "We unloaded the pieces of eight from the Spanish Fleet onto our piraguas, as Jennings loaded treasure from d'Escoubet's sloop onto his flagship, the *Barsheba*."

Hornigold burst out laughing. "That was incredibly ballsy. I must say, well done, lads." Bellamy stuck out his chest in pride. "We would like to express our gratitude for protecting us. It worked out perfectly."

"And it worked out perfectly for me, Sam, for I detest Jennings and Vane."

"Vane is just a varmint, period," hissed Bellamy. "The man is as insane as a bat in the daylight."

Hornigold pointed to his temple. "*Loco en la cabeza*, unquestionably. I've known him for a while—"

Williams interrupted, "The man functions like an eel, not knowing his next move."

"Look, gentlemen, I need a couple of brazen sailors like you two, men of courage and fortitude. Would you two be interested in joining the crew of the *Marianne*?"

"I would consider it an honor, Captain," said a surprised Bellamy. "Your widespread reputation serves you well."

"Likewise." Williams nodded. "What do you expect of us?"

"Do everything that you ask of those you command," Hornigold stared into the eyes of Bellamy. "The men see your soul if you walk in their shoes."

"If I do my full duty, Captain, the rest will take care of itself," replied Bellamy.

"I like the way you think," Hornigold grinned. "We'll do just fine."

The three men shook hands in agreement. The *Marianne* had a new force of men to be reckoned with on the high seas. However, the relationship only lasted a couple of months. Bellamy and Williams soon tired of Hornigold's refusal to attack English ships.

"Paulsgrave, we need to go on our own again," said Bellamy irritated. "This is nonsense. We are missing one opportunity after another."

"I agree. His crew is restless and ready to remove him," said Williams.

"He has a fine aptitude of the seas and loves his men." Bellamy hesitated. "But, Hornigold told me that he was about to retire to Nassau." Bellamy's thick, black, unruly eye brows pinched together. "I find that odd."

Williams shook his head back and forth and leaned on the thick, wooden mast. "His unwillingness to attack English ships defies logic."

"I admire his allegiance though. England is his home country." Bellamy grabbed a frayed line and tied a knot. "Like this rope, Paulsgrave, his loyalty to the king cannot be broken.

"Why? What have they done for him?"

"Nothing." Bellamy shrugged.

"Exactly.

Chapter Six
Maria Hallett

Beads of sweat poured out on Maria Hallett's forehead as she gripped the low-lying branches of a pine tree. She gasped as pain rippled through her body. Her blue eyes widened with each agonizing surge. The contractions came faster. She squeezed the branches tighter, leaving bark under her fingernails and ridges in her palms.

Steady. Once this baby comes, everything will be better.

The pain eased for a moment. Maria bowed her head and looked through her matted blonde hair at her open legs.

Oh God, why do you do this to me?

A beautiful, unwed fifteen-year-old, pregnant by an absent no-account sailor, was a severe liability for the well-to-do Halletts, living in a Puritan community.

Banished from Eastham and disowned. How could my parents do that? How could they! And even if Sam should return, my parents will never forgive us. Preacher man says God will never forgive us, too.

Maria's heart felt empty. She blinked as tears filled her eyes. *Sam's bin gone for so long now, and he don't even know about this here baby. Will he ever come back for me? He doesn't know, I've been abandoned by everyone, even God.*

Maria looked away as another wave of pain overtook her and another thought crowded her mind. *Preacher don't know ever'thin'. Next time you feel that pain, you jus push hard 'n' slow 'n' long as you can. Jus push that critter out, and everythin' will be awlright."*

An unbearable, excruciating surge of pain shot through Maria's body, triggered by another spasm. Maria had a seizure and passed out.

Maria woke to a torrent of rain pounding on the thatched roof and small rivulets of water pooling on the dirt floor. The threadbare quilt used to cover her was damp with rain, sweat, and blood. She looked down at the baby boy wrapped in rags, lying in the crook of her arm.

He has black hair, like Sam.

She didn't want to touch him or hold him. She slid him from her arm and moved her body away from the little bundle of rags. He didn't open his eyes or cry. He just lay there, only the rags moving slightly with his baby breath.

Maria asked herself in a panic, *What am I supposed to do with him?*

She closed her eyes and shuddered. That is when she heard it, a slight movement in the dusky corner of the hut. She opened her eyes, expecting to see her mother, but instead focused on the figure of a dark-skinned man. His features were shrouded by the weak light of the misty, chilly morning.

"What to do with him, indeed. That is the question." The Dark Man seemed to smile at her, though she couldn't see his features. "You could suckle him, as any mother would do. But ya don't want him, do ya?"

Maria stared at the stranger. She detected a heavy West Indies accent. *How does he know my deepest thoughts? Why is he here?*

The grin on the stranger's face widened, showing extraordinarily white teeth. I'm here to help till your Sam returns."

"Ye know Sam?" she whispered.

"Not as well as I'd like." The stranger reached into a pocket to produce an apple and a pipe. He leaned toward Maria, offering her the apple, then filled the pipe with dark, green grass. He began to smoke the weed of Jamaica.

"You, my dear, are in a predicament. But every predicament has a solution, and I'm here to offer one."

"And how can you help me?"

"I bring you nourishment."

The Dark Man set a small iron cauldron inside the dilapidated hut. The ingredients of the heavy pot sloshed back and forth. Steam rose from the fish-smelling kettle. "Here, smoke this and drink the magic brew." The Dark Man sat beside Maria with crossed legs and spoon fed Maria until she became dizzy. "Repeat after me: 'Death to the li'l one,'" whispered the West Indies voodoo man.

The top of the straw roof of the hut started to spin out of control.

"Death to the li'l one," chanted Maria, time and again.

Her fingers of frost gripped his tiny throat. Maria blacked out.

The dirt floor of the hut showed no signs of a struggle, but Maria was gone. The newborn baby, abandoned on the floor, was not breathing, bits of straw protruding from his mouth.

Sam Bellamy's baby was dead.

Maria ran swiftly between the barren trees of the woods. Zigzagging through the underbrush, dead needles from pine trees stuck to her muddy feet. She tripped and fell to the ground, out of breath. Her face was covered in a pool of mud. She lay there, helpless.

Oh, where is my Sam. We are all doomed to hell without him.

In the hot, steamy summer of 1716, Hornigold was deposed as captain of the *Marianne*. The ninety-man crew elected Bellamy to replace Hornigold. Reluctantly, Hornigold accepted the decision and returned to Nassau.

Captain Samuel Bellamy, now known as Black Sam Bellamy, was a dashing, handsome young man. In the wintery months, he wore his deep-cuffed black velvet coat to fend off the nor'easter winds. His black knee breeches and silk stockings were tucked into his silver-buckled shoes. Instead of wearing a tricorn hat, his long black hair was pulled into a pony tail and tied with a black satin bow. He dare not wear the fashionable powdered wig.

"Sam, Hornigold's crew needed someone like you. And we've made a name for ourselves on *Marianne*. The crew members like you, not only as a captain, but as a man."

"More importantly, we've plundered over fifty vessels, regardless of flag." Bellamy laughed. "I think the crew liked that much more. They've been yearning to plunder English ships for a long, long time."

"It's more, Sam. It's your manners, the way we were brought up in New England. And your fairness, you let the men vote on important decisions."

"Hornigold did the same. I watched him. I bet he learned that from his privateering days."

"The men have a new name for you."

"And what may that be?"

Paulsgrave smiled and said, "Robin Hood of the Seas."

Bellamy became known for his mercy and generosity toward those he captured on his raids. Time and again, Bellamy would take from the wealthy and give to the poor.

"Kindness, I learned from me mum. It's a forbidden pleasure on the seas, for some reason."

Bellamy placed his hands onto his favorite weapons—dueling pistols, four in all—carried in a black sash inside of his fitted, long black coat. A sword slung on his left hip. He had a menacing profile and a heart of gold. Williams, with his white wig and tanned face, was in stark contrast to the persona of Bellamy.

"You give away more than you keep. The men and others appreciate the generosity. The crew members refer to themselves as Robin Hood's men."

"We deprive ourselves of pleasure, Paulsgrave, fundamental to our sense of who we are."

Bellamy had long relinquished the crack in his armor. He immersed himself with sympathetic identification for those who had less than him and made up for it by giving silver and gold.

"I prefer 'Prince of Pirates,' instead." Bellamy grinned.

"Call yourself whatever you please, Sam. The men love you more than you know."

"Well, let you and I do this. We have two ships now. *Marianne* has many cannons and the second has speed but too small for battle. The next large ship we plunder, you take *Marianne,* and I'll take the new one."

"We can double our takes," Williams said sharply. "Do you think the crew will object to me as their captain?"

"I think not. Put it to a vote, you will see."

It didn't take long for Bellamy to spot another ship. The *Sultan* was a twenty-six-gun British ship. Bellamy raised the skull and crossbones on the *Marianne.* Attack was imminent near the small Caribbean island of Saba, a Dutch-owned colony in the British Virgin Islands. The captain of the *Sultan,* John Richards, gave up easily. He was nursing serious wounds from an earlier battle and was in no position to defend his ship. The capture was easy and uneventful.

With the approval of the crew, Bellamy assumed command of the *Sultan.*

"Paulsgrave, you now have control of the *Marianne.* A vote wasn't really necessary; all the men trust you."

Bellamy and Williams, the ultimate captains, were in control of two large, powerful ships. The New Englanders could do some serious damage on the high seas.

Maria Hallett peered out the iron bars of her cell in the Eastham jail. The throng outside had dispersed with the incoming evening fog, and with the judge's decision that the testimony on how the infant died was not sufficient for Maria to be held for murder.

Indeed, there was controversy as to whether it was murder or simply neglect that had led to the infant's death. Her father's hefty bribe might have had something to do with the leniency of the decision, although some people in the community whispered it was just outright murder.

"Come on, you," the jail keeper called to her as he rattled his keys. "The judge says yer to live in Wellfleet, and no longer to bother the likes of us Christian folk in Eastham. So the sooner ye get out of my jail, the easier my sleep'll be. Dark fella signed for ye. Promised he'd see ye safely to Wellfleet, keep th' Christian ladies from tearin' ye ta bits."

Maria stepped from the cell and stared directly at the jail keeper, remaining silent. He glanced away quickly and stood aside, pressing against the wall as she passed.

Taking up residence in Wellfleet, Maria moved into a tiny cottage across from a field of poverty grass. With the shunning in effect, people were forbidden to talk to her. But Maria wasn't totally alone. Village folk occasionally reported seeing Maria in the company of a dark man, who appeared some evenings on the edge of the woods. Tales and rumors surrounding Maria took on new life.

"James, I'm warnin' you, stay farther and farther away from Goody's Hallett's cottage. The woman taint right in the 'ead, and she's the devil's bride, for sure. Missy Carpenter saw her tyin' fairy lights onto the tail of a deer, and just a talkin' and talkin' to that deer like it was a person. She'll murder you in a flash o' lightnin' if you get too close."

"Oh, Mama, I forgot to tell you. Christopher told me in school he saw her last week, naked as a buck, in the woods, eatin' the heart of a baby from Eastham. Christopher said it was to do with black magic she's learnin' from the Dark Man."

"Now, James, don't be exaggeratin'. The Dark Man might be teachin' her the likes of magic, but it was too cold last week for even Goody Hallett to be in the woods without her petty coats. Now, ye go on home the long way, and don't be cuttin' across that field by her house."

Chapter Seven
The Whydah

In February 1717, a three-hundred-ton, 110-foot powerful English slave ship, called the *Whydah Galley*, sat in Port Royal Harbor, Jamaica. It was arguably the equivalent of Blackbeard's *Queen Anne's Revenge*. The captain, Lawrence Prince, had just delivered nearly five hundred African slaves to Jamaica. He was preparing for the most dangerous and last leg of the lucrative "triangle trade," loaded with cargo of sugar, indigo dyes, and most importantly, four and a half tons of gold and silver.

Captain Prince waited until the last week of February to sail back to London. As the *Whydah* passed through the eastern edges of the Bahamian islands, a lookout saw two ships closing in on the horizon. It was apparent to Prince that the two ships were catching up and on an intercepting course.

Bellamy placed his hand on his quartermaster's shoulder. "Well, Nolan, we anchored off the Exuma Islands, and lo and behold, an enormous slave ship appears before us."

"Captain, it could not have been planned any better," replied Nolan.

"Order the navigator to take a deeper angle and cut off their escape route."

Captain Prince saw Bellamy's intentions and ordered full sail on the *Whydah*. The chase was on. The intercepting angle that the *Sultan* and the *Marianne* worked, trapping the *Whydah*. Bellamy's greatest capture was in striking distance.

"Fire two cannons in their direction," ordered Prince. The percussion shook the wooden deck beneath the feet of Prince's crew. The pungent smell of gunpowder and white smoke filled the air of the *Whydah's* deck.

Prince pulled out his spyglass. *Damn, both shots fell short.* The broadside fell harmlessly into the water.

As he peered closer, hundreds of men on the deck of the *Sultan* and the *Marianne* were shaking their fists at him. Bellamy had taken a play out of Hornigold's book to use intimidation. Crazed-looking men, including slaves, waved spikes and cutlasses. This time, however, the slaves were without shackles, clutching swords and axes.

"Raise the Jolly Roger," ordered Bellamy. "Do not fire until ordered."

Bellamy sailed directly at the *Whydah*. Without incident, Prince surrendered, having fired only two shots.

The *Sultan* and the *Marianne* pulled alongside the *Whydah*. Bellamy and Williams boarded without a fight from Prince.

"Captain, I wish no harm to you or your crew. I only want your ship. I offer you the *Sultan* in exchange."

"I have never heard of such," sputtered Prince. "Well, well . . . thank you."

This act of Black Sam Bellamy built his reputation for generosity.

"One more thing, Captain." Bellamy handed a canvas bag to Prince. "It's yours."

Prince lifted the heavy bag and looked inside. It was filled to the top of the tie bag with pieces of eight.

The battle was over. No damage was done to the ships nor were any men killed. It was Bellamy's trademark.

Bellamy and his crew removed all cargo and provisions from the *Sultan* onto the *Whydah*.

"Paulsgrave, my friend, we have more silver, gold, and jewels than would last us for many lifetimes. I have an idea."

"And what might that be?"

"Let's turn northward along the eastern coast of the Carolinas and sail back to New England."

"Well, there is only one reason for that," said Paulsgrave, smiling.

"You know me well, my friend. I have enough wealth to prove to Maria's parents that I am worthy as a husband."

"Likewise, Sam, I want to go home for a while. I wish to visit my family in Rhode Island and spread my newfound wealth."

"We may not have hit the big haul with the Spanish Treasure Fleet in Florida, but the double-cross with Jennings worked out well. It garnered the respect we needed on the high seas."

"Let's take a vote from the men," Williams said.

Black Sam stood at the helm and called for an aye from the crew to sail onward to New England. It was unanimous. "Lads, we've gotten enough," Bellamy said. "It's time to go home."

Just two months after acquiring the *Whydah*, Bellamy sailed her to Cape Cod with Williams following on board the *Marianne*. Everyone needed a break from being on the seas for so long.

"Sam, let's meet up in Maine. That will give us a month or so to spend with our families."

"Excellent idea, my friend. I can't wait to see the look on Maria's face. And especially her parents."

The *Whydah* and the *Marianne* set sail for New England.

Maria ducked into the brush, hunkered down, and waited until the group of children passed by on the path. As much as she would have liked to talk and play with them, hiding was necessary, if she didn't want stones thrown at her. Once they were gone, Maria leaned back to rest against a tree. On a branch above, a squirrel chattered at her.

"You hate me, too, don't ya?" she asked the squirrel.

Maria heard words expel from the squirrel's mouth. "Are you to kill me, too?"

This cannot be happening. Maria pulled on her long, blonde hair. *God, the devil has taken control of me. Please make this go away.*

The effects of the Jamaican weed and porridge wore on Maria's judgment. She slumped against the bark of the tree and fell into a sound sleep.

When Maria awoke, she saw the squirrel running up and across the limbs of the tree and shaking its bushy tail at her. Her mind started to clear from the intoxicating mix.

Maria blinked but her tears wouldn't leave. She shook her head, remembering her last night with Sam, the feel of his black, silky hair under her hand, the scent of his skin.

Are ya comin' back for me, Sam, like ya promised? It's been so long. Still alive out there somewhere? Could ya not 'ave sent word to me by now? Could ya not 'ave come for me by now?

So engrossed in her thoughts, Maria didn't hear the young boys sneaking in the brush behind her. She never saw the piece of firewood until she felt it crash against her skull, the pain spiraling her downward into a dreamless pit. The older children of Eastham wanted to make a name for themselves . . . by killing the witch of Wellfleet.

Hours later, Maria staggered to her feet. Dried blood crusted her face and fierce pain pierced the right side of her head.

An angry, vengeful resolve was about to replace her innocence.

In April of 1717, Bellamy and Williams arrived off the coast of Massachusctts. The skies darkened as the *Whydah* and the *Marianne* sailed along the coastline. The morning broke and the warmer inland air stretched into the cooler seas creating a thick fog. Bellamy and Williams lost sight of each other.

"Ring the ship's bell," ordered Bellamy. "Maybe Paulsgrave can get some idea of our location."

Quartermaster Richard Nolan wrapped the line of the bronze bell around his thick wrist and yanked it hard back and forth. The clang of the bell was deafening as was the silence of the *Marianne*.

Increasingly concerned for his friend, amid the dense fog and bad sea conditions, Bellamy made a decision. "Nolan, let's anchor out and wait for *Marianne*."

Separated by bad weather, Williams had made the decision to anchor at Block Island, only twelve miles from land. As the fog lifted the next morning, Williams pulled out his spyglass. He could see the hillsides of his home town in Rhode Island.

He scoured the horizon in hopes of seeing the *Whydah*. Bellamy was not in sight.

Can't imagine one of us without the other. Maybe Sam sailed onto Maine. How do I explain this to the men, especially when most of the booty is on the Whydah?

On the morning of April 25, 1717, Maria sat on the stool in her tiny cottage and pulled on her favorite shoes. The red shoes held memories of better days. Sam had literally swept her off her feet. *Oh, I remember when Momma bought these for me. I wore them so Sam could see me all grown up. But today is so different.* Bitterness, despair, loneliness took the place of joy. *I need to find the list of items the Dark Man gave me for a stronger magic potion.*

Standing, she heaved a wicker basket over her arm and pulled a tattered shawl over her shoulders.

Once down the path from her home, she turned onto a track that led to the highest dune line. Struggling up the sandy slope, she thought of the many hours she'd perched on that cliff, hoping against hope that she would spot Sam's ship in the distance. Each time she had been disappointed.

At the hill's apex, Maria unloaded a basket filled with dried dill weed, anise seeds, and bits of clover. She lit a fire and sprinkled the mixture onto the bonfire. Maria watched the smoldering residue filter into the air.

I send the ashes to avenge my suffering. Cause my enemies to suffer as I have suffered at the hands of those who should be my family, friends, and neighbors. Cause them harm until I release them.

Maria spun slowly to the left and chanted, "Oh great Oya, always your supplicant. Listen to my plea. Send the ashes to avenge your humble servant."

The sound of her chanting carried across the sands. Below the cliff, fishermen returning from the sea glanced up the hilltop.

"There goes that crazy woman again. What's the Witch of Wellfleet up to this time?"

"She's wavin' her arms in the air, but what's she sayin'? Cain't make it out from here."

"Don't know either, but it can't be good. Nothin' but craziness comes from that woman."

"Look at her, crazy, just plain crazy." The fisherman removed his hat and scratched his head. "But no matter, lookin' like a nor'easter brewin' out there. We ought to be getting back 'n stowing these nets before waves start pilin' up on us."

Maria, immersed in her storm spell, did not notice the fishermen. She wouldn't have cared if she saw them anyway. Hypnotized by the ever-increasing wind overhead, she spun like a water spout, head thrown back, arms flailing at the sky. Her shredded petticoat flared out as she twirled around and around.

"To hell with you, Puritans. I dance widdershins with torn skirts." Maria frantically circled her fire and screamed curses to the clouds. "Behold, the day is coming, all of you will burn in hell."

All the anger and rejection Maria endured at the hands of the Puritan community spewed back out in ritual chants; "who, who, who . . . who are ye to judge me? I shall set you ablaze, for sure."

Maria's arms flung wildly into the sky. Her bloodcurdling screams became louder.

"May you drown in your arrogance, insults, and persecution of me. You shall suffer in the fury of my storm."

Hours passed while a surreal quiet fell on the dune. Maria collapsed to her knees.

Williams rowed on shore to visit his mother and sister. Williams's mother embraced her son and would not let go.

"Oh, my Paulsgrave. I thought you died on the seas, Hallelujah. Bless the Lord."

She held Sam tight and kissed his cheeks.

"Mum, I have missed you, too. And while at sea, I thought about father . . . a lot. I was a little boy when he died, but I miss him so much." Williams stared at the wooden floor. "A hole was left in me heart, Mum. He didn't spend much time with me, though."

"Your father was the attorney general of Rhode Island and didn't have much time for either of us, Paulsgrave." His mother looked him in the eye. "But that don't mean that he didn't love us."

"Do you think he would be proud of me now?"

"Your father loved you dearly. Yes, of course, he would."

"Sam Bellamy and I have come into great wealth, Mum. But, you cannot tell anyone. I'm giving you one hundred pounds of silver and gold. I do not have the time to travel to see my wife and children. Will you make sure they are taken care of?"

"I will see them soon," she said softly.

"Send my love to them, Mother."

"How long will you be on shore, my dear son?"

Williams hesitated. "My ship hangs off Block Island. I'm sorry, but I must leave tomorrow."

After spending a day with her, Williams returned to Block Island and waited for Bellamy. The crew was getting anxious. Williams broke out all the wine and food to keep the crew from growing impatient. Another week went by and still nothing was on the horizon.

"Captain, let's move on," said the navigator sharply. "We can look northward."

"I agree. Prepare the ship and tell the crew we're leaving within the hour."

Williams sailed well off shore in hopes of finding Bellamy. Unknown to Williams, Bellamy was about 150 miles northeast and sailing toward his home in Eastham, Massachusetts, near Cape Cod.

On the afternoon of April 26, 1717, the skies grew darker. A storm was brewing, again. Black, menacing clouds hovered off Cape Cod, over the Atlantic Ocean. A powerful wind blew the *Whydah* sideways against the angry white caps. The sails started to rip apart from the masts.

"Light up the lanterns and set anchors." ordered Bellamy. "It's going to be a rough night."

"Captain, I've battened down the racks of cannonballs and barrels of spikes," said one of the gunners. "Me crooked leg was caught under a barrel once. I could not free myself. It won't happen again, I assure you."

At about midnight, the weather turned vicious. The men were soaked as it rained sideways. Heavy winds, strong squall lines, and massive lightning strikes surrounded the *Whydah*.

"Navigator, turn the bow of the ship into the wind," commanded Bellamy.

"Aye, sir." The shrieking winds keep changing direction, from the north to the northeast. "We need to move the ship again if this continues," hollered the navigator. "The rain stings against my face. It feels like small spikes piercing my cheeks."

The lines grew taut and dragged the bow of the ship downward. Water rushed aboard. The wind howled through the ship, drowning out any orders from Bellamy.

"Cut the cables with the axes; turn the bow forty-five degrees. Do it now!"

"Aye, sir." nodded the navigator. "The screaming winds . . . I can't . . ."

The *Whydah* would not turn.

A lightning bolt struck nearby and lit up the shoreline. Bellamy saw the cliffs of Eastham, Massachusetts nearby and realized the *Whydah* was only five hundred feet off shore. The gale force nor'easter drove the *Whydah* toward the shoreline. The crew was held useless by the power of the storm.

"I'm praying," said a gunner to the cook. "Mother of God, please help us."

"I'm not a religious man, but I sure am hoping we can get through this," grimaced the cook. "It's hard to breathe."

"Captain Bellamy can get us through this."

Then the unthinkable happened; twenty- to thirty-foot seas crashed violently over the deck. Both the gunner and cook were swept over the deck into the raging water. The sixty cannons broke loose smashing through the decks trapping, maiming, and crushing anyone in the path.

Bellamy looked around in astonishment, slipping on the rain soaked deck. He tried to help as many of his crew as possible. *The captains from the Spanish Treasure Fleet felt helpless, like me, their galleons crashing against the reefs and rocks of Florida. I'm powerless, like them.*

The *Whydah* was doomed.

When the hull struck the sand bar with shocking force, many men were thrown overboard. The main mast snapped and hit Bellamy in the back, knocking him to the deck. The gale force winds mercilessly drove the *Whydah* onto the shoal, stern first.

"Grab on to anything you can," yelled Bellamy. "Try to-"

Sam Bellamy lost his grip on the slippery side rail and was swept overboard, head first. The undertow sucked him down under and out to sea. Sam battled to the surface, gasping for air, only to be pummeled again by another foamy, giant wave.

Whydah capsized, rolled with the giant, breaking waves, and quickly sank, in only sixteen feet of water. The *Whydah*'s spine of timber broke and split the vessel into the bow and the stern. The cargo, including four and a half tons of silver and gold from fifty ships, spilled across the ocean floor.

The hurricane took 145 of his loyal crew, while only two survived.

Black Sam Bellamy was not one of them.

As the storm raged, bodies were strewn on the beach, churning back and forth in the surf. Waves broke on shore, into sharp, grayish, jagged rock. Many crew members were caught on the rocks and could not escape. Their lungs burned from inhalation of the salt water.

Another massive lightning bolt hit some trees on top of the hill. Thunder clapped repeatedly. A silhouette of a young girl was visible on top of the dune line encompassed by a pale gossamer fog. It was Maria with outstretched arms flung above her head. Clouds swirled above her and grey mist crept in from the sea. Tears filled her eyes and her voice grew hoarse as the screaming chant continued, "I beg you to send out Sluath. Cause my enemies to suffer as I have suffered. Cause them harm until I release them."

Coming out of her trance slowly, turning to the sea, Maria spotted the ships of Sam's fleet for the first time as lightning filled the vast New England sky. Her heart leapt with joy to see the familiar flag flying aloft.

"Sam," she screamed. "Ye're back. You've come back for me, my love."

She began running toward the cliff for a better look, when she saw the hull of the *Whydah* strike the sandbar. The men aboard were strewn like broken dolls, and she saw the mast snap and topple.

Maria knew the men were in terrible trouble. Suddenly, she realized that it was her storm that put them in such jeopardy. Paralyzed for a few moments, she stood helpless at the clifftop, arms outstretched, unable to utter a sound, with only one thought in her mind. *This is my fault. The fearful hand of death, I've killed my Sam.*

Disregarding the wild wind and the surging surf, she clamored down the side of the cliff, and ran along the waterline. *Oh no, please don't let this happen. I can no longer take any more unexpected suffering.*

With superhuman strength, she pulled body after body out of the churning waves, dragged them higher onto the dunes, checked each to see if he was Sam before moving to the next. Most were dead, but she saved two men, a young Indian and a carpenter.

With each dead body, Maria's mind cracked a little more. She ran up and down the beach through the wreckage and drowned corpses only to fall to her knees and sob. The sobs turned to wailing and screaming. The escalating guilt for each death, the uncertainty of whether Sam was alive or dead, proved too much for her fragile state of mind.

The Dark Man stood at the tree line and watched.

Part 5

Benjamin Hornigold

and

Edward 'Blackbeard' Thatch

ALLEN BALOGH

Chapter Eight
The Mentor

In the winter of 1716, several ships were exchanging cargo in Port Royal, Jamaica. There were hundreds of masts in the harbor. Like Nassau, the taverns and brothels littered the shoreline, eager to serve the desires of young buccaneers. The seamy, bustling harbor-city was known by merchantmen as the richest and wickedest city on earth.

Edward Thatch stood alone on the rock ledge overlooking Kingston Harbor. He pulled a book and a pen out of a leather bag from his school in the mid 1690's. He began taking notes on the ships. After marking a few notations, he stared at a ship's captain on the dock as if he were a long, lost friend.

The master of the seas, Captain Benjamin Hornigold, was watching. He waved to Thatch to join him on his dock.

"You bin watchin' me like a vulture o'er a dead seagull. What's the name, young man?" Hornigold asked.

"Edward Thatch."

"And where ye from, Thatch?"

"Near Bristol, England."

"Rest assured, mate, you be in good hands. I hail from Norfolk. Ye must have heard of me before," boasted Hornigold.

"Yes, sir, I have. Your home port was the coastline of England—King's Lynn, I believe, a fishing port with large catches of herring." Thatch grinned and held his nose. "Who in their right mind likes herring?"

Hornigold wiped away the sweat on his forehead with his sleeve. "A man has to eat, Thatch."

"Aye, a man must make a living, for sure."

"A lot of Englishmen got rich working the Triangular Trade—leaving England with guns and sailing to West Africa. Hell, the slavers do all the work for ye, roundin' up all the slaves, tradin' the guns for slaves, simple."

"That second leg of the trip from African to the Caribbean can be dangerous, Captain," said Thatch. "A lot of bad weather between Africa and the Caribbean, and the disease on board those ships . . . just not for me."

"Aye, same way with the third leg; the slaves produce sugar, molasses, and other foodstuffs for distribution back in Europe. That sailing back in wicked weather can tax the innards of any sailor."

"What about the Americas?"

"Tobacco, cotton, rice, that's it . . . no gold," said Hornigold wryly. "Certainly nothin' like the Spanish Treasure Fleet that sails along through the Florida Straits."

"I need work, sir. That slave trade may be enticing to some, but not me, Captain."

"It's big business, Thatch. Consider it."

"From whence came you, to start your life on the seas, Captain?"

"I was a privateer. Easier to take from an enemy than to work as a shipmate for another. My first piracy was in the cold air of 1713 off the coast of Nassau. I had some piraguas. You know what piraguas are?"

"I've seen them, but tell me about them."

"It's a dugout canoe with one or two masts, carries up to thirty men who can row against the wind. I had several of them, along with a sloop. I harassed and boarded every merchant ship possible with them."

"And where did ye harass, only the islands?"

"Off the coast of New Providence, mostly; its capital, Nassau; and thereabouts. It's perfect."

"Aye, sir, I know that."

"That's what's special about you. I saw you readin' and writin' in a book at the dock. And I'm sure that you navigate with the best. Not one crew member can do both. Were you from wealth in Bristol?"

"No, not from wealth, Captain, but I had schooling. The old man died when I was sixteen years of age."

"What happened after your ol' man died?"

"Me mum remarried. Her new husband gave me most of these scars that I wear."

Hornigold looked concerned. "You ran away?"

"I couldn't take it anymore—too many fisticuffs with the bastard. The last time we fought, he choked me, but I got free. I knocked him to the ground and got on top of his chest."

"Who won, mate, you or the old man?"

"I beat him half to death with my fists."

"That's why you seem ready for the sea. You got nothing to live for but what's in front of you. Once you lost everything, all you need to do is take everything."

"When people found out about the beating, I fled to the seaport in Redcliffe. I hopped on the next ship that would take me anywhere. It didn't matter. I signed on as a cabin boy sailing to Port Royal, Jamaica."

"That's it? A cabin boy?"

"I learned quickly and moved up. I became a full-fledged sailor. With some sea experience under my belt, I became a privateer. Besides, I had an allegiance to my country. It was the respectable profession of Queen Anne's War."

"Queen Anne's War made an impression on you, Thatch," surmised Hornigold. "England declared war on France and prevents the union of France and Spain. I can't stand either. To hell with both of 'em, mate."

"We're always on the high seas and at war with those blokes."

"Their next stranglehold will be in the Americas. I've seen it already. The French, their Indian allies, and the Spanish constantly take land in the settlements."

"That's good for us. We take from them."

"You're a smart young lad, Thatch. What did you learn that would be helpful to me and my crew?" Hornigold asked.

"My specialty is navigation—winds and currents. I see wind-driven surface currents miles away. I know how to use the trade winds to my advantage."

"Give me more, lad."

"I'm dead on with the hourglass and compass. I navigate with the stars and the moon. Even you would be impressed. Give me a map with the latitude line, and we're on our way, dead reckoning or not."

"Well, lad, I'll give a try soon."

"How soon, Captain?"

"I'm about to seek out a merchant ship from France." Hornigold thought for a minute. "We can do it then."

"Captain, I'm not like Columbus. Hell, he left Spain heading due west. He missed the entire land mass of North America."

"He ended up in the fookin' Bahamas somewhere. I think San Salvador. And he thinks he is in China for Christ's sakes," Hornigold laughed. "In my eyes, Columbus was the first real pirate. He certainly was a privateer."

"I wonder why did Queen Anne put so much trust into Columbus?"

"I wouldn't have." Hornigold pointed to a wooden barrel. "Spain controlled the spice trade in the Far East. That barrel is worth more than rum."

"Me mum loved her silk scarf. When I was lil, she told me it came from the Far East," said Thatch.

"Just like now, Spain wanted more riches." Hornigold scratched his head. "Things just don't change with those Spaniards. But that's good for us. We just take from them."

Thatch shook his head. "How that Italian flew under the flag of Spain is beyond me."

"He promised riches to the greedy bastards. Columbus pillaged San Salvador and the outer islands. The Arawak Indians were gentle people," Hornigold explained. "Probably like an auntie of yours from Bristol, kind and gentle."

"What happened to the Indians?"

"He bullied them, took their jewelry and gold nuggets, and forced them to look for more. Columbus took whatever he wanted, whenever he wanted. Even the Queen had him arrested. He was a cruel bastard. Sounds like a pirate to me."

"Captain, the mistakes Columbus made in navigating will not be made by me."

"That may be true. You have much to learn," said Hornigold.

"You are the master of the seas; everyone knows that. Even your enemies respect you. But I need to know what you think and how you think."

"I worked my way up from wartime. We were legalized pirates, really no difference, mate. We protected any favorite nation's cargo and pillaged the others. The Spanish Treasure Fleets were our prime targets."

"I hate those fookin' Spaniards," said Thatch as he pounded his fist on the desk.

"That makes two of us, mate. But none denying, Spain is a force in searching new routes. The Spanish Treasure Fleets sail from Cartagena, South America; Veracruz, Mexico; and the Caribbean Islands. They met in Cuba and returned in numbers. They're afraid of us."

"It's getting ruthless," said Thatch. "Rival nations send ship after ship to grab their fair share of the riches." Thatch paused. "Like us, they understand that it's better to rule on your own rather than at the orders of a captain."

"The Letters of Marque were no good when the war was over. What's a mate gonna do?" Hornigold looked Thatch in the eye. "The royalty sold us out, the bastards. The temptation to turn into what I am now became inevitable."

"You must have made a lot of money being a privateer."

"I did well. I purchased the piraguas and this thirty-gun sloop. It's called *Ranger*. It's the most heavily armed ship in these waters. I have superior firepower. I seize ships with little effort. They are afraid of me."

"You instill fear and rule by intimidation?"

"It's in sight and sound, mate. They see the *Ranger* and the black flag. I fire off thirty guns in their direction. They are petrified. No man wants to die. Let them think death."

"What do you do when you board their ship?" asked Thatch.

"Depends on the flag the ship is flying. I put on me best accent. I tell them. 'Don't make me have to cut ye.'" Hornigold smiled. "And especially the Scots, I tell, 'I'll bash ye fookin' head in. I swear on me mum.' Then, I bring me ax out."

"How do you know, for sure, if they fear you?" asked Thatch.

"The frightened man stands like a statue. I can see his heart beating through his eyes. That's when you know a defeated man, Thatch. His mouth shuts and his head bows down."

Mesmerized, mouth agape, Thatch hung on to every word Hornigold spoke.

"They must fear you first. That's the key. The more fear I strike into the crew of a ship, the more likely they'll surrender without a fight. Then intimidate the wretched souls, catch yourself on fire if need be," Hornigold said with a smile.

"And my crew?" asked Thatch.

Hornigold placed his hand on Thatch's shoulder and stated, "Make them fear you as well, but also let them think for themselves. When the time's right, seek the votes of your mates. But never be on their level when voting; you stand tall. You stand on the top of the quarterdeck, looking down."

"I'm taller than any man on the islands. My father was tall and lean."

"You have the right mettle, Thatch. I like the spirit in you."

"Thank you, Captain. I feel it to be a privilege."

Hornigold pulled out a long cutlass from his waistband and placed the tip against Thatch's jugular vein. "When you board another ship, point the tip of the cutlass against the neck of the most insolent on board and make 'em bleed. Tell him, 'I come from hell, mate.'

Thatch stepped back as if he were next.

"Everyone must fear you, Thatch. Everyone."

Chapter Nine
A Promotion in the Making

In the winter months of 1716, the ships rolled on top of the ocean from the northeastern winds cutting across the Caribbean in the Bahamian chain of islands. Hornigold recognized Thatch was able to learn from him. After a fierce battle in the Caribbean, Hornigold rewarded Thatch with a sloop, a small crew of seven men, and the title of captain. Thatch was now the second-in -command.

"I admire your fighting skills and the thirst for blood you showed from the last skirmish," said Hornigold. "You have the eye of a marksman and the steely heart of a vulture. You showed no mercy to anyone. Most important, you were relentless in pursuit of the enemy. Let's port in Nassau, raise hell, drink rum, and find some whores."

"Captain, my lips are thirsty and my heart yearns for a lass."

Nassau was referred to as the "Republic of Pirates," a mecca of pirate pleasure. Gorgeous crystal-clear turquoise waters outlined the harbor. The docks were loaded with dozens of masts. And nearest to the docks were taverns and brothels. It was a supply-and-demand economy of rum, gambling, and prostitutes. Tucked away behind the busy streets were the quieter areas of locals. And near the northern ridges of the island were a couple of plantation homes and respectable private homes. It was a colorful blend of Old World, colonial architecture, and a busy port. In the center of the island lay several shallow lakes tidally connected the moon.

Thatch was known in Nassau as a hard drinker. He was a hell-raiser and womanizer by any standard.

Hornigold and Thatch walked into a favorite watering hole along Nassau Harbor, an open-air structure. The roof was haphazardly made of canvas from old sails. Vines ran up the walls. A couple of whores walked freely around the tavern, up and down the stairs, soliciting their next customers. Women flocked to Thatch. He was charismatic, daring, and rich.

A lonesome, obnoxious sailor was getting too rough with one of the lady employees of the bar.

"Leave the maiden alone," said Thatch as he walked past.

"Fook you, mate."

"I don't give more than one warning. Now take your hands off her."

The sailor spit on the floor near Thatch's boots. "And I don't relinquish my freedom while on shore."

Hornigold grabbed the sailor from behind and placed a choke hold on him. The sailor's face turned red. Thatch removed his flintlock from his waist. He struck the sailor in the jaw with the wooden butt. Hornigold released his grip. The sailor gagged, spit out two teeth, and collapsed to the ground. The bar grew silent.

"Thank'ee," said the West Indies wench, blushing. "Maybe I cun repay somehow?"

"Let us have drink of rum and we can talk about that," Hornigold smiled.

Several pirate patrons approached Hornigold to give him a slap on the back. Thatch stood tall with Hornigold, proud of their fight together.

"A bottle of rum, please, for me mate," Hornigold told the barkeep. "The best that you have."

The wench tried to squeeze herself in between Hornigold and Thatch, not to show favor to either.

"Thatch, sometimes these whores can make a man marry 'em." Hornigold placed his arm around the wench. "Sometimes they can take your heart."

"Aye. I know well they can," said Thatch. "My fourth bride was a whore." He smiled and placed his arm around the West Indies wench as well. She looked up at Thatch and grinned.

"Well then, Thatch. I didn't know you're a taken man," replied Hornigold.

"Every time I port, I get married. I've got a few of them now." Thatch grinned ear to ear. "Whores, taverns, and gold. Now, what's better than that?"

"Another rum," ordered Hornigold.

"What kind of whore do you prefer, Captain?"

Hornigold gulped the last few drops of rum in his tankard. "How about Queen Anne?" As soon as the words left his mouth, Hornigold wished he could retract the statement. He had high regard for the queen and would not even attack an English ship out of respect for her and his homeland. "Forgive me, mates, for speaking ill of the queen. That comment will not leave these doors unless you want a dagger in ye eye."

The tavern's owner, a maiden named Lazue, walked by with a broom, sweeping the floors. She bent over in front of Thatch to pick up some empty rum bottles. She pulled back her long black hair to partially expose her voluptuous breasts. Thatch placed his foot on one of the bottles.

"Pardon me, missy, I haven't seen ya in the past. What's the name?

"Lazue." She smiled at being flirted with. Her deep dimples cut into her cheeks.

"Would ya mind if I fired me cannon through your port hole?"

Lazue swung the straw broom and hit Thatch in the back of the head.

"You're a toad," Lazue shouted.

The rogues leaning against the bar broke out in laughter.

"You've been on the seas too long," said Lazue teasingly. "Your takin' a leap of faith sayin' somethin' like that."

They made eye contact that lasted a few seconds, each enjoying the other's gaze. He took her hand and bowed. "May I see you at a later time?"

Lazue cocked her head sideways, showing a sincere interest in his inquiry. "No, I can't, maybe another time. I'm already taken by a local merchant."

"Never mind him." Thatch opened her fingers, and pressed something into her palm. "We can meet atop the hill this evening, near the outlook, and watch the stars."

"Maybe, maybe not," teased Lazue. "We'll see."

Lazue continued to clean the floors. She walked away, glancing back one more time. She opened her hand; inside was a gift of a beautiful black pearl.

"I have more to give you where 'at came from," Thatch yelled.

Across the table, the West Indies wench had her eye on Hornigold. She brushed her black, braided hair away from her high cheek bones. In broken English, the pretty West Indies said, "Thank for rescuin' me from a pig, Cap'n. He's a scourge."

"Only a foolish man would disrespect or taunt me."

"Sum way I repay you?" She lifted her white skirt. "I have somethin' you may want to buy, no?"

"It's been a while, lassie." Hornigold stretched his arms outward to welcome the wench. "Do ya think you can scrub the barnacles off me rudder first?"

The couple of blokes at the bar overheard their conversation and broke out in laughter. Within moments, the word spread that Hornigold and Thatch were at the tavern and spending money freely. The tavern quickly filled with gamblers, she-devils, and beggars.

"Let's talk about whores, Thatch." Hornigold grinned. "Which do you like the best?"

"I like the one sitting across from you, the West Indies mulatto, the half-breed," said Thatch. "It would be my honor, a present to you for your graciousness. May I buy her for you?"

The pretty West Indies lass smiled and said, "I'm in th' game if you ar'."

"All this talk, Thatch, I miss me Viking lass," said Hornigold. "I need to find her." Hornigold's heart lay with a beautiful blonde-haired teen from Norway. "I haven't seen her for months."

The wench grabbed the hand of Hornigold. In broken English, she whispered, "Come wi' me. I sure that I make you forget about 'er."

"You, my dear, resemble the West Indies lass of my dreams." Hornigold smiled and then finished off his drink in a gulp. Taking her hand, they slowly walked up the steps into an open-air room.

In the corner of the open-air tavern, another pretty, young half-breed gazed at Thatch as he sat alone at the wooden table. She approached him in a seductive walk and bent over to reveal her breasts in front of his face.

She gave Thatch a deep kiss and smiled. "Eros seizes me, Cap'n."

Thatch gulped his last drop of rum. Uncharacteristically, he shed his outer armor of crassness and melted in his own desire.

"Your slender waist and bubblies are as revealing as the stars at midnight, lassie." Thatch kissed her right hand.

"I overheard you say that you like West Indies ladies the best. I am from Montserrat. Is that to your liking?

"My sweetheart has the most delicious lips." Thatch smiled.

"Lay your heart against my heart, Cap'n. Lay your lips on mine. Let me lie in your arms. I want to cover you in love."

Thatch, for a second, revisited his mother's words: *Treat ladies like you treat your mum.*

Thatch embraced the lady from Monserrat. "I want to gorge on you, lassie, but not like most. Let me make love to you, like a midnight storm off the coast, lightning and thunder in our hearts."

"Oh Cap'n, I never expected such words uttered to someone like me."

"Let me give you the prize of love," Thatch said softly.

Hand in hand, the lady of Monserrat escorted Thatch up the stairs and into her private room. A breeze from an open window carried in the perfume aura of jasmine. She inhaled deeply and removed a locket from her braided hair. Thatch caught his breath as the braid fell apart onto her chest.

"Now ye're are under my spell, Cap'n."

In late afternoon, Thatch's prized wench stood on top of the second floor and watched her lover walk down the stairs into the tavern. She leaned over the bannister and clutched a canvas bag.

Thatch turned around and hollered, "Look inside."

The wench opened the bag. She gasped at the sight of an uncut emerald. "Thank you, Cap'n." The sensuous lady of Monserrat clutched the emerald to her heart. "I shall miss you."

"You never know what happens in life, missy, even in matters of the heart." Thatch looked up the stairs and saluted her. "Thank you."

Hornigold was standing at the bar waiting for Thatch. He smiled and placed his hand on Thatch's shoulder and said, "You're right, the half-breed is incomparable."

"I know, for I have just returned me-self from an afternoon of delight with a French half-breed from Monserrat." Thatch smiled. "I rode the waves of rapture."

"The half-breeds, Thatch, they really are delightful and beautiful," said Hornigold.

The barkeep placed a bottle of rum on the wooden bar. Thatch filled his tankard to the top with the best rum in the tavern. He reached into his side belt for a leather bag filled with gunpowder and then sprinkled a handful into the rum. He pulled out some flint, lit the gunpowder, and set the rum on fire.

Thatch held his tankard high. "Listen, scalawags, I drink this toast to me newfound mentor and only captain. And by me own blood, ye have me allegiance, Captain Benjamin Hornigold, forever." Thatch looked into Hornigold's eyes and toasted, "May I drink a bowl of brimstone and fire with the devil."

Thatch threw his head back and guzzled the fiery mixture of rum and gunpowder. He wiped the remnants off his chin with his sleeve. He slammed the empty tankard on the wooden counter and ordered another one.

Hornigold watched in disbelief.

In the spring of 1717, Hornigold and Thatch sailed together, but this time as business partners. They left Nassau en route to the Americas, amassing a fortune in silver, gold, and jewelry by capturing ships along the way. Some of the merchant ships carried flour, textiles, and wine. To most that seemed useless, but they knew it was valuable.

"Mate, we have done well. We plundered six ships between Bermuda and the colony of Virginia. We did damage to their trading. The governor of Virginia will be none too happy with us." Hornigold laughed. "He'll probably want me head."

"Aye, and the ships in the Delaware Bay were the easiest pickin's," said Thatch.

"The Royal Navy will be on our tails in no time. We need to head south."

"I agree. Good timing, Captain. I feel the chill in my bones of late. The winds are shifting out of the northeast. We should make good pace."

"It's time to sail back to the Caribbean and enjoy our riches. Tell the crew."

"Aye, Captain. The seas are magnificent there, blue-green. I have a tower on the high hill outside of Nassau. That's th' closest place that I can call home."

Hornigold placed both hands on his cheeks.

"What else are ye thinkin?"

"It's time for me to get married again," Thatch said with a grin.

"Since we left Nassau, I've been thinking a lot of a beautiful lass there. She has me heart," revealed Hornigold. "She is of Viking descent, blonde hair and blue eyes."

"But, I thought you liked the West Indies mulatto?"

"I like 'em all, but this one is special. Like you, she can read and her accent puts me under. That raspy accent, maybe Norwegian. I find her delicious."

"My only true love is gold," Thatch said with a smile.

"Be careful, mate; not all treasure is silver and gold."

"I have me eye on Lazue, Captain. High cheekbones, dark skin, long black hair. She is beautiful as the nighttime heavens."

"Was that the lass in Nassau, the tavern owner's daughter, the one sweeping up? I saw her on the beach as we sailed out of the harbor. She was waving good-bye. I didn't know why then."

Thatch's eyebrows creased. "I didn't see that."

"She was by herself, jumping up and down on the shoreline. She was a young'n, maybe half your age."

"Yep, that's Lazue. She just looks young for her age." Thatch leaned against the stained wooden rail. "I never stay at port long enough to call home and find a permanent wife.

"Do you like her enough to settle in?"

"She met me that night atop Nassau hill."

"I thought you were with the youngin' from Monserrat."

"I was, but that was in the afternoon. Lazue is different. She knows what I love. We were swept out to sea in our thoughts."

"For Christ's sakes, Thatch, is that all you think about? Gold and fookin'?"

"And Jamaican rum. You forgot the rum, Captain."

In November 1717, Hornigold and Thatch approached the Abacos, a chain of islands north of Nassau. By this time, Hornigold had amassed a sizeable fortune and simply wanted to retire.

I have no use for piracy anymore. And the new governor of New Providence, Woodes Rogers, is offering pardons to all pirates. He may give me a new home. It's time to leave this life. I have all the riches a man needs for a lifetime.

Hornigold placed his hand on Thatch's bandolier and looked him in the eye.

"What are ya thinkin', Captain?" asked Thatch.

"It's time to depart and go our separate ways. I hope you learned from me. I saw fire in your soul when we first met—one that doesn't need me to light it anymore. It's time to live a different life, Thatch. Woodes Rogers's pardon is just too good to be true. I get to keep my fortune, ask the Viking mermaid for her hand, and lead a planter's life on a beautiful island."

"Woodes Rogers will be a happy chap, knowing you're done. Have a rum on me when you see him. And let him know, I will remain on the high seas."

"He'll be lookin' for you, mate. And he has the British Naval frigates to aid. You'll need a bigger ship and more firepower."

"Tell the good chap this: Edward Thatch will go through any ships, regardless of flag, like crap through a goose. May God have mercy on him and his allies, because I won't!"

Thatch was quiet, and Hornigold considered his face, which seemed to reflect confusion, or perhaps anxiety.

"Tis it, mate?" Hornigold asked.

"Hmm." Thatch paused. "Why do I know this name, Woodes Rogers? Is he from Bristol?"

"Could be, I don't know." Hornigold became inquisitive. "What's next for you, mate?"

"I may sail past New Providence toward the Lesser Antilles. I can just take me time and wait for those sugar ships to sail by. It's an easy sail from here. I'll just lie in wait and be patient. You taught me that, Captain."

"I have some buccaneer mates in Tortuga. They call themselves the Brethren of the Coast. It's been a stronghold. You can always hide out with them. Like us, they love gold and hate Spain."

"Do any disfavor you?" asked Thatch.

"No, a lot served with me when I was a privateer."

"How did the buccaneers end up in Tortuga?"

"To be rid of them, the Spaniards slaughtered their pigs, their only food. They were forced to leave Hispaniola. No more boars, so they sailed to nearby Tortuga. Spain regretted that. Those buccaneers retaliated. It was a massacre."

"The next ship that I attack, Captain, will be of Spanish flag."

Hornigold smiled. *I taught this man well.*

"Quartermaster, have all of the crew members on deck," yelled Hornigold. "And have 'em bring their tankards filled with rum."

The quartermaster looked at the first gunner. "This must be important. Seldom does the captain talk to everyone at the same time. Help me get everyone at deck."

Hornigold went to his quarters and exited a few seconds later with the best rum on his shelf. He stood on the bow overlooking the flat deck below. A couple hundred men stood before him, waiting to hear his speech.

"I bring you here today to announce my separation. I will be leaving here soon."

The entire ship was silenced by those few words. Shocked and in despair, the crew remained quiet.

Hornigold embraced Thatch like a father hugs a son. "Well, mate, it's time to depart for better seas."

Thatch's eyes welled up with tears. Hornigold proposed a toast to Thatch for the last time. All of the crew raised their tankards, and the clinging of the cups echoed through the deck.

"I say to you, Captain Edward Thatch, one last thing: never let the enemy pick the battle site. Here's luck and a fair wind to ye. May good fortune attend ye."

"And here our ways divide, Captain Benjamin Hornigold. And a long life to you. I bid thee farewell."

The two pirates heartily shook hands, never to see the other again.

Chapter Ten
The Services of the Devil

In November 1717, Thatch continued and arrived off the coast of Martinique. He lay in wait in the transatlantic shipping lanes. Thatch's ship rolled gently in the light, lazy wind of the Caribbean. The sun started to shift in the afternoon, playing odd tricks with the clarity of the water.

The quartermaster scratched his head. "Gentlemen, stay in the shipping lanes. Keep your eyes on the horizon; leave no chance to running aground." He carefully looked at the depth of the water beneath the ship.

The lookouts sat on the high perch to observe sea-grass and water color. One of the lookouts spotted a sail.

"Captain, there's a large vessel on the horizon!" yelled Blackwood.

Christopher Blackwood was Thatch's first mate. The crew referred to him as "Blackbeard's Claw." He was feared and a ferocious fighter. He led many of the boardings on enemy ships.

"Er be damned. Hand me your spyglass and let me see firsthand. And be quick about it," said Thatch.

He peered through the spyglass and clearly saw a large merchant vessel flying under a French flag. The ship of Thatch's dreams was about to sail into full view.

Thatch looked again, but this time with a naked eye. To the southeast, a massive ship sailed toward him. The spyglass fell onto the deck, his jaw dropped, and he thought, *This must be a slave ship.*

"Blackwood, what is our exact location?"

Latitude 14 degrees 27 minutes north, nearly sixty miles west of Martinique."

"Makes perfect sense, mate; the French control Martinique. Prepare the crew to attack immediately. And raise the black flag."

"Aye, sir."

Captain Pierre Dosset, pilot of the slave ship, pulled out his spyglass and looked back over the sea. The sails on Thatch's ship grew larger and larger inside the lens. They were getting closer.

"Lieutenant, I don't like what I see!" Dosset exclaimed.

"What, sir?"

"Take a look through my spyglass. What do you make of it?"

As François Ernaud zeroed in on the sails, his stomach went into his throat.

"What do you make it to be?" Dosset asked anxiously.

"Two pirate ships with black sails—one large and a smaller sloop. Both have their black flags raised now. I'm guessing a couple hundred men. You better take a look."

Captain Dosset was stunned as he peered through the spyglass again.

"You don't suppose . . ."

"I think so. None other than Blackbeard, Captain."

"Tell the helmsman to change course and turn a hundred and eighty degrees."

As the crew adjusted the rigging, the sails tilted leeward and the ship lost ground. The wind no longer supported their getaway.

"Damn it to hell! They are pursuing, and we slow down. The black flags are less than fifteen minutes away. Ernaud, what do you suggest?"

"Can't outmaneuver, sir. We are about to be pinned from opposing quadrants."

Thatch took dead aim at the massive French ship and ordered the attack.

"Stand by. We'll all fire together. All ports. Cannons ready. Guns forward. Fire! Attack, mates; keep pursuing."

"In the name of the queen, we're going to murder and pillage those fookin' French bastards. We don't stand by—we attack. Don't let up," said Thatch as he stood on the upper deck.

The echo of "aye, aye, sir" circled the ship.

"And listen, mates," Thatch yelled. "Ye got to spill their blood, or they will spill yours! When shells are hitting all around you, wipe the dirt off your face and realize that instead of sea salt, it's the blood and guts of your mates."

Thatch waved his hands above his head and motioned for Blackwood to see him. In all the chaos, Blackwood ran the length of the ship weaving in and out of crew members.

"You call, Captain?"

"Blackwood, once we board, order the men to rip 'em up the bellies with the daggers and use the flintlocks to shoot them in the guts."

"I hate those whiney French almost as much as the lyin', filthy Spaniards."

The Queen's War of England against France and Spain was ingrained in every sailor's bones, including Blackwood's.

"We're not going to just shoot the sons-of-bitches, we're going to rip out their living goddamned guts and use them to swab the deck. We're going to murder those lousy French Hun cocksuckers by the bushel basket," said Thatch.

With twelve guns on one ship and eight on the other, the firepower of both ships unleashed a splattering of cannonballs toward the French ship. The swivel cannons exploded with a deafening sound. White plumes of smoke engulfed the ship. Some cannonballs splashed alongside the French ship as others hit the bulwark, and some flew over the deck.

"Continue to attack, mates; do not let up. Gunners, prepare for another volley!" Thatch barked.

The French cannons fired back, missing each time. Thatch smiled and laughed at the futility of their response.

A second volley of cannon fire was launched from the flat trajectory cannon.

"For Christ's sakes, don't shoot at the waterline. I need this ship intact. Do not sink it. All those with small armaments, align to the starboard and fire when ordered," commanded Thatch.

The prized ship was the twenty-six-gun *La Concorde*. And it was loaded with a rich cargo of gold dust, money, plate, and jewels. *La Concorde* was built to haul slaves from the Congo River in Africa to Saint Dominique. Four hundred fifty-five slaves were on board.

"Small armaments, fire away!"

Captain Cole, the pilot-navigator, placed the ship perfectly parallel to starboard and boxed in the French vessel. Cole was the best on the open seas, especially in battle. No one doubted his skills. Thatch was very fortunate to have him; he was loyal and smart. He was worth his own weight in gold.

"Captain Dosset, we are outmanned and outgunned. For the rest of us, please raise the white flag and surrender, in the name of God. If not, we shall all perish," Lieutenant Ernaud pleaded.

A cascade of musket balls penetrated the hull, and the French crew members started to fall on deck and into the water. Now within fifty yards, the captains could see each other, eye to eye. Thatch looked at Dosset, laughed, and made a hand sign, as if to cut his throat.

Dosset wisely acquiesced. "Ernaud, launch the flag now."

'Prepare to board, mates! And this take is for Hornigold," ordered Thatch.

Cole continued to get as close as possible without ramming the sides.

"Throw the grabbling hooks overboard. Latch on to the sides and don't miss," Cole commanded to the starboard crew. "All others, take the crow's feet and throw them on their deck."

Crew members tended to work barefoot to avoid slipping on a wet deck. Crow's feet were small iron spikes that looked like stars. They inflicted terrible pain when stepped on and at the very least, created confusion.

"Blackwood, go first with fifty men," Thatch yelled.

Blackwood boarded and observed the mangled carnage of crew and slaves. Blood and partial limbs lay about on the deck. Wherever he looked, men screamed in pain.

Ernaud approached from behind and startled Blackwood, who pulled out his flintlock pistol and pointed it at the forehead of Ernaud.

"I'll blast you out to sea if you make a move."

"You have no right to be on *La Concorde*," Ernaud boldly stated.

Blackwood looked Ernaud in the eye. "I'll choke those words down your throat. Blame yourself for your own death."

Blackwood placed the end of the pistol between his eyes. Ernaud winced, the sun lines on his neck and eyes tightened. He felt the uneven iron of the barrel against his forehead. His daughter's face, Adrienne, flashed before him.

Ernaud closed his eyes and whispered, *"Our Father who art in Heaven, hallowed be thy name . . ."*

Blackwood pulled the trigger on the flintlock pistol. Ernaud gasped. Yellow smoke repelled into his face. The smell of burnt sulfur filled the air. The pistol inexplicably misfired.

Cole, the pilot-navigator, watched closely nearby as Ernaud fell to his knees, sobbing.

"Take your death like a man; quit crying like a li'l wench. Cole, have someone retrieve Black Caesar."

Three crewmen scampered down the deck to find the enforcer, Black Caesar. Caesar was known for his towering size and strength. He made merchant sailors quiver in their boots.

"Lieutenant, you're amid a scurvy savagery; it'd be smarts of ya to keep your langy-loving tongue where it belong, from here on out," Blackwood quipped.

"But—" Ernaud decided not to finish his thought, for fear of being beaten.

"I'll feed yer pagan liver to the seas yet. Shut up, fool."

Blackwood removed his cutlass from the scabbard. The cutlass was different from most, one side for striking and the other for cutting. He placed both hands on the guard and raised it above his head to split Ernaud's skull.

Simultaneous to the skull splitting, Thatch and other pirates boarded the ship.

"Blackwood, stop. I need the lieutenant and his captain," bellowed Thatch.

Blackwood shook his head and placed the cutlass inside his belt and not the scabbard. "Frenchman, you must have a black cat's eye in your pocket," snarled Blackwood. He was annoyed by Ernaud's extreme stroke of fortune.

Thatch pushed Ernaud out of the way and confronted Blackwood.

"You and Caesar round up the surgeon, the pilot, gunsmiths, and the master carpenter. Interrogate all of them, especially the carpenter. Do not harm them. I'll smack these two Frenchmen about the ears."

"I'll rip them up the gut if need be, Captain," said Blackwood.

"No, hell no. You won't need to."

"Why, Captain?"

"The Frenchmen, they are all cowards—always have been. They laugh like frogs; their Adam's apples bulge out of their necks."

Blackwood thought about the image and said, "Maybe I will slice one out and see."

"Only if they don't tell us what we need to know. But do not, unless I tell you. They will spill their guts, you'll see."

"Blackbeard's Claw . . . I like me name, Captain. It befits me reputation."

After a few minutes of searching, Blackwood and Caesar returned. The men lined up on the main deck for everyone to see. On their knees, each was interrogated and hit about the head with pistols.

"Surgeon, there is a lot of carnage about your ship. And you may be the next," threatened Caesar. He removed a scalpel from a medicine bag and placed it against the neck of the surgeon.

"I may put an inch of your knife into your veins. Where is the gold on board?"

"I do not know," replied the surgeon.

Caesar inserted the knife deeper into the tissue and cuts his skin from right to left. Blood spurted onto his hand.

"There is no need to go further," the surgeon muttered. "I may be the one who saves your life someday."

Caesar knew the value of a surgeon from his own pirating days in the Florida Keys. He lost many men during that time.

"Surgeon, would you be listed in the services of the devil?" asked Caesar.

"You spare my life, and I will save yours, when in the need," the surgeon replied.

"Thatch appreciates the skill of a surgeon as well. I know this firsthand. Tend to any of our wounded and leave yours and the slaves to die."

Caesar looked to the front deck. He saw two others hanging *La Concorde's* navigator from the bowsprit.

"We have no need for that navigator; make him wince with pain. Hang him by the thumbs from the yardarm," Caesar ordered.

Cole looked in wonderment and thought, *That may be me some day if captured by the British Naval frigates.*

"I plead, do not hang me; let me be a part of your crew. I will serve you faithfully."

The navigator was strung up with rope wrapped tightly around his thumbs only. His legs wiggled back and forth in the air.

Caesar asked for the gunsmiths next, two in total.

"Where is the gold?"

Terrified, one of the gunsmiths stated, "We do not know."

"I'll have none of this. Gunsmiths, proceed to commit suicide."

The gunsmiths were forced to place their pistols into their throats. The hard steel choked and gagged each one. Vomit flew up around the barrel and out their mouths.

"Pull the trigger or I will do it for you," demanded Caesar.

Neither of the gunsmiths would attempt suicide.

One at a time, Caesar stood over the gunsmiths. He placed his dagger against their eyelids. The dagger was slowly inserted into their eyeballs.

Neither could tolerate the pain of their eyes being cut out. Each of them pulled the trigger, blowing out their esophagus and torso. Blood spewed; bits and pieces of human flesh lay on the deck like sawdust.

The cook stepped forward next, shaking uncontrollably.

"Where is the gold?"

"Like the others, I do not know."

"I will carve up your gizzard and fry it for supper. Now, where is the gold?" Caesar demanded.

"I don't know. But I do know who does."

"Who?"

"The cabin boy knows."

"Blackwood, save the cook. He tells no lies. Unlike the navigator, we can always use him."

"Step aside, cook; life has been spared."

The last to be interrogated was the master carpenter. Blackwood and Caesar took part in the questioning.

"Master carpenter, you have built a beautiful ship. If you do not tell, I'll keelhaul you all the way back to Nassau," threatened Caesar. "I'll tie that line around your neck and drag you under the ship. The barnacles will cut you like a razor."

"I built a special compartment in the hold. But I am too big. Find the cabin boy; he is small enough to crawl in the hole."

"You best not be a lyin' or a split tongue you will have."

"It will be there. Find the cabin boy. I request that Blackbeard be told of my honesty and that my life be guaranteed."

"Master carpenter, the captain requested to speak with you personally. Do you wish to join us?" Blackwood asked.

"I am tired of being on a slave ship. There is a lot of disease and bloody flux on board. It smells. Had I known beforehand, I would not be here," the master carpenter replied.

"Let me give you a hint, mate. Tell the captain that you will help repair the ship. That will be good news for him. And don't torment me and I will assure your place."

The only men to escape the wrath of Black Caesar were the surgeon, cook, and master carpenter. All others perished at their own hands.

The cabin boy, Louis Arot, hid in the hold and overheard the conversations. He lifted the trap door and fled to retrieve the gold. He returned by himself and approached Caesar.

"I have a bag that you asked for. But it's gold dust, not gold bars. Please spare my life," pleaded Louis.

"That's it? Gold dust?"

"Yes, it's in this leather pouch. It has a lot of value."

Caesar took the pouch and placed it over his shoulder. It was surprisingly heavy. The dust felt like a bar of gold.

"It's time for us to see the captain. Everyone on their feet," commanded Caesar.

The hostages walked toward the front deck awaiting their fate from Thatch. Despair and death were in their eyes.

"Captain, the surgeon, cook, and master carpenter convinced us to save them and volunteer their services to your ship," stated Caesar with a smile. "The cabin boy asked for your friendship."

"I will speak to them later. Take them to Dosset's quarters. I need more time with this captain."

Dosset stood by himself, in shock.

"Captain Dosset, you are a coward," said Thatch. "I know that because it's in your blood. Tell me about this vessel, or I'll filet your skin like my favorite sea urchin."

"First, please don't kill me. I will tell you whatever you want."

"Stop with the quibbling, Captain."

"It's been a horrible journey." Dosset's broken English was difficult to understand. "We endured many strong storms to get here. I lost most of my crew to disease and death."

"I wondered why your attack was held so useless, your ship slowed."

"I could only bluff my war with you. I had twenty-five men who could fight."

"No one escapes my grasp. But why did you slow?"

"As you came closer, my first mate and I felt a growing sense of terror," said Dosset. "Your sails grew larger and larger. I saw your sloops raise the black flag with the death's head. I ordered the helmsman to swing. But we lost wind and drifted slowly to a stop."

"You should shoot your helmsman and throw him overboard."

"When you boarded, I knew it was you. I heard that you look like the devil with fire and smoke clouds around your head."

Thatch lit hemp and saltpeter pellets tied to his hair and beard to heighten his terrifying appearance. He commandeered ships with little to no struggle with the appearance as a devil incarnate.

"Most on board are African slaves, Dosset. Captain Hornigold told me of this new business called the Triangle Trade. Now, I see. This is the biggest ship that I ever laid me eyes on."

"Her owner is going to be very angry with me," said Dosset. "I ask that you not burn her to ashes and ambers."

"Who is the owner of this magnificent vessel?" inquired Thatch. "Its design is none that I have seen before."

"A French slaver, Monsieur Rene Montaudoin of Nantes. He and his family build the best vessels on the sea."

"I do not know of Nantes; tell me."

"Nantes is a French port, located on the Loire River. The Montaudoins are the principle ship owners. Three quarters of the ships carrying slaves are from Nantes."

"So the French control the slave market?"

"We did a lot of business with the colonies. But the slave market grew and grew. That's where the best ships are built to haul slaves. I need to get these slaves to the market. It's my duty and what I was paid for. Please let me do that."

"I have bad news, Dosset. *LaConcorde* is now mine."

Dosset looked on in disbelief. "I'm happy to be alive, but my ship? It's all I have."

"I will spare your life, the lives of your slaves. Take my smaller sloop to Martinique. It's an even trade. One last thing: your best slaves will go with me."

"My owner will have my blood."

Thatch knew this was going to be his ship as soon as he set eyes on it. *La Concorde* was bigger and better than Black Sam Bellamy's *Whydah*. It was large enough and powerful to fight the British Naval frigates.

Thatch and Dosset walked throughout the ship's slave hold, separated into pens. Thatch wanted the strongest. He could not help but notice marks on the backs of the slaves.

"You have branded all the slaves with the initials of *La Concorde*. You have the instincts of a pirate—torture and control."

"A lot of the scarring was already there, Captain. In Africa, body markings are a ritual. The deep skin cuttings show what tribe they belong to."

"The skin has the initials of *La Concorde*."

"We have no other way of establishing our property than to place our name on their backs."

"Point out your best slaves, Dosset. They need to be young, no scurvy or mouth disease, and strong. And no women, they are not allowed on my ship."

Thatch and Dosset walked throughout the pens. The wooden hold reeked with the odors of urine and excrement.

"I counted sixty-five in total. Keep them in chains. I will have Caesar take control of them."

"Caesar? Who is Caesar?" asked Dosset.

"He is also African, as big as a whale, my friend and enforcer."

Dosset and Thatch walked down the steps into the hold of the ship. It reeked of spoiled food and contaminated water.

"Your food supply is rotten. Maggots and worms crawl in and out of the feed. The water barrels have dead rats in them. My goodness, at least throw them overboard."

"Now you know my plight."

The ship had been on the seas for nearly eight months. Most of the crew on *La Concorde* suffered scurvy and dysentery; the men would be useless to Thatch.

Thatch walked by a large room filled with textiles. "Where did you get these fine materials of textile?"

"The cloth was from India," boasted Dosset.

"Me buxom beauty Lazue will love and cherish the colors. I will give all of it to her as a present."

"What shall I tell the authorities?"

"When they ask, I traded you ships." Thatch smiled. "Take the remaining slaves to Martinique. Your owner should be pleased with that."

"Monsieur Montaudoin will be outraged that you have his vessel. He will come after you."

"I will be long gone. Tell them Thatch has a heart, but I may cut his out if messed with. Ever hear of a French pirate by the name of François L'Olonnais?" asked Thatch.

"Of course, we are both French. But that was years ago. He terrorized the Spaniards and Portuguese along the coastlines of South America. I don't know how he tells the difference between them."

"He beheads Spaniards when he boards. He leaves one alive who can tell the story. His last board, he drew his sword, sliced into a Spanish prisoner's chest, pulled out his heart, and ate it."

"I heard he bit and gnawed it with his teeth, like a ravenous wolf," said Dosset.

"Tell Montaudoin that. Your owner has no idea who he's fookin' with. I will do the same to his. Do you know how he died . . . L'Olonnais?"

"Never did hear."

"His vessel ran aground near Panama. The Kuna Indians tore him in pieces . . . alive, throwing his body limb by limb into a fire and his ashes into the air. Not a trace nor memory might remain of such an inhuman creature. The pirate Charles Vane is much like him."

"If it not for my allegiance to France, I would join you."

"Dosset, you're dreamin', mate. Never. I hate your cowardly blood and what you stand for. Now, leave before I change my mind."

Thatch sailed further south with his new ship to the island of Bequia. It was a long-established watering hole for privateers and buccaneers. The island had better protection than the other outlying chain of islands. Unlikely to be bothered there, Thatch retrofitted *La Concorde*.

"Master carpenter, it's now time to put your skill to use. You have my crew to assist. *La Concorde* will be my flagship."

"What do you require?"

"I want speed. Strip the upper deck with a lot of space to maneuver. I want all forty swivel guns placed there. And remove the wooden holds and pens for the slaves."

"It's a French design by the owner, Monsieur Montaudoin. He wanted the ship to be built for weight, not speed. I can cut the stern as well; it will be swifter."

"Cut some of the forecastle if need be. There is no need for the upper deck to be so large. I want at least three masts, and alter the rigging with larger square rigs. Speed. Make it fast . . . my newfound friend."

"Brilliant, Captain. Absolutely brilliant."

"Use my crew to scrape the hull. It's loaded with growth and worms. I have sulfur and tar to give it a complete makeover. By the way, do you know anything about the navigation instrument we found on board?"

"No," said the master carpenter, "but the navigator that was strung on the yardarm did."

Thatch winced. He now regretted the order to string up the navigator.

"Captain, Monsieur Montaudoin will never recognize his ship. It will be a maritime fortress after I am done. You will be pleased."

"I want the best."

After the master shipbuilder was done, Thatch had a massive three-hundred-ton fighting ship, more than one hundred feet long. It allowed for a fast attack and getaway. Nothing could compare to its speed and maneuverability, not even Black Sam Bellamy's *Whydah*.

Thatch now commanded one of the largest warships on the seas and developed an even more of a fearsome reputation. He was a person and pirate to be reckoned with.

"Master carpenter, one last thing. Rid of the name *La Concorde* on the back of the ship. It will now be known as the *Queen Anne's Revenge*."

The combination of Thatch's appearance and the largest warship on the water was incredibly disturbing to every merchant captain sailing on the high seas.

Chapter Eleven
Physical Appearance and Intimidation

Blackbeard in Smoke and Flame, Frank Schoonover, 1922

Blackbeard's image—a tortuous pirate from hell—was constructed to perfection. So effective was it that his persona has lasted three hundred years. He was a dazzling producer and director of battle. And he learned well from his mentor, Captain Benjamin Hornigold, that fear and terror were everything.

The ladies of Nassau and Port Royal knew differently. To them, he was a generous man who had a way with words. They liked his swagger—dashing and unapologetic. He was welcomed at every tavern in every port.

Part of Blackbeard's show of intimidation and dominance was the flag on the *Queen Anne's Revenge*. It depicted a skeleton spearing a heart and toasting the devil, while blood dripped from the heart. Before attacking a ship, the flag was raised to forewarn his enemies that a boarding was imminent.

The devil incarnate was about to strike again.

The *Queen Anne's Revenge* sailed north from Martinique, boarding more and more merchant ships along the way: the *Great Allen*, the *New Division*, the *Montserrat Merchant*, and the *Margaret*.

The boarding of the *Great Allen* was typical of the viciousness becoming more frequent. Thatch was about to inflict fear and maim on those who did not abide by his requests. It was time to perform again.

"Men, board the ship and do it quickly. Caesar, put the captain of the *Great Allen* in leg irons," Thatch snapped.

Thatch jumped onto the ship and approached the captain in a terrorizing manner. He placed his right hand on the inside of his long black coat. His belt left an indelible impression, showcasing an assortment of sharpened knives and daggers.

He tugged on his long, black beard and asked, "What's the name?"

"Captain Taylor."

Thatch looked around the deck and observed a timid crew. Taylor was taken back by and furious about the intrusion.

"What do you carry?"

Taylor stated abruptly, "Nothing, we are empty, headed back to port."

"And where is your harbor?"

"Boston."

"Caesar, shackle the captain and whip him soundly."

"Why? I tell the truth. I am abiding by your questions. I have done nothing wrong."

"You are from Massachusetts. Your governor wants me dead. Let him know what my crew did to you."

"I refuse to be treated like this," Taylor stated defiantly.

"Hold your tongue, or I'll bring bloody death to you."

"You will regret this."

"Caesar, beat this man senseless. Blackwood, take five men and search for any valuables. Pillage and take all valuables on board."

It didn't take long to search the ship's quarters and hold. The crew was broke, and there wasn't any cargo. However, Blackwood fumbled through the Taylor's desk and made a startling find.

Hurriedly, Blackwood ran back to the front of the ship, "Captain, the only thing I could find of value was this cup. It's made of gold, of all things."

"It's worthy for sure. I'll use it to toast on the next taking."

"Shall the beatings begin?" Caesar asked.

"No. The captain was a sufficient beating."

Caesar smiled. "Let me take my cutlass out and I'll see the color of his insides."

"It's more important for the captain and his crew to remain alive. I want his governor to know what we did."

Caesar reluctantly obeyed the order.

Thatch wanted the governor of Massachusetts to hear a firsthand account of how treacherous he could be. And a warning that he was not a man to be chided.

"Caesar, lift the anchor and spread the sails. Tell Blackwood to take a course to the nearest island. We will put the crew on shore there."

"Shall I place any others in leg irons?"

"No, leave them be."

Within the hour, the *Great Allen* and the *Queen Anne's Revenge* were off the shore of the beautiful island of St. Vincent. Placid waters, blue-green in color, with the bottom visible to the eye.

"Captain, I gave you my Bible oath. I harmed no one on your ship. As we stand here, I release all of you. I bid you farewell."

"What about my ship?"

"It's mine now."

Taylor was devastated and could not believe what he just heard. He spent his entire life at sea and yearned to command such a vessel. And now it was gone in a second.

"It's too bad that you're from Boston, mate, or I would have left you go."

Taylor was on his knees, moaning in pain. He wiped away some blood dripping down his lip.

"You beat me, take my ship, and then leave us stranded on an island? What kind of person are you?"

"I'm the devil, Taylor."

"So you beat me to uphold your reputation? Be done with it; let me perish, and go to your eternal hell."

"I will let you live. It's the best way. Your governor would do more than a bloody face to me."

"All of this because you don't like my governor?"

"Sorry, mate, you don't understand, but the governor of Massachusetts will."

Motionless, Taylor asked, "Now what?"

Thatch towered over Taylor and looked down at him. He then scanned the *Great Allen* sitting off shore.

"Tell your crew to move the goods onto my smaller sloop. It's called the *Revenge*. Another pirate, Stede Bonnet, will oversee the transfer."

"How will I know him?"

"He is the only pirate that wears a dress. It's white; can't miss him, mate."

Thatch placed his boot against Taylor's back and kicked him forward. Taylor fell down on the beach, face first, mixing blood and sand on his face.

All of the provisions were moved onto the *Revenge*. It took Taylor's men more than a half day in the hot sun.

Tired, hungry, and thirsty, Taylor's men were hopelessly stranded on a deserted island.

And the *Great Allen* was empty. It appeared to be a ghost ship.

"Are we going to add this to our fleet, Captain?" Blackwood asked.

"No . . . burn it."

"Captain Thatch, this is such a useful vessel. We have a couple hundred men now. It's perfect. I ask that you permit me to command it and become a captain."

"BURN IT, I SAID."

It was December 5, 1717, Crab Island, Antiqua. Another take was on the horizon. The massive *Queen Anne's Revenge* unloaded a single shot at the *Margaret*.

"Raise the flag and fire one over the bow," Thatch ordered. Wisps of white smoke emerged from the cannon. The captain, Henry Bostock, chose not to fire back. He recognized the black flag and immediately surrendered.

Captain Cole carefully placed the massive ship adjacent to the sloop. Now, within shouting distance, Thatch yelled, "I want you and your best five; row over and board my ship."

The crew threw grappling hooks onto the *Margaret* and pulled it closer.

Like long lost friends, a couple of crew members on the *Queen Anne's Revenge* helped Bostock up the side of the ship and onto the deck.

"Blackwood, while I speak to the good captain, ransack his ship. Put anything of value onto Stede Bonnet's sloop and any excess onto the *Queen Anne.*"

"Aye, sir, and if there are beatings to do, let me know."

"Blackwood, why is everyone on Bonnet's sloop wearing grease and soot under their eyes?"

"Bonnet called it kohl. The Indians wear it. It shields their eyes from the sun and makes them like warriors. It works."

"A dress and now cosmetics? What is wrong with that chap? Tell fookin' Bonnet this, real pirates don't wear dye on their eyes.'

Blackbeard was a gargantuan man with wild, maniac eyes and unkept, long black hair. His beard ran down his chest intertwined with pigtails and tied with twists of ribbon.

"Captain, your eyes stare through me. I have no quarrel with you," Bostock stated.

Thatch removed his large feathered tricorn and stated, "Welcome aboard the *Queen Anne's Revenge*."

He placed one hand on his cutlass and the other on his bandolier of pistols. Yellow smoke circled about his head from lit, embedded pellets in his black hair and beard.

"What do you carry on board?"

"Animals."

"Animals—that's it? Where is your gold?"

"There is none. We aren't that type of merchant ship."

"Don't lie or I will peel you like a fresh mango," threatened Thatch.

"Look around for yourself."

"I see that. You bring me no argument, Captain. Come, drink rum and eat turtle with me. We can talk."

Bostock was an Englishman as well. Most of their conversation was about the England's war with Spain and France. In reality, Thatch wanted to know the whereabouts of the Spanish Armada Fleet. Bostock avoided any conversations of other merchant ships.

"Captain Thatch, I've been told that King George issued an Act of Grace, pardoning all pirates for their crimes, provided they surrender. What do you make of it?"

"Yes, I know. Captain Hornigold told me of such. He was going to abide by the act and seek a pardon from Woodes Rogers."

"And you?"

"Like I told Hornigold, I'll go through any merchant ship, regardless of flag, like crap through a goose."

"Well, we have one thing in common."

"What's that?"

"We need to stop the Spanish control in La Florida and the Caribbean. None denying."

"The 1715 Spanish Plate Fleet perished off the coast of La Florida," Thatch reminded Bostock. "There wasn't much treasure left after the hurricane. That crippled Spain."

"I heard. Eleven or twelve Spanish galleons went down. Hundreds of thousands of pieces of eight and gold bars were lost at sea along its coastline."

"The Spanish recovered some treasure near Palma de Ays but were unable to protect the wrecks. The pirates Vane, Jennings, and Black Sam Bellamy got there before me. Vane and Jennings did well."

"Charles Vane is a mad man," Bostock emphatically stated. "Maybe the French disease got to his brain."

"I know him. He is crazy regardless of disease. You should have been a pirate, Bostock. Instead you choose to carry smelly animals, cows and pigs; what is wrong with you?"

"It's safe and profitable."

"I enjoyed your company throughout the day. It's time to depart. Bostock, you may leave whenever you wish."

Bostock felt relieved. Unharmed, he and his crew returned to Saint Blackwood Island (St. Kitts) after spending the entire day eating and drinking Jamaican rum on the *Queen Anne's Revenge*. It was a reprieve of sorts for him; a spacious ship, good food, tasty rum, and an intriguing conversation with Blackbeard himself.

Bostock sailed back to Antigua and immediately reported the pirate act to Governor Hamilton.

"Your Honor, I have grave news. Our ship was boarded by pirates. The captain was a frightening man, but he did not harm us. I have not seen anything like it."

"What was taken off your ship?" Governor Hamilton inquired.

"He did not want provisions but he seized our cattle and hogs. Our cutlasses and firearms were taken from us. He took possession of my books and navigational instruments."

"Were there secrets inside?"

"No, but just as important, the book was years of work. It had the mathematical tables of the sun's shadows. And my instrument was the best to work out latitudes. It cannot be replaced."

"You will need to give a deposition. List the details in an affidavit before a judge. I will send it to London."

"Of course."

Historically, this was the first recorded account of Thatch's appearance and is the source of his cognomen: Blackbeard.

"What did this pirate look like?" Governor Hamilton inquired.

"He was a tall, spare man with a very black beard, which he wore very long."

Governor Hamilton was concerned and asked, "What about his crew? I'm interested in them as well."

"He had a crew of three to four hundred men. There was a lot of silver on board, as well as a 'fine cup' taken from a Captain Taylor."

"Did he torch any of the crew?"

"On his last boarding, just the captain. A Massachusetts chap by the name of Captain Taylor. A crew member told me an interesting story. When he boarded, the navigator had a diamond ring on his finger. Blackbeard took a fancy to it."

"And?"

"He argued and resisted Blackbeard. To set an example, Blackbeard chopped it off, finger and all, and took the diamond ring."

"Brutal, this pirate."

"Even his own men fear him. I saw a gent by the name of Israel Hands. He walked with a limp. I asked him why. He looked down and away and did not respond."

"Probably a leg wound from one of their battles," the governor guessed.

"Another mate told me this story. They were off the coast of Charles Town looking for medicine. One night, Blackbeard and another man sat at a table in the captain's quarters. Rum was being guzzled down. Israel sat down and joined in the conversation. Within a couple of hours, all three were drunk. For some unknown reason, Blackbeard drew out a pair of pistols and cocked them under the table. Blackbeard blew out the candle, crossed his arms beneath the table, and pulled the triggers of both pistols. One misfired, but the slug from the other tore through Hands's knee and crippled him for life. When the pirates on board asked for an explanation, Thatch's only answer was a curse: 'If he did not now and then kill one of them, they would forget who he was.'"

Governor Hamilton pounded the table with his fist and stated, "The Royal Navy needs to find this barbarian and hang him at the nearest port."

In a defensive manner, Bostock stated, "My impression, Your Majesty, is that Blackbeard could be merciful to those who co-operated, but woe to those who did not."

Governor Hamilton looked into Bostock's eyes and stated, "You must be mad man yourself. You're out to sea too much; the sun and sea effects your thinking, Captain. You're lucky to be alive."

"Possibly."

"Go and complete the deposition, then come back. I have some rum and delicious boar from Jamaica. We can talk some more then."

While their talks proceeded, Thatch sailed out of the English territory into Spanish-controlled countries. He spent the winter of 1717-1718 cruising the Gulf of Mexico, especially the coastline near Veracruz, Mexico, and the Bay of Honduras.

It was perfect. No one knew him there.

Chapter Twelve
Home Away from Home

Word had not reached the Americas about the death of Benjamin Hornigold and the arrest of Woodes Rogers. Thatch was en route to Topsail Inlet with two sloops and Stede Bonnet's *Revenge* trailing behind. As the *Queen Anne's Revenge* sailed deep into the Atlantic Ocean, Thatch scanned a map of the Carolinas lying on his splintered desk. He walked out of his cabin and peered over the side of the ship.

The Caribbean means death to me at the hands of Woodes Rogers. And the only place I may be welcomed is North Carolina. Hell, even the governor of Virginia wants my head for Christ's sake. Time to move a li'l north to see my old friend Governor Eden.

Thatch was alone in thought as he walked along the port side of the ship. He saw Hands and Caesar sitting on a wooden box, talking and drinking rum.

"Hands and Caesar, we need to talk," said Thatch firmly. "I've studied the maps. Topsail Inlet in North Carolina should be our new haven. There will be talk among the crew. I need your support."

"What is so unique about Topsail, Captain?" asked Caesar. "It has a good protective harbor, but it's certainly not Nassau."

"I thought the same thing, Caesar. Ocracoke Island gives us an outlook onto the seas. If we need to conceal, we can sail the smaller sloops into the backwaters on the Pamlico River and up a back creek into the town of Bath."

"We love Nassau, Captain," said Hands disappointedly. "In all my travels on the seas, nothing compares to New Providence."

"I will forever miss the waters, the whores, and me mates at the taverns as well. But we can never go back. Woodes Rogers is waiting to hang us all."

"Hands, that's a fact we need to face," said Caesar. "We need to be a lookin', for better or worse."

"I saved the best for last, lads. Governor Eden of North Carolina offered a pardon the last time. I trust him."

"If that's the case, I think we are all in agreement, Captain," said Caesar. "So will the crew be when they know the alternative. Living is better than dying at the end of a noose."

Hands smiled and nodded in agreement.

"It's settled then. Topsail is our new Nassau," said Thatch. "Make sure the crew understands why."

"Aye, Captain. I think we can all agree to that," replied Hands.

Thatch stood on top of the quarterdeck and looked out over his crew. An orange summer sun started to set on the horizon in the west. His imposing figure cast a large black shadow over the deck below as the end of the day neared.

"Mates, a meeting is in order to decide our next stop. I propose we lay low at Topsail Inlet by Bath Town. It's safe and peaceful. And the good governor of North Carolina will welcome us. I have a chest of goodwill for him."

"We rely upon you, Captain Thatch," blurted out a first mate. "You haven't steered us wrong yet."

Much to Thatch's surprise, the crew was in support; all were looking forward to a new place to call home, where they were free to spend their plunder and get off the high seas for a while.

The entire crew raised their tankards in a salute. Once again, "Aye, Captain" was heard all around.

"To all of you, every last one, I owe my gratitude. And you should take great pride in being a shipmate of a son-of-a-bitch named Blackbeard. You are the best crew ever, on the best ship ever."

A first gunner hollered out, "And we think you are the best captain ever."

"Mates, you can look your grandson in the eye and tell him, 'I trained and fought with the best.' Let them know, no one fooked with Blackbeard. You won't have to look down and say, 'I shoveled horse shit in the governor's barn.'"

Laughter was heard throughout the ship.

"Aye, another toast to our captain," yelled another gunner.

"And lastly, I am personally going to rip out the belly of that son-of-bitch Spotswood. Just like I'd rip the belly of a sea turtle. Ye governor of Virginia wants me head for Christ's sake."

A loud cheer broke out as the crew members slapped one another on the back.

"Mates, in show of me appreciation, let's drink merrily all the way to the Carolinas," said Thatch loudly. "I toast to my crew, the best in the Caribbean. Cooks, feed the best that we have on board. And break out the rum . . .all of it."

Thatch learned from Hornigold that with great risks come great rewards. Life was either a daring adventure or nothing at all.

Set the sails full; let's move on to Topsail," commanded Thatch. "And enjoy the sights. It doesn't get any better. We will drink, eat, and dance all the way."

The fiddlers and singers on board broke out in a triumphant sea shanty, "The Drunken Sailor." The voyage to the Carolinas was going to be fun.

Black Caesar stood nearby, awaiting his personal orders. Israel Hands walked along the outer edge of the ship. He eagerly spread the word to the crew that Topsail Inlet would be their new harbor and haven.

Thatch heard a single fiddler playing an Irish love song in the midst of the night. He was lost in thought.

I wished me Lazue was here. The buxom beauty has me heart, like none other. I love when she looks o'er the side of the ship in the darkness of a moonlit night and plays the violin.

"Captain, are you okay?" asked Caesar.

"Caesar, stay behind. I need to talk with you," Thatch said softly.

The two men had become the best of friends, though one was from Bristol, England, and the other a tribal war chieftain from the Congo. Both understood torture and death. Thatch relied on Caesar as much as Caesar relied on Thatch.

"Caesar, when we first met, you lost your ship and crew north of Key Largo."

"I did, sir. But I fought and gouged all the way to keep it. We were outmanned by well-armed sailors. I left my soul and harem of one hundred on a rock island there. Even had my own prison. But most died, for I could not feed them."

"Then you will certainly understand what I'm thinking. This is a new challenge for all of us. Caesar, if anything happens to me, burn the ship."

Caesar was taken aback by Thatch's resignation. "That would be a shame, Captain. It's the *Queen Anne's Revenge*, the most admirable ship on the high seas. It would be pleasure to command such a beautiful vessel."

Thatch glared at Caesar. "None of your reflection on the matter. Burn it, I said! Do you understand?"

"Yes, sir, you have my honorable word. I will burn it in all of its glory."

"One more thing, Caesar, you're now the lieutenant of the *Queen Anne's Revenge*."

Rum was Thatch's downfall. Uncharacteristically, he would stammer, falter, and lose his sense of judgment and intuition. As they sailed the Atlantic, everyone on board was totally inebriated. Even in daylight hours, the crew lay on deck, passed out in the hot summer sun.

On June 3, 1718, things started to go terribly wrong as the *Queen Anne's Revenge* and the adjoining sloops approached Topsail Inlet. Their judgment was impacted by the amount of Jamaican rum in their blood after days and nights of drinking.

Thatch signaled for Bonnet to pull adjacent to his ship. He hollered across the bow, "Your vessel drafts less than me. Go first; navigate through the shoals so I can see the depth. Either signal or put out markers for the navigator to see."

Stede Bonnet's sloop, the *Revenge*, and two other sloops attempted to navigate the inlet; the *Adventure* commanded by Israel Hands and a small fifteen-ton prize Spanish sloop followed. All three sloops were successful in navigating the comma-shaped entrance of the inlet.

"Navigator, run full sail on the south side of the shoal," commanded Thatch. "Keep the bow on centerline of their rudder markings."

"But we will be unable to see, Captain. A lot of the water is discolored. We should wait for more clarity."

Thatch focused his eyes on the navigator with an evil stare. "I said, stay on centerline!" Thatch relaxed his jawbone as the navigator looked away toward the inlet.

The *Queen Anne's Revenge* followed the three sloops in full sail. Within minutes, the flagship shuddered to a stop. The ship hit a sandbar at the shallowest part of the inlet. The wooden hull jumped on top of the shoal.

"I cannot believe this happened," cried out Thatch.

The force awoke drunkin' crew members as they were thrown forward from the immediate halt onto the sandbar.

"You lards need to get with it and grab onto the main lines and pull tightly." With his teeth clenched, Thatch bellowed, "Get us off this fookin' sandbar, now!"

As soon as Thatch gave the command, the main mast cracked from the force of the hull running up on the shoal. Old wooden timbers crashed on the deck and trapped a drunken crew member underneath.

"We're taking on water, Captain," screamed the boatswain. "It's gushing in on the portside."

Furious, Thatch jumped onto the second deck and looked to the open inlet.

"What in the hell are you doing, Bonnet? You were supposed to warn us," yelled Teach across the bow of the ship. "You will need to pull us off this shoal now."

"I did warn you. You weren't paying attention, Captain."

"You stupid ass, Bonnet," shouted back Thatch.

"Fook you, Captain."

For the first time, ever, Bonnet showed insolence toward Thatch.

"Hands, bring your sloop over and pull me off," yelled Thatch.

"Aye, Captain," said Hands hurriedly.

Thatch was furious. "Throw the ropes and grappling hooks; try to free her off the shoal. And move quickly; the tide is starting to shift back out so sea."

Afraid to make the next move, Hands asked, "Then what?"

"Drag her off the sandbar. We can beach and repair the hull and fix the main on the island."

Hands's crew scrambled on the deck to attach the stern of the *Adventure* to the bow of the flagship.

"All set, Captain," said Hands.

"Ready on this end," Thatch yelled back.

Hands ordered full sail. The *Adventure* caught a burst of sustained southeasterly wind.

"Stop! Stop!" yelled Thatch. "You're pulling me farther onto the sandbar."

The weight of the flagship pulled the *Adventure* downward. Hands also ran aground, tearing enormous holes in the hull, creating more pandemonium.

"You damaged the keel and lower haul. I can see it from the quarter deck. For Christ's sake, what are you two doing to me?"

Both vessels were damaged beyond repair. Two stranded wrecks with water pouring into the hulls. It could not get any worse. The *Queen Anne's Revenge* was doomed. It was simply too massive.

Only Bonnet on his *Revenge* and the prize Spanish sloop were still afloat inside of Topsail Inlet.

"Bonnet, come closer," yelled Thatch. "Leave the *Revenge* behind and go into Bath. See if Governor Eden is there. Let him know what happened."

Bonnet and several of his men took a longboat and rowed up into the swamplands of the Pamlico River into Bath Creek.

"Caesar, after Bonnet is out of sight, board his ship."

"For what purpose?"

"Remove all the treasure, provisions, and armaments off the *Revenge*," ordered Thatch. "Then I will personally take whatever those stupid bastards left on his sloop and maroon them. I cannot tolerate stupidity, drunk or not."

"You takin' his supplies, Captain? Bonnet will be livid." Hands laughed. "Should be about £2500 of plunder on there."

"I'm not done. Caesar, count out the best of the Africans on board," said Thatch in an irritated voice. "Hands, bring the best of the other crew."

"Aye, Captain," said Hands.

"Both of you, listen: young, no rotten teeth, and a broad chest. Let me know how many you have."

"Bonnet is going to be none too happy, Captain," said Caesar.

"Do it quickly before he returns."

Hands and Caesar jumped onboard the *Revenge* and ordered Bonnet's best off their own sloop at gunpoint. There was no resistance from Bonnet's crew.

"Captain, I have sixty from my homeland. And Hands has forty of his own," said Caesar.

"Perfect. Have everyone board the prize sloop. I knew this sloop would come in use someday. That was an easy capture off Cuba from a few months ago."

"For sure," replied Hands.

"Incredibly, it's the only thing I have left. I'm back to where I started. Let's get out of here," ordered Thatch. "There is more on the horizon."

In a cramped fifteen-ton sloop, Thatch left Ocracoke Island to hide for a couple of days. It was a quiet summer evening. He looked back and saw the *Adventure* and the *Queen Anne's Revenge* listing starboard, lifeless.

When Bonnet returned from Bath, everyone was gone. Astonished, he could not figure out what happened. The *Revenge* was left intact inside the inlet with only a few scrappers left onboard.

"Captain Bonnet," said the cook with his head hanging down, "Thatch took everything you had and sailed away. At least he left your ship behind."

That rotten son-of-a-bitch, he takes everything I have and disappears. My ship will truly be vengeful someday. He may be the devil, but I'm the religious man. And Revenge is mine said the Lord.

On the way out of Topsail Inlet, Bonnet spotted part of his crew marooned about a mile north. He picked them up and headed south along the coastline.

Two men were of equal importance: David Herriot, Bonnet's captain, and Ignatius Pell, the boatswain. Both were furious with Thatch.

Herriot, dehydrated from a couple of days without water, wanted revenge. "Captain Bonnet, Thatch is the hole of an ass. He left us here without food and water. He knew we might die. I will relinquish my next plunder if we go after them."

"I feel the same, but we have the upper hand," said Bonnet. "He has only the small prize sloop overloaded with men. He may maroon them as well," said Bonnet.

"You know, Captain, I think Thatch ran his ship aground on purpose," said Herriot. "He got rid of everyone and kept the plunder for himself."

Pellagreed. "He split us up. We just weren't in his plan, Captain. It's that simple. He's a rotten sort."

Bonnet thought for a moment, then stated, "There is no way Thatch would intentionally run the *Queen Anne's Revenge* up on a shoal. His ship represented him and everything he plundered for. Drunk, yes—with more of a drunk crew on his hands, probable. But not intentional, in my mind."

"Sir, I think you are wrong," said Herriot. "Mark well my words, Captain."

"Herriot, let's take a heading of south toward Charles Town. Let's see what their harbor looks like. I don't need captains like Thatch nor his kind anymore," said Bonnet. "We can board and plunder well

Chapter Thirteen
Ignorance Is Bliss

The fall of 1718 was gorgeous. An occasional thunderstorm or a breeze off the ocean cooled the air. The northern winds made their way south into the Atlantic Ocean, creating clear skies and moonlit nights. Fresh air permeated the Carolina coastline.

Thatch lay in wait at Topsail Inlet, adjacent to Ocracoke Island, watching for merchant ships to pass by. He peered through his spyglass and saw a three-mast warship with square rigs out of the southeast. It was approaching the mainland.

"I don't like what I see," Thatch said to a gunner. "Fire a warning shot in their direction." The cannon repelled backward with a puff of white smoke from the starboard side of the sloop. The warship fired one back.

Who in the hell is firing back at me?

The cannon from the warship retracted three more times: *Boom! Boom! Boom!* echoed across the calm waters. Cannonballs fell about one hundred yards in front of Thatch's sloop, intentionally not to cause any damage.

Who is this maniac that dares to fire at me?

The sails grew larger as the ship approached Ocracoke Island. Thatch pulled out his spyglass again from his belt. Three black flags waved briskly in the air from the masts.

It was the insane Charles Vane.

Vane sailed northwest out of Nassau directly to the Americas. There was no trickery on the part of Vane to outwit his pursuers after all.

Mysteriously, Vane stayed offshore of Topsail Inlet, watching Thatch and his crew from his spyglass.

"What is this man up to?" said Thatch to Caesar. "Let's stay put. Let him make the first move."

"He probably doesn't trust what he sees, Captain." Caesar peered over the inlet. "I wouldn't, either."

Soon, more and more notorious pirates sailed into Ocracoke Island. All were seeking shelter to avoid the British Naval Fleet. None of them knew that Governor Rogers had been arrested weeks before and was sent back to England. And no one knew that Captain Benjamin Hornigold perished at sea.

It was the largest pirate fest of all time: eating, drinking, and dancing on Ocracoke Island throughout the day and night. Israel Hands, Calico Jack Rakham, Robert Deal, and Black Caesar were all there. Even Charles Vane finally sailed in. Thatch and his crew jumped off their ship onto the beach and joined in the merriment.

An old buccaneer was on the beach underneath some palms. He fired up some wild boar. Fish and local berries were abundant. Fiddlers played sea shanty songs. A couple of hundred pirates were having the time of their lives.

"Mr. Deal, I hope you had a good voyage," said Thatch. "How are things in Nassau since Rogers took over?" Thatch looked out of the corner of his eye, distracted by a group of pirates walking up the island's shoreline. "Look over there, Deal; here walks the wizard of insanity."

Vane approached with a huge grin on his face. His eyes were wild with anticipation at seeing Thatch. Drenched in sweat, he smelled of salt, tar, and body odor.

"Thatch, quite a time since I clapped my eyes on you last," stated Vane in a soft, raspy voice.

"Vane, you always have a wicked story. What do you have today?"

"Wait till you fookin' hear this one." His demonic stares were enough to shake anyone. "Hornigold turned traitor. He's coming after us," said Vane sharply.

"That's crazy talk, Vane."

"Ask my crew; ask Calico Jack . . . he was there. Hornigold took the pardon."

"I already knew about the pardon. He told me."

"This part, you don't know, Thatch. After Hornigold took the pardon, he cut a deal with Woodes Rogers to hunt down all pirates. You and I are on the list, as number one and number two."

"Are you worried about your life?" asked Thatch.

"No, but he's about to take yours, mate." Vane laughed in his face. "Fool."

Thatch's black, bushy eyebrows squinted with concern. "Does Hornigold know that you're with me?"

"Probably not. I sent a fire ship in the middle of Rogers's fleet, including some man-o'-war. Caught them by surprise, cut through a passage, and sailed directly here."

Thatch grabbed Vane by the collar. "You're the fool. Hornigold will figure out your northwest departure from Nassau. I do not want any confrontations. I gave word, more than once. I would give me life for him."

"Fook Rogers and fook Hornigold. All of us must regroup, Thatch," cried Vane.

"You don't understand—"

"I understand well," Vane interrupted. "We can go back in numbers and retake Nassau. My crew will slaughter those in opposition. A good plan, violently executed now, is better than any plan next month."

Thatch looked at the serenity of the ocean. The water's edge was lapping as the evening waves broke on shore. "I don't know." Thatch pulled on his long, black beard as if to entertain Vane's proposal.

"Look around; everyone is here. It's the best one could ask for," Vane said emphatically. "Have you lost nerve? You have the best captains; the most ferocious, battle-worn crews; and the most firepower on the seas. And here you stand . . . idle."

For once, Vane makes sense.

Thatch scanned the waterline along the beach on Ocracoke Island. Hundreds of pirates were on shore, partying and releasing pent-up tension from being on the seas for too long. Jamaican rum flowed freely, food was abundant, and the fiddlers played the best songs. This fest was a one-and-only.

"What is wrong with you?" Vane grabbed Thatch by his arm. He repeated, "Everyone is here for Christ's sake."

"None denying, Vane. But I want no part of it. I want to retire. I'm done."

"You always listened and followed Hornigold's way," Vane said. "You followed him like a shark on the trail of a bloody, wounded fish."

"Well, like Hornigold, I want a new way of life. Take the plunder, find me Lazue, and rest on the banks of the Pamlico River. Besides, I can take merchant ships off of Topsail when I get bored."

"Why not Nassau?" inquired Vane. "You runnin'?"

"I have too many enemies on both sides of the ocean. I feel safe here. Look at the protective inlet and waterways. It's the next best to Nassau."

Vane turned to his left and looked over his shoulder to see who else was on shore.

"Where is Stede Bonnet?" asked Vane. "I know he'll join in."

"He was here but floated away," said Thatch, annoyed by the inquiry.

Deal walked over to Thatch when he overheard the comment. "We heard he's pissed at you, Thatch." Deal grinned.

Thatch looked at Deal with cold eyes. "As for Stede, I have no idea nor do I care."

"I bet he went back to Palma de Ayes off the coast of Florida," said Vane. "He always seemed to think there was more gold and silver at Sebastian Inlet."

"There must be more, Thatch. It carried all the queen's jewels and tons of gold and silver out of Cuba." Vane had always been intrigued by the disappearance of the 1715 Spanish Fleet.

"I've been at Palma de Ayes as well. Any remaining is certainly at the bottom of the ocean," said Thatch. "It can't be retrieved."

"It must have been a monster of a hurricane to drown all eleven ships. The galleons had to roll and break up in the surf once they hit the first reef," Vane speculated.

Thatch nodded his head. "I would think so. How did you fare?"

"Henry Jennings and I had taken with ease 350,000 pesos on site, then another 60,000 pesos from an unsuspecting Spanish boat near Cuba. Nice haul, eh?"

"Good thing you got there first. Rumors were rampant in Nassau. Every mate that had a sloop was on his way to Florida to pillage."

Vane became wild-eyed and regressed as he recalled his presence the year before. "I made a poor Spanish guard kneel down on his knees, put the muzzle of his own weapon into his mouth, and fire down his throat."

Thatch gazed at the sand below his feet. "You're the worst, Vane." Thatch looked back up into the deep-set eyes of Vane. "And no one defended the encampment?"

"The Spanish soldiers guarded the treasure on the shoreline," Vane said excitedly. "They ran up the dune line like ducks. I picked them off one at a time. I killed the Spanish guards like rats on my ship." Vane laughed in one of his psychotic episodes. "It was easy takings after that."

"Like I said, you're the worst."

"They reminded me of the French . . . crying and gutless."

Thatch's sixth sense told him that it was time to move on and separate himself from the others, especially Vane.

"Mates, I am going to adjourn for the evening. I wish everyone well. As for me, I'm taking the Hornigold route, retiring with all my loot and mates. I love Nassau, but unfortunately I cannot return."

Thatch looked around at the scourge of the earth lying drunk on the sand. *I don't want any part of this anymore. Nor do I want to lead to retake Nassau. It's certain death for me, either in battle or by noose.*

"I bid thee a good evening, mates," Thatch continued, "I have a look-alike Lazue awaiting upstream. Please give Hornigold my best, even though he wants me head. Tell him I hope he finds his Norwegian beauty as well."

As the sun fell below the horizon, each captain boarded his ship, one by one, and sailed out of Topsail with their crews. It was a beautiful night; the moon's reflection gleamed off the ocean, and a slight wind blew in from the northeast. The largest pirate fest of all time came to an end.

The crews and their captains were disorganized, drunk, and undecided on what to do. Vane looked back at Ocracoke Island as he sailed north. His face was blank.

Chapter Fourteen
A New Way of Life

Bath, North Carolina, was a hamlet off Pamlico Sound. Access was through Topsail Inlet onto the Pamlico River. A creek veered north from the river and meandered into town. Bath was an early settlement with a population of one hundred. It was a good day's sail from the Atlantic Ocean, safe and secluded.

It's time to see Governor Eden. Let's get this pardon out of the way. Time to get back to business.

Thatch sailed west on the Pamlico. The sluggish water was discolored, a strong contrast to the blue-green clarity of the Caribbean. Large cypress trees, indigenous to the swamps, hung over Bath Creek, creating a cool shade along the banks. It was a welcome relief from the scorching summer sun.

At midafternoon, Thatch spotted Eden along the shoreline of the Pamlico River at the entrance to Bath Creek. Eden flung his hands in the air in a gesture of welcome, and Thatch returned a hearty wave. An aide of Eden's ran down the embankment to help Thatch tie up his vessel.

"Good afternoon, Gov'nor; great to see you once again. It's been awhile." Both men shook hands, hugged, and exchanged pleasantries. "I love the cypress and oak trees along the way. It was a pleasant sail here."

"Thatch, good to see you, old chum. Welcome to my home," Eden said.

Eden smiled from ear to ear. Thatch knew what the governor was thinking: *I bet my friend from the seas has pillage to give me.*

"Governor, I'm here to seek a pardon, not only for me, but for my crew as well. Do you think that's in the stars?"

"Absolutely. I wanted to discuss that with you anyway. We can help each other a lot."

"And how is that?"

"Bath is a small town, Captain. We can use your resources. You have more men than we have population. I need your men to spend money with our residents and merchants."

"That's not a problem. My men will spend their take. More importantly, we need a place to call home besides Nassau. They love to spend money and have fun. You'll see."

"There are two more requirements. Your men must not harass our citizens."

"And the other?"

"You have a lot of armaments. Your crew must defend the citizens from attacks by the Yamasee Indians. The women and children are frightened beyond belief. The savages are wiping us out."

"Governor, you have my word. We will meet all three of your requests."

"Thatch, it's not a request. It's a demand. This will be a good reason for your presence and pardon before the Crown."

"It will be something we will pledge to do: spend our take in Bath, no harassing the married women, and protect the fearful citizens from the Yamasee."

"Then I will draw up the papers for the act of grace. You may consider yourselves pardoned. Feel free to pass the word on to your crew."

Thatch smiled. "I am much relieved, Governor. I owe a debt of gratitude."

Governor Eden came through for Edward Thatch and his crew. Everyone received an official pardon. His new Nassau was in the backwaters of North Carolina. The added benefit was observing ocean-going vessels passing by at Topsail Inlet.

Thatch walked toward the bank of the river and inexplicably turned around and walked back.

"Governor, the most difficult will be the behaving." Thatch grimaced. "You must know that my men raise hell whenever possible. Don't get me wrong, they're the best, but they are a motley crew."

"Thatch, Bath is full of widows and orphans. A lot of their men were killed from attacks by the Yamasee. Just make sure the crew stays away from the married women and no harassing their daughters," Eden said sharply.

"Governor, I pledge my loyalty to you."

"I believe you."

"My crew will unload some gifts in a token of our appreciation."

"Do it at nighttime, when Bath is asleep."

"The supplies, cargo, silver, and gold represent my appreciation and not a bribe, sir. Over the past couple of years, I have felt safe and comfortable here."

"Likewise, Thatch, I consider you a friend as well. I own some property across from my residence on Bath Creek at the juncture of the river. If you like, I can have a house built for you on the east side. We can become neighbors as well."

"That would be wonderful, Governor." Thatch beamed. "It is an idyllic part of the river—high elevation, cypress trees, and overlooking the bay. It's a splendid view."

"You can clearly see who sails in and out." Eden smiled.

"That is a generous gift, thank you." Thatch extended his hand to accept his offer. "I would like to do that."

"Then consider us friends, neighbors, and protectors of one another."

"In your honor, Governor, I would like a gathering tonight. All of the best rum Jamaica has to offer, a boucan of wild boar, and fine entertainment. The fiddle players are the best from Ireland."

"I haven't danced a jig since I was a lad," Eden reminisced. "I know of a young lass, sixteen years of age. I'll bring her for you."

"Please do. Bring your wife and all of your friends from Bath. We shall dance till the moon turns o'er to the sun. What is the lass's name?"

"Mary Ormond," replied Eden. "You will like her."

"I have a lass but have not seen her for a long time. Her name is Lazue, a gorgeous wench from the West Indies. You should hear Lazue play the violin, Governor. She is not a fiddler but a classical violinist. Her chin is held high, arms stretch outward with long bowing, and her fingertips play with ease."

"Lazue sounds special. I must meet her. Is she in the Bahamas?"

"I have been told she is in the Americas. My last night with her in Nassau was exquisite and unforgettable. The strings played softly as she overlooked the harbor on a moonlit night. Lovely, just lovely, Governor."

"You talk as if you miss the lass. Does she have your heart?" asked Eden judiciously.

"Oh, I do miss her. She has me heart, for sure. And she fooks like a whore. Wonderful, mate, just wonderful. Everything a chap could ask for."

"Thatch, about your reputation. Is it all true?"

"Such as?"

"Killing and maiming your enemies and the innocent."

"I kill where I choose and whom I choose, Governor. I slay when offended. I slay sometimes for pleasure and when not at all offended. I boarded a Frenchman's ship off Martinique. He had not offended me. Do you know what I did to him anyway?"

"Obviously not."

"I sliced off his nose, both ears, and both lips with my dagger. My cook fried them in a French wine while he watched. I made the captain eat his own ears and nose and lips. Then, I shot him in the bowels."

"Why?"

"I ordered him to smack his lips, but he had none to smack."

Thatch was stone-cold silent. His demonic stare went through Eden like a shooting star. Eden, for the first time, saw the evil in his eyes. Would the governor be next on the list some unsuspecting day?

"That's not exactly what I wanted to hear, Captain."

Thatch burst out in laughter and slapped Eden on the back. "A hearty tale for sure, Governor, believe in what you want."

Eden backed up a couple of steps half expecting to be the next victim. He stumbled and fell down the bank to the water's edge. "You're crazy," he said shaking.

Thatch extended his hand to help Eden climb back onto the bank.

"That's what I want others to believe."

Eden adjusted the waist of his pants and brushed the dirt off his sleeves. "Maybe I should govern the colony of North Carolina the same way—through fear and intimidation."

"Maybe. It works for me." Thatch shrugged.

Eden and Thatch walked toward Plum Point, an area of quaint homes along the creek. Eden had a surprise of his own for Thatch.

Within the week of the pardon, the pirates were spending their loot and having a good time. Most of the crew behaved, but as predicted, some of Thatch's crew was out of control.

"Captain, your men must quit harassing the plantation owners along the river," hissed Eden. "I'm getting too many complaints."

"I will take punishment to those responsible."

"Also, one of your men washed up on shore. Apparently, he was drunk and fell in the river and drowned. Do you want him buried in the desolate mud flats on the back side of the creek?"

"No, it's customary that a mate be buried on shore between low tide and high tide. I will have one of my men take him back to the sea."

"Some of the snobbish plantation owners are talking of getting assistance from Governor Spotswood in Virginia instead of me. And that man hates both of us."

"Fook Spotswood. He's having his own problems. The citizens of Virginia are about to oust him anyway."

"I know. He spent a fortune of the people's money on the mansion in Williamsburg." Eden stepped closer to Thatch.

"What you don't know, Captain . . . he's putting up his own money to capture you. If he is successful, then he becomes the hero and not the one who squandered away tax money."

"I apologize for my men. I'll punish those who violated their pledge. I do not want to give reason for Spotswood to be invited into either of our lives. But, I must admit, I long to feed his pagan liver to the fish at sea."

"I do not want sentiment of the local citizens against me." Eden sighed.

"Their wayward acting will not happen again, I assure you," replied Thatch

"Good, let's survey some of the land that may be to your liking."

Eden and Thatch continued their walk along the banks of the creek. Thatch drank rum out of his gold-laden tankard taken from a captain in the Caribbean. He picked a high and dry parcel across the creek from the governor, called Plum Point. Spanish moss, cypress, and oak trees covered the area, providing protective shading during the hot, muggy afternoons of Bath.

"I think this will do splendidly, Governor."

Thatch saw Mary Ormond picking berries nearby and summoned her. She held her beige linen dress in her hands and scurried over to meet him.

Mary was so excited to see the new man in her life. After all, he was the most powerful man in town, even more powerful than the governor.

Mary Ormond was a quiet, young girl of Irish descent. Her long, red hair draped over her freckled face. She enjoyed the attention, not only from Thatch but from locals who attended the party. She was someone now.

Mary stood in front of Thatch and looked up. "Hi, Captain. It's so nice to see you. I had such a lovely time with you."

Thatch leaned over and brushed Mary's bangs away from her face. He placed his left hand against her cheek and kissed the other cheek.

Mary blushed. "Oh, thank you, Captain."

Thatch placed both of his hands on her rose-colored cheeks and looked deeply into her blue eyes. "Mary, I had a lovely time the other night as well."

"Thank you so much for treating me so nicely. I loved your stories." Within a short period of time, Mary became intoxicated with Thatch's demeanor and sway.

"Mary, I will be building my house here at the point. Do you like the location?"

"Oh yes, it's perfect. I love to sit by the bank of the river and watch the water flow quietly by. And the deer come here to drink at nighttime."

Governor Eden stood close by, and nodded silently in agreement.

"It's special, Captain," Mary continued. "In the evenings, you can see the lanterns lit from the local homes and hear the cicadas sing. And right before the sunrise, a lone owl will awake you with her calling."

"That sounds just delightful. But I need someone to share that with."

"Captain, don't you have anyone in your life?"

Thatch quickly thought of his Lazue and how he missed her. He shook his head sideways to be rid of the thoughts. It was time to move on. "I have a question." whispered Thatch to Mary.

"Yes?"

"I would like for you to be my wife and live here with me. Would you?"

"Well, it's awfully—"

Thatch interrupted. "Governor, would you be so kind as to marry us here at Plum Point?"

"Of course. I'm legal enough as a governor. Mary, do you accept the captain's proposal of marriage?"

Without batting an eye, Mary exclaimed, "Oh yes . . . yes."

Thatch and Mary stood under the shade of a cypress tree, awaiting the vows. She beamed with delight; a lonely heart soon disappeared.

Eden stood before them to begin the ceremony. The river ran slowly behind them as the trees whistled with a light breeze. He lifted his arms to the sky, palms turned up.

"By the power vested in me, in this great state of North Carolina, I now pronounce you husband and wife," said Eden forcefully.

"Brush your lips with mine, softly, like a light breeze, Captain." Mary's tongue wetted her lips in anticipation of a kiss. "Kiss me, like you've kissed no other before."

Thatch pulled aside his cutlass and bandolier of weapons to make room for an embrace. He became amorous as he looked into her blue eyes. His long arms engulfed Mary.

"You're beautiful, Mary."

"Oh, thank you. And you're so handsome, Captain."

Thatch leaned over and kissed Mary on the lips for a long time. Mary melted into his arms and returned her affection by giving Thatch a long hug around his chest.

"Will you protect me forever, Captain?" asked Mary.

"I give you my Bible oath, no harm will come to those young tits."

"Oh, Captain, you mustn't talk that way." Mary blushed.

"Lift your skirt, Mary. Let me see what me new wife has awaiting."

Mary's freckled face turned red again as she looked away.

"Not now. I will be glad to show you later, though. It's still daylight out."

"Prepare to be boarded, Mary." Thatch smiled. "Ye want to see me coxswain?"

Governor Eden stood by in shock with his head forward and his mouth agape.

Thatch leaned and whispered into Eden's ear, "Mary is wife fourteen."

Chapter Fifteen
Cape Fear

In the distance, Thatch noticed a small boat up river. As it approached, he saw that it was Israel Hands. Hands jumped off the boat and ran up the bank. He was clearly out of breath from rowing.

"Sir, we have dire news."

"And what could be so dire as to interrupt the marriage of me life?"

"Really, Captain?" Hands was taken aback but not surprised. "Congratulations, but what I have to say is more important. We wanted you to know immediately."

"And ye say?"

"We have good word that Stede Bonnet was hung in Charles Town. And they are looking for you."

Thatch bowed his head in sadness "How did this happen?"

"After we abandoned him, he sailed south along the coastline. The fool attempted to raid Charles Town like you did. The man thought he was you for Christ's sake."

"Stede had a heart of gold. I truly liked that man, even though he never had the right innards. He caused too many unnecessary problems."

"I liked him, too, but a strange fellow, though. I've never seen the likes of a little, fat man walk around with a dress on and claim to be a pirate to everyone."

"I would like to retrieve his library of books, if possible. See what you can do about that," Thatch ordered. "What else have you heard?"

"The governor of South Carolina sent patrol after patrol looking for Vane. A Colonel William Rhett was assigned to find him. Rhett sailed from the Carolinas to Cat Cay in the Bahamas and back. He found nothing."

"I have heard of this Colonel Rhett. He is a danger to all of us." Thatch looked concerned. "Maybe even more of a danger than the Nassau governor, Woodes Rogers."

"Rhett blocked his ship on Cape Fear River, thinking it was Vane. It turned out to be Stede instead."

The governor shifted nervously to Thatch's private conversation with Hands.

"Captain, I am going to excuse myself. The good governor of South Carolina and I know each other. I do not want an accusation of conspiracy. I will take Mary with me until you are done."

Thatch nodded to the governor, kissed Mary on the cheek, and turned back to Hands. "Bad luck for Stede. May his soul rest in peace."

"It was a bad trade. I'm sure Rhett would have preferred Vane over Stede," Hands replied.

"I took that chap under my wing when he left his wife and children in Barbados. He was an educated, wealthy bloke. And his only dream was to be one of us . . . go figure."

"Captain, Stede once told me that he thought God might be a pirate," said Hands.
Thatch burst out laughing. "Was he crazy?"

"He showed it to me in the Bible. Look, he wrote it down for me."

Hands reached in his back pocket. He pulled out a small leather case. A salty, wrinkled piece of paper was folded inside.

"Here, read this, Captain."

The wind blows where it wishes, and you hear the sound of it, but cannot tell where it comes from and where it goes. So is everyone who is born of the Spirit (John 3:8).

"Who else would know that, besides us and God?"

"The secret of the sea is in the wind. But Stede met his maker at the end of a noose," said Thatch. "I'm more concerned about this Colonel Rhett. He makes me a li'l nervous. We don't have an equal amount of crew or armaments."

Hand grimaced. "I smell trouble, Captain."

"Me, too."

"Th' word must be out that you are nearby. Colonel Rhett wants you as well."

"Blast his eyes, for what? We took some medicine from their city. That was about it."

"I'm sure he sees it differently," said Hands nervously.

"We pillaged some citizens on their way back to London. Hell, they were already on their vessels. I could have burned Charles Town down, if I wanted."

"Th' governors of South Carolina and Virginia will be coming after you, too," advised Hands. "Everyone wants me, Hands. That's why I chose Bath. It's isolated. Vane told me that even Hornigold was coming after me. That disturbs me."

"I don't believe that, Captain."

"Me neither, mate. But Hornigold can make the Pope believe he is a Protestant."

Hands was uncharacteristically nervous. His eyes darted back to the river. Shifting back and forth he stammered, "Ahhh, ummm, Captain one more thing."

"Yes." Thatch's eye lids started to twitch, a tale-tell sign that he was agitated.

"Lazue was in Charles Town."

"And?"

"They hung her, too."

"Where in Charles Town? Was she in plain view like a common pirate? Tell me the details," insisted Thatch.

"Word is they were after her to turn witness against ye', and when she wouldn't, had planned to torture her to get back at ye'. But she jus' started a-chantin' one of her bloody curses, and the men, well, they were too a feared to carry it out. When the hangman put th' noose round her neck, she spit in his eye and put her knee in 'is groin."

Hands paused and swallowed, waiting for a response back from Thatch.

"Continue . . ."

"She ended at the hangin' tree at th' garden. Th' other pirates were at th' gallows by the harbor. They twisted in th' breeze fer days, cut down, and thrown into Vanderhorst's creek."

Thatch's thoughts raced out of control. Images of love making flashed in out of his head from their days in Nassau. Thatch could not rid of the images of Lazue's dark eyes, long black hair, and high cheek bones.

"Captain! Captain!" Hands repeatedly shouted.

Thatch came out of his trance. The blood in his veins began to boil. *I'll beat that man to a pulp, just like I did me mum's husband. He hurt me Lazue. I'll torture that bastard. He will convulse to his death.*

"Bastards . . . no good rotten bastards. They will all pay for this, I guarantee, Hands."

"Th' eerie cry of swooping sea birds thought the same thing, Captain. At th' end, they circled Lazue to protect her."

Thatch let out a blood-curdling scream.

"Retribution and treachery, Captain," stated Hands. "It's th' only way."

"He fooked with the wrong pirate! I'll piss in his skull when I'm done." Thatch's eyes turned evil and deadly. The devil incarnate was about to seek revenge for the hanging of his Lazue. "I might have the satisfaction of slipping a couple of feet of steel into his vitals. That man will be a bloated tick when I'm done with him."

"I'll sharpen your knives to cut his thickened skin," Hands said eagerly. "I will help if need be—maybe pour boiled water in his ears first."

Thatch paced back and forth, biting the inside of his lip.

"Hands, no mention of this to me new wife."

Chapter Sixteen
The Hunt Is On

News spread quickly throughout the colonies of the impromptu pirate fest at Ocracoke Island. The largest gathering of the most notorious pirates was in the Americas. The feast scared the bejesus out of everyone along the coastline.

The governor of Pennsylvania heard the pirates were going to burn down Philadelphia. He sent out two sloops to capture them, but they were unsuccessful. However, it was Lt. Governor Spotswood of Virginia that gathered the intelligence and manpower to capture the pirates.

In July 1718, Spotswood met with the governor's council and his new attorney general, John Clayton, inside the people's mansion in Williamsburg.

"Gentlemen, it is my contention that these thieves be put out of their misery and ours as well. They are killing our commerce," proclaimed Spotswood. "I propose we capture and hang every last one of them, especially Blackbeard. By last account, Blackbeard is good for plundering fifty ships."

Spotswood, an Oxford graduate, was a religious Jacobite known for his sermons on Sundays. His favorite passage conveyed a message of anger and indignation. Resentment toward the Virginia House of Burgesses and exasperation with the public was apparent on Sunday mornings.

There are issues that need to be resolved, and you do not know how to bring them to resolution. But, I say to you that if you will release your offense and trust Me to take care of this, I will. I will lead you in the way of righteousness and bring peace not only to your own heart but to your situation, says the Lord. All you need to do is let go and put your faith in Me. Mark 11:22 So Jesus answered, "Have faith in me."

He ruled robustly in the absence of Governor George Hamilton and felt untouchable since Queen Anne signed his commission. However, his unbridled contempt for members of the Assembly of Virginia, unpopularity with the citizens, and arrogance began his rightful demise.

Attorney General Clayton was new and cautious. "Sir, I don't know if we have the jurisdiction to do so. They reside in North Carolina, not Virginia."

Spotswood was clearly agitated by the logic of the law. "The governor of North Carolina is weak and corrupt."

"We may need to wait till a pirate is inside our waters or on our land, Governor."

A portly man, Spotswood stood and adjusted his pants before making his point. "I have little faith in his ability. We cannot depend on him, John."

"I agree, Governor. Eden is absurdly deficient. We need to act quickly and judiciously."

Spotswood raised his chin in righteousness and placed his hands on the lapels of his long, golden, embroidered vest. "I want Blackbeard eliminated even if it's outside our jurisdiction. Clayton, damn it, find a legal reason. He's too close for comfort."

Spotswood limped back to his desk as he bragged about being severely wounded in battle. A four-pound cannonball was on his desk as a souvenir.

"I want Blackbeard to feel what I felt when I was injured—pain and agony. The wound felt like a hot poker piecing my skin. He needs to feel the same."

"What would you like for me to do, Governor?"

"We need to find out where they are and bring them in. I do not want any miscreants living in Williamsburg. Do you hear me, Clayton?"

Clayton shrugged and did not like the condescending voice of Spotswood, who spoke as if Clayton were personally responsible. "The acts of piracy occurred after the cutoff date for pardons. We may be able to use that to our advantage," replied Clayton.

"You're the attorney general of Virginia; you figure it out."

"Governor, may I suggest some type of ordinance be passed?"

"Such as?"

"That all pirates make themselves known to our authorities and give up their arms. I would also suggest that they not be allowed to travel in groups of more than three."

"Yes. That makes perfectly good legal sense. Draft the ordinance. And do it quickly for a vote," ordered Spotswood. "How we enforce the ordinance is another issue."

On November 24, 1718, an "Act to Encourage the Apprehending and Destroying of Pirates" was passed by the council. A surprise addendum was added by Spotswood: a reward of £100 for the death of Blackbeard. Spotswood called for a special meeting in his office, which was opulent enough for a king.

"The proposed ordinance is law, gentlemen. We need to pursue and hang these vile men," growled Spotswood.

A council member abruptly interjected. "Governor, I overheard an intriguing conversation from one of the slaves. He stated some of Blackbeard's former crew was living in our seaports."

"Who is that?" asked Spotswood.

"The slave was the greeter at your door. He said the pirate's name was William Howard, a quartermaster on the *Queen Anne's Revenge*. Supposedly Howard has been seen in the taverns and on the docks."

"Clayton, have the authorities verify the slave's story. If it's true, find Howard. He should have every piece of information that we need."

Within the week, Virginia authorities found William Howard at the docks, attempting capture of a vessel that he could use to resume pirating. The authorities arrested Howard and brought him to the mansion in Williamsburg. He immediately appeared before the governor and his ad hoc council.

Howard stood before the council defiant and stared down Spotswood. He was cagey, calculating, and remained silent. His reputation was as feared as Blackbeard; Howard was a muscular, handsome man with a weathered face and was well respected on the seas.

"Are you William Howard?" Spotswood demanded to know.

"Yes, I am."

"You have been arrested as a vagrant seaman attempting to steal a sloop. How do you plead?"

Howard scratched a star-shaped scar underneath his eye. "I plead nothing."

Spotswood looked at the council members, confused by his statement.

"Are you now or have you ever been the quartermaster of the *Queen Anne's Revenge*?"

"Yes, I have."

"Were you the highest ranking officer on the ship?"

"Yes."

"Quartermasters have the power to veto a captain's decision. Did you ever call for a vote or veto any decisions made by Blackbeard?"

"No, never."

"Did you lead the boardings onto merchant ships for the purpose of theft?"

"No." Howard winked at the council. He lifted the sleeves of his dirty, white linen shirt to show the scars on his fingers and arms. "I was a working quartermaster."

"You have two choices, Howard," said Spotswood. "Spill your guts, or we will spill them for you at the end of a flintlock." Spotswood became more aggressive in his speaking. "I've had it with your ilk. As a matter of fact, it would give me great pleasure to pull the trigger myself."

"What do you need of me?" asked Howard.

"I want Blackbeard, period."

"That I cannot help you with."

"Howard, I have deep contempt for you. Your boorish and aberrant behavior disgusts me," gloated Spotswood.

Howard laughed. "Governor, you are a practitioner."

"Sergeant-at-arms, take this man away and place him back in his cell," ordered Spotswood. "Clayton, get a court date set, the sooner the better."

Still chained, the guards escorted Howard away. He stopped and then turned around to look at the governor. "I find you contemptible as well, a luxuriant life on the backs of the Virginia taxpayers. You, sir, are the boor."

"I will not quibble with villains of your likes."

"Governor, you have stolen taxpayer money and deeded thousands of acres of land back to yourself. How do you plead for the crime of theft from the people?"

Spotswood was outraged with Howard's insolence and disrespect. "Remove this animal," he cried.

"May your mother and daughter be on board my next ship, Governor." Howard spat on the marble-tile floor and smiled in the face of the council. "All of you, damn to hell, for you are the repugnant ones."

One of the guards removed his weapon and struck a gash on the back of Howard's head. The knees of Howard buckled and he fell to the marble floor.

Howard looked up. "I'll be seeing you again, mate, outside someday. You'll regret that."

Early the next morning an attorney visited Howard. He was dressed in a long, black wool coat. The visitor surprised the jail keep when the attorney asked for Howard. Out of respect, the jailor escorted the attorney to Howard's cell.

"Are you William Howard?"

"Yes, I am."

"My name is John Holloway. I will be representing you at your trial before the Virginia court."

"And to what do I owe this opportunity?"

"Governor Eden and I are longtime friends."

The wind has brought favor to me, finally.

"Is Captain Thatch still in Bath with Eden?" asked Howard.

"I can't say at this time, Howard. More importantly, Eden and I put in place a pardon for you. It should arrive any day."

Howard began to laugh uncontrollably. "Really? Am I a free man?"

"Not yet. We need to act quickly. Spotswood wants to hang you, expeditiously."

"Holloway, that man represents what we fight against, corrupt nation-states. It would be my honor to draw his blood on a cold piece of steel."

"I will write the legal work for your release. Do not talk to anyone unless I am present. Do you understand?"

Howard nodded. "Me lips are sealed by tar."

Ironically, William Howard was defended by John Holloway, a prominent attorney and the mayor of Williamsburg. Exasperated with Spotswood's abrasive power grabs, Holloway would take pride in making a political fool of Spotswood.

Unfortunate for Blackbeard, other pirates in jail talked too much about their captain.

Spotswood had spies throughout the town and as far south as North Carolina. Conversations about Topsail and Eden were overheard in the cells and the taverns.

"I knew it. I just knew it," Spotswood said emphatically. "Eden has been in on this from the start."

"So, what do you propose?" inquired Clayton.

"There are two British warships at Hampton Roads Harbor. I propose we meet with the captains. They are here to serve as officers of the court."

"I'll track them down and bring them to the governor's palace," stated Clayton.

Within the day, Captains Brand and Gordon were inside the most opulent room in the mansion. The floors were made of Italian marble with Parisian chandeliers hanging from the twenty-foot ceilings. A long mahogany table made in London sat twenty-four chairs.

"Gentlemen, welcome to the people's mansion." Spotswood stood at the head of the table, pulling on his favorite golden vest. "I need your services."

"In what manner may we assist?" asked Captain Gordon.

"I desperately need you to extirpate this nest of vipers attacking our merchant ships and ports. We know Blackbeard is nearby at Topsail Inlet."

"That's not possible, Governor. The *Pearl* and the *Lyme* are too large for that type of mission," said Gordon emphatically. "They cannot navigate the shallow and difficult channels around Topsail Inlet."

"If you can find some men and smaller vessels, I will pay for the venture myself."

Once Blackbeard is in my hands, I can always take his plunder to repay myself from his hidden silver and gold.

"Isn't it illegal to go into another colony's territory for this purpose?" asked Captain Gordon. "We don't have jurisdiction in North Carolina."

"None you mind, Captain. I am not concerned with that. I will handle the legalities." Spotswood sneered, "You sound like the Virginia House of Burgesses, always questioning my authority."

"Is Blackbeard at the inlet on Ocracoke Island or inland on the backwaters?" asked Captain Brand.

"I don't know for sure. But I already thought of a strategy I used years ago. I will send a two-prong advancement of troops: one by land and the other by sea."

"Exceptionally clever, Governor," said Gordon.

"Captain Brand, I need for you to go by land." Spotswood became more convincing with the show of his leather wallet chained from his hip. "I will supply the men and horses. It will be worth your while; I promise. It's only a six- or seven-day journey."

"I will, Governor. But you must protect me if something goes awry—not only financially but politically."

"Guaranteed," reassured Spotswood.

"There are two sloops available at the docks," Gordon interjected. "Neither is associated with the Majesty's Crown. I can make the deal for those two sloops."

"What are we waiting for?" Spotswood smiled. "Let's move quickly."

Captain Gordon thought for a minute. "Governor, I recommend my first officer, Lt. Maynard, lead the expedition. He is an experienced officer and gentleman of great bravery and resolve."

"That's what I need, someone like myself, a gallant leader," gloated Spotswood.

"We appeal to your good judgment, Governor. Please remember us in the future."

"Thank you, gentleman. Your acceptance and experience is invaluable to me." Spotswood was elated. "Maybe I can get the Assembly of Virginia to add an additional reward for you. I will inquire as to what the Crown may have to offer as well."

"We are all in agreement then. I will speak with Maynard about our agreement and tactics," said Gordon. "However, I will remain behind, Governor. I want political protection for my men; I hope you understand."

"I guess so."

"The Assembly of Virginia will be more apt to help me than you. These are my men. I protect them and they protect me. It's a code, Governor. You know that."

Lt. Robert Maynard of HMS *Pearl* was given command of two sloops and sixty men from the warships: thirty-five from HMS *Pearl* and twenty-five from HMS *Lyme*.

Maynard had extensive experience and was the oldest naval officer in the Americas. Dressed elegantly in a long, blue frock with gold buttons and epaulets, he commanded respect from his men for his bravery, more than for his title of lieutenant. His lips were parched and cracked, and he suffered a deep-lined face from the season's winds. Maynard wore a frock opened to show his weapons of choice.

The hired sloops were the *Jane* and the *Ranger*. Maynard took control of the larger sloop, the *Jane*, with an ample supply of provisions. However, much to his distress, the sloops were too small to carry cannons. Muskets, swords, pistols, and small armaments had to make due in attacking the most feared man on the seas. Maynard knew that the element of surprise would be crucial in capturing Blackbeard.

The other twenty-five crew members were commanded by one of Maynard's officers, Edmund Hyde of the HMS *Lyme*, who took control of the *Ranger*.

On November 18, 1718, the two sloops sailed slowly along the James River, out to Chesapeake Bay en route to Topsail Inlet, North Carolina. It was a chilly day, with heavy winds on the seas of the Atlantic.

On the land side, Captain Brand set out for North Carolina several hours later. The cold air smacked Brand in the face as his horse galloped through the woods of Virginia.

Brand rode side by side with a fellow officer. "Sergeant, I cannot help but to see the beauty of Virginia by horseback,"

"This is different for me also," replied the officer. "The seas held my interest, but the mountains hold my heart."

Brand never saw the beautiful landscape of Virginia before, the earthy rolling foothills and tobacco fields in the valleys. Old cut leaves of tobacco lay along the roadside as his detachment trotted through the crooked trails. The temperature was getting colder as they traversed the mountains. The air from the horses' lungs poured out of their nostrils like frozen mist as they crossed into the foothills of North Carolina.

"I've never seen such poverty, Sergeant. The people are illiterate, very few that can read and write, even of the justices of peace."

"Captain, I could not help but to observe what they ate as well. At the last stop, salt pork and Indian cornbread. The bread was still dirty from the mills."

"There seems to be a big difference between the wealth of Virginia and the poverty-stricken colony of North Carolina."

Around midnight on November 23, Brand arrived in the coastal lowlands of Bath. He picked up additional support from a number of North Carolinians, including Colonel James Moore and Captain Jeremiah Vail. Their job was to explain the presence of English naval troops to the locals in the backwoods.

"Colonel Moore, it may be best if you go into town by yourself. I am too obvious," said Brand. "See if Blackbeard is there."

Within the hour, Moore reported back. "Captain, Blackbeard wasn't there. However, I was told that he was expected at any hour with another load of cargo."

Brand rode his horse to Governor Eden's plantation home. With him were two of Eden's local political enemies, Maurice Moore and Edward Moseley, an accomplished attorney.

Eden looked in shock at the appearance of the three on his porch.

"Who in the hell do you think you are awaking me at this hour. What brings you to my house?"

"Governor Eden, my name if Captain Brand with the Majesty's Royal Navy. I have come to capture Blackbeard."

"He is not here. Nor do I know of him. And you need to leave my house, now." The gull of their presence was maddening to Eden.

"Then I will sit her till dawn and wait. If need be, I will put more logs on the fire."

Eden slammed the door on their faces.

Unknowingly to Eden and Brand, Blackbeard stayed on Ocracoke Island that night, drinking rum and partying with his crew.

Chapter Seventeen
The Last Battle

Lt. Maynard stopped northbound vessels on the Atlantic to gather intelligence about Blackbeard's location. He surmised that Blackbeard's sloop, *Adventure*, was anchored on the inner side of Ocracoke Island, facing the sheltered waters of Pamlico Sound. It was an ideal refuge protected by numerous shoals and sandbanks.

Maynard arrived at dusk on Thursday, November 21. Unfamiliar with the local shoals and channels, he decided to wait for the tide to rise and make the attack at dawn. Maynard did not want to take on Blackbeard in the midst of night. Maynard could see remnants of a campfire on the west side of the beach. He posted a lookout on both sloops, *Jane* and *Ranger*, to ensure that Blackbeard could not escape to sea.

Blackbeard was drinking hard and stumbled around on the sand. Israel Hands was in Bath with twenty or so crew members. His crew was reduced to a few, thirteen white and six Africans, including Caesar. Blackbeard and his men were far from prepared to engage in the battle of their lives.

It was a gray morning with very little wind. Maynard's men had no sleep in anticipation of the battle. As morning unfolded, the sun was trying to break through the overcast skies. A mist arose over warmer waters from the cold air. Maynard's sloops pulled anchor and crept toward the island and the *Adventure*. Only the lapping of the water on the side of the hull could be heard.

As they entered the channel, Capt. Hyde's *Ranger* ran aground on a sandbar.

"Damn it. Men, throw some of the ballast overboard," ordered Hyde. "We need to lighten the sloop to get us off this bar." Racing to obey Hyde's command, the crew passed ballast stones to one another and dropped them overboard. As the sloop rose with less weight, a brisk wind caught the sails of *Ranger* and moved it off the sandbar.

"Gentlemen, there is little wind. Break out the oars. It's now time to row as hard as one can. Pass the orders." Twenty-five of Hyde's men rowed toward the *Adventure*.

Hyde looked through the mist and saw the *Jane* adjacent to the shoal and shook his head in disbelief. Maynard had run aground as well.

One of Blackbeard's crew saw the two sloops sneaking up on them and raised the alarm. "Captain, I think that we're being attacked."

Blackbeard was hungover and not expecting any battle in the early morning hours. He threw down his tankard of rum and jumped over two drunken mates laying on the deck. He was alarmed at the closeness of both sloops.

"Caesar, cut the anchor cables," ordered Blackbeard.

The rum intoxication was wearing off rapidly.

"First gunner, prepare all nine cannons. Get ready to fire."

The unknown sloops were playing into Blackbeard's hands. He knew the shoals and channels better than anyone.

"Navigator, take us into the narrow part of the channel."

When Hyde's *Ranger* got within a pistol shot, Blackbeard signaled the gunners to fire.

"All cannons, fire away."

Flames blasted from the muzzles of the cannons. Four-pound cannonballs tore across the *Ranger*, demolishing the foresails. Then six-pound cannonballs flew onto the deck, crippling the *Ranger*.

When the chaos dissipated, Edmund Hyde lay dead in a pool of blood, along with his second in command, Allen Arlington. Officers and crewmen cried in pain from severed arms and legs. Others convulsed, their bodies withering on the blood-soaked deck, as the *Ranger* slowed to a stop.

Now it was Maynard's turn. A lucky shot from a small arms fire of *Jane* caught the jib and severed the halyard of the *Adventure*, causing her to slow as well. Blackbeard and Maynard were now within shouting distance of each other.

"Damn you for villains, who are you? And from whence came you?" hollered Blackbeard.

"You may see by our colors we are no pirates," said Maynard.

"Send your boat and board, that I might see who you are," Blackbeard replied.

"I cannot spare my boat, but I will come aboard you as soon as I can."

Blackbeard held up a tankard of rum, high in the air, in a salutation to Maynard. "Damnation to you and your men, ya cowardly puppies. Seize my soul if I give you quarters, or take any from you."

"I expect no quarters from you, nor should I give you any."

"Caesar, hoist the Black Death's flag and swing into position on these fools."

The starboard guns on the *Adventure* faced the enemy. Blackbeard waited patiently for point-blank range. The vessels were now within four hundred feet of each other. Three hundred feet. Two hundred feet.

Blackbeard's patience paid off.

"Cannon, fire away," yelled Blackbeard. All of the cannons repelled backward, sending violent tremors over the *Adventure*. "Mates, open fire with the muskets and grenades."

Phillip Morton, the master gunner, and others, unleashed grapeshots of spiked nails, lethal at short range. Empty glass rum bottles filled with gunpowder and bits of old iron were thrown on board the *Jane*. Blood-spattered bodies fell one after the other as shards of glass slid across the sloop's deck.

When the smoke cleared, the broadside barrage crippled the *Jane*. The deck was devastated and littered with bloody bodies from the deadly barrage. Twenty-one of Maynard's men were killed or severely wounded. Only two men were standing.

Blackbeard removed and tipped his hat. "Splendid job, mates. Navigator, pull alongside their sloop for the last blow. Secure the grappling hooks and pull tight."

The gap between the vessels narrowed as the sides banged into each other.

"What do you see, Captain?" asked Morton.

"All knocked on the head, except three or four. I need ten men to board and cut them to pieces."

Maynard's crew was in apparent defeat. However, rum still clouded Blackbeard's judgment. He underestimated the number of men on the *Jane*. Maynard used a simple military tactic of hide and seek.

Maynard's few remaining crewmen disappeared as they scurried down the steps into the hold of the sloop.

"Await my orders to charge with cutlasses and be ready to fire with pistols," ordered Maynard. "Stay close to the hatch. I will signal when they are on board."

As Blackbeard led the charge onto the *Jane*, Maynard's men emerged from the hold, yelling and firing their pistols.

Maynard screamed, "Take no prisoners; kill the bloody bastards."

In the frenzied encounter, men spilled out of the hole like rats, surprising Blackbeard and his crew. It was an absolute horror of fast and furious hand-to-hand combat: decks slick with blood, the men's hearing dulled by noise of the cannon and grenades, thick smoke obscuring their sight. It was a brutal no-holds-barred fight to the death. Pistols, cutlasses, hatchets, knives, clubs, fists, and even teeth were used.

Against superior training and advantage in numbers, the pirates were pushed back toward the bow, allowing the *Jane*'s crew to surround Maynard and Blackbeard, who was by then isolated from the rest of his crew.

Maynard and Blackbeard singled each other out and began the fight with swords. Maynard thrust the point of his sword against Thatch's cartridge box and bent the hilt. Blackbeard, known for his physical strength as well as his terrifying appearance, swung his large, sharpened cutlass with incredible force. He broke the guard of Maynard's sword and wounded Maynard's fingers. Blackbeard knew he had the advantage. Maynard was bleeding and vulnerable.

Blackbeard smelled death and moved in to finish his opponent. Maynard jumped back and pulled out a flintlock from his waistband. A puff of smoke expelled from the chamber, grazing Blackbeard in the shoulder.

As Blackbeard raised his cutlass for the final blow, the *Jane*'s helmsman, Abraham Demelt, made his way in to protect Maynard. Wielding a sharpened sword back and forth, Demelt slashed the face and neck of Blackbeard.

Blood spraying from his jugular vein, Blackbeard remained standing, swinging his cutlass like a wild man.

Blackbeard was running out of strength. The swings with his sword became less powerful and slowed to a halt. He looked over his shoulder and heard his crew moaning and falling onto the blood-stained deck. The will to survive was at an all-time high.

More of Maynard's men aimed and shot at Blackbeard. His resolute spirit to survive was like none seen before. He staggered on, swinging his sword at Maynard and Demelt, blood gushing from his face and chest. More musket balls struck his tall frame as the sailors surrounded him, swords drawn, circling a defeated Blackbeard.

One of Maynard's men, a young Highlander officer, circled from behind and engaged Blackbeard with his broadsword. He cut the pirate's neck.

"Well done, lad," Blackbeard said breathlessly.

The young officer replied, "If it be not well done, I'll do better."

The Highlander placed both hands on the hilt and swung full strength from right to left. He cut completely through Blackbeard's neck. It lay flat on his shoulder only held in place with jagged skin. Blood from the jugular veins squirted on the deck as he fell, cocking his pistol. Blackbeard collapsed to his knees into his own pool of blood.

Edward Thatch, the infamous Blackbeard, died on the chilly morning of November 22, 1718.

Maynard needed the head as proof that he had killed the notorious pirate to claim the reward. "Men, before you dispose of the body, I need to inspect it."

Maynard examined Blackbeard's body, noting that it had been shot no fewer than five times and cut about twenty times. He also found several items of correspondence, including a letter from Tobias Knight, the Lt. Governor of North Carolina.

"Now, hang his head on the bowsprit. I want all to see from Beaufort Inlet to the St. James River that Blackbeard is dead."

Maynard's first mate shimmied up the bowsprit with the head of Blackbeard tucked underneath his arm and secured it to the very edge. It was a grotesque warning for others not to commit piracy on the high seas as they sailed back to Virginia.

All was quiet on the blood-soaked deck. The air was thick from smoke. Pandemonium suddenly turned to calm. "Men, lift this poor, wretched soul and throw him overboard," Maynard said softly.

Two naval officers picked up the headless torso saturated in blood. One grabbed Blackbeard by the legs and the other underneath the shoulder blades.

"Heave him overboard," Maynard repeated.

Blackbeard's body free fell and splashed into the Atlantic.

A strong, cold gust of wind came across the bow of the *Jane*. The sails turned black and the sloop shuttered.

"Come quickly, everyone," hollered out the first mate. "You must see this, Lieutenant."

Maynard and his crew ran to the portside and peered overboard into the depths of clear water. Their mouths were agape in astonishment.

Blackbeard's headless corpse swam around the *Jane* in his final act of defiance. A swirling, vortex of iridescent green water surrounded Blackbeard as the devil incarnate sank to the bottom.

Lazue, is that you?

Yes, Edward, it's me. I've been waiting for you.

Chapter Eighteen
Black Caesar

The remaining pirates put up a desperate fight. To help expedite the final blow, the *Ranger* came alongside the *Adventure* to finish her off. The decks on three sloops were overflowing with blood and strewn with dying men. Many of Blackbeard's crew jumped overboard into the water.

"Aim, fire. Aim, fire," was repeatedly heard as crew members were shot as they swam away. One by one, their bodies floated until the air was gone from their lungs.

By midmorning, the final death toll was counted. Lt. Maynard lost eight men with twenty seriously wounded. The pirates lost twelve with nine badly wounded and taken as prisoners. But there was one final scare for Lt. Maynard. Where was Caesar?

"Find the black pirate," ordered Maynard. "I saw him when they boarded."

Maynard's crew became anxious one more time. "Find him, now." A frantic search ensued from bow to stern.

"I need two mates in the water." Without hesitation, two officers dove into the cold, morning water; one on the portside, the other on the starboard side. "Look under the rudder and hull," ordered Maynard. Caesar could not be found.

In a bizarre twist of fate, two men from a trading ship were hiding on board the *Adventure*. They were drinking with Blackbeard the night before all hell broke loose. The two merchantmen chose to hide instead of fight. As they climbed out of the hold, the door to the powder room creaked open.

One of the men opened the door and saw an African slave crouched behind powder kegs.

"What in the hell are you doing?" asked one of the men.

Caesar lit a small candle stick. The *Adventure* was about to be blown to smithereens. *Blackbeard's last command, in the event of defeat, blow up the ship. Do not let it be captured.*

A ferocious struggle emerged between the two merchants and Caesar. "Grab his arm," shouted one of the merchants. "Break it if need be."

Caesar easily threw off one as the other jumped onto his back.

"Good Lord, you're about to blow all of us up," screamed the wide-eyed merchant. "What's wrong with you?"

One of the merchants repeatedly punched Caesar on the back of the head. None of the blows bothered him. Three of Maynard's officers scrambled to the powder room after hearing the commotion. As the officers entered, Caesar leaped to light the fuse with the candle. The candle brushed the fuse and ignited. Seconds seemed like eternity. The fuse sparkled from the heat as it became closer and closer to the keg of gunpowder. A gunner officer grabbed a piece of cloth and smothered the wick.

Caesar continued to fend off all attacks. He took a pistol from an officer's waist and pointed it at him as they struggled on the floor. Maynard entered the door and put his right leather boot on Caesar's fingers while another officer dismantled the armament.

"Shackle this man until he cannot move." It took five men to hold down Caesar. Three officers wrapped rigging from his feet to his neck while leg irons secured his ankles and wrists behind his back. The same piece of cloth that put out the fuse was stuck into Caesar's mouth. He gagged and choked on the burned cloth.

Caesar could not fulfill his last order.

Maynard and his men searched the *Adventure* for the accumulation of Spanish gold and silver. They found very little, only some gold dust. Where was Blackbeard's accumulated wealth?

After the battle, Lt. Maynard sailed across the sound to Bath to get help for the wounded. He remained several more days at Ocracoke Island making repairs to the sloops before sailing back to Virginia.

The remainder of Blackbeard's crew were in Bath and did not know about the last battle. Captain Brand gathered up the pirates and transported them to Williamsburg. They were jailed on charges of piracy. Many of the crew members were African, prompting Governor Spotswood to ask his council what could be done about "the Circumstances of these Negroes to exempt them from undergoing the same Tryal as other pirates."

Regardless of Spotswood's inquiry, the men were tried with their comrades in Williamsburg's capitol building, under admiralty law, on March 12, 1719. Fourteen of the sixteen were found guilty. One of the merchantmen proved he was on Thatch's ship only as a guest at a drinking party the night before and not as a pirate.

Israel Hands successfully claimed that he should not be prosecuted. During a drinking session, Blackbeard had shot him in the knee, and he was in Bath at the time getting medical treatment. He also claimed that he was covered by the royal pardon. The remaining pirates were hung and left to rot on gibbets along Williamsburg's Gallows Road, including Caesar.

The arguments between Eden and Spotswood over jurisdiction raged back and forth between the colonies until Eden's death in March 1722. His will named one of Spotswood's opponents, John Holloway, a beneficiary. In the same year, Spotswood, who for years had fought his enemies in the House of Burgesses, was replaced by Hugh Drysdale.

Because of his fearsome reputation, the death of Blackbeard and the subsequent execution of his crew were regarded as a major coup in the war against pirates. For the British authorities, it was as significant as the trial and hanging of Captain Kidd in 1701.

When Blackbeard took over a vessel, if everyone did exactly as he ordered, there was nothing more to fear than the theft of property. With the exception of his last day on earth, Blackbeard had not so much as killed one man . . . until The Last Battle.

Thirteen-year-old Benjamin Franklin wrote a stanza in his father's paper in Boston.

Its better to swim in the sea below
Than to swing in the air and feed the crow,
Says jolly Ned Teach of Bristol

Chapter Nineteen
The Templar Knights?

On January 3, 1719, the *Jane* sailed up the James River toward Williamsburg. The *Adventure* was tucked in behind. It was a cold winter's day with strong northeast winds and white caps on the river. Lt. Maynard ordered the anchor to be dropped, opposite HMS *Pearl*. Maynard was anxious to report his success to his commanding officer, Captain Gordon.

"Men, it is highly appropriate for a nine-gun salute. Fire away at will." Maynard grinned as the small cannon retracted and shook the deck of the *Jane*.

The HMS *Pearl* answered back with deafening explosions heard even at the governor's mansion several miles away.

Maynard was at the bow and waved to get everyone's attention on the dock. "Look at who we got," Maynard said sharply. The sailors and merchantmen gazed at the bowsprit with their jaws dropping onto their chests. Blackbeard's head was slung below the bowsprit. The gruesome trophy was very much in the spirit of unusual punishment.

"This reminds me of the days of impalements," said a merchant to a fisherman. "The hands of traitors were tied behind their backs and the anus sliced out with a razor."

The fisherman winced. "My grandfather and I fished along the Thames. Every day, I saw impaled corpses strung along at the London Bridge.

"A sharpened stake, as long as a man's arm, was thrust up the body until the stake came out of the mouth. A horrible way to die, my English friend."

"I'd rather be that man hanging from the bowsprit," added the merchantman.

Lt. Maynard jumped off the *Jane* onto the dock. He was immediately escorted by naval officers to the governor's palace in Williamsburg. The horse-drawn carriage slowed as the lead horse trotted through a guarded gate. On one side of the entryway was a stone unicorn and on the other side, a stone lion. Several servants scurried to meet the escort at the carriage house.

"This is the most spatial and luxurious mansion that I have ever seen," stated Maynard to driver. "The front lawn, gardens, even the orchards are meticulously maintained. Exquisite, even the queen would be impressed."

The same slave who mentioned that pirates were in port was at the portico. He opened the massive double walnut doors into the governor's office for Maynard. The slave was unaware that his previous, seemingly insignificant, comment carried the weight of death for Edward Thatch, known as Blackbeard.

Governor Spotswood limped into the opulent portal, which was decorated with a display of bayonet-tipped muskets.

"Lt. Maynard, good to see you. I heard the cannons go off at the port to greet you. What was that all about?"

Maynard concealed the skull inside of his embroidered frock. "Governor, I have a present for you."

Spotswood was unaware of the last battle. "And that may be?"

Maynard pulled the skull out and held it high in the air. Long scraggly black hair was pulled taut from the weight of the head hung from Maynard's hand. "I give you the head of Blackbeard."

Spotswood was stunned. "I don't know what to say. This is reminiscent of the days of King Henry the Eighth." Spotswood stepped backward and raised his eyebrows with a look of incredulity. He'd never seen a severed head before.

Maynard lowered the head to his chest and placed both hands on the sides.

"Sir, a gift for you. May you rejoice and receive honors from Her Majesty."

"I am very pleased, Lt. Maynard. It is a sight to behold." With his air of superiority, Spotswood adjusted his gold-embroidered vest and asked, "Where is the rest of him?"

"We decapitated him and threw his torso overboard. I watched him sink to the bottom of the Atlantic Ocean at Ocracoke Island."

Spotswood was elated. He was vindicated by Maynard's skill and could now reestablish himself as a worthy politician. "Let's toast, Lieutenant."

Maynard held the head with both hands out in front of his chest. "Governor, may I suggest we use the skull as a drinking mug?"

Spotswood looked baffled but smiled. "Hell yes, let's do it. If you are willing to drink out of it, so will I."

"Sir, I placed his head on the ship's bowsprit for all to see. His mangy, long, black hair and beard blew in the wind as we sailed north."

"It appears to be clean; there's no brain."

"His skull was cleaned by the salt air and dried by the cold air and the sun, Governor."

"Let me get the best rum. This is a glorious day indeed."

Spotswood removed a bottle of dark Jamaican rum from his elegantly engraved desk and poured it into the inverted skull.

"Governor, Blackbeard's head was waving from side to side. It was a sight to see. All the locals from Bath, North Carolina, to Hampton Roads, Virginia, looked on in amazement. It was a lesson for all viewers; do not usurp the power of the Royal Navy of England."

"I toast to you and your crew, Lieutenant, for doing such a marvelous job." Governor Spotswood gloated as if he were on board the *Jane*. "You remind me of myself in battle."

Spotswood turned the skull sideways and sipped some rum from the forehead side of the skull. "Long lived Blackbeard." The governor laughed.

"Yes, long lived Blackbeard," repeated Maynard.

"You will receive a much higher ranking, Lieutenant." Spotswood handed the skull of rum to Maynard for his turn. "I thank you in the name of the Colony of Virginia and the Crown of England."

Maynard turned the skull upside down and gulped the rum until he ran out of breath. "And may the Crown elevate you as well, sir; we're both certainly deserving. What would you like for me to do with his head?"

Spotswood thought for a minute. "Let's put it on display much like on the bowsprit."

"Any ideas?"

"Put it atop a pole at the entrance on Hampton Roads. Let every Virginia citizen and sailor see that it was I, Governor Spotswood, who brought down Blackbeard."

"I will do that immediately. It will also serve purpose that the great governor of Virginia will not tolerate piracy."

Spotswood shook the hand of Maynard.

"Good day, Sir. I am off for the final tribute," said Maynard.

Maynard and his escorts traveled back to Hampton Roads by carriage. He picked the best possible viewing site for all to see; citizens, sailors, and merchant men stood at the bottom of the pole to gawk upward, as if Blackbeard was the devil himself.

A little boy held a small Jolly Roger flag on a stick in his hand. He placed it on the ground in front of the pole.

The skull and crossbones that the little boy placed at the bottom of the pole had an unusual origin.

Legend portrays the Templar Knights as a lost, secretive society. The order was associated primarily with the Christian Crusades in 1095. Their purpose was to protect Christian pilgrims en route to Jerusalem and secure the Holy Land against Muslims. Well trained, vicious, and fearless in battle, these warrior monks wore distinctive white mantles with a red cross. Their battle cry was said to be, "No quarter asked, no quarter given."

The Great Lady of Maraclea, of what is now Syria, was loved by a Templar Knight, the Lord of Sidon. Sadly, she died at a youthful age, but her legacy lived on in a most unusual manner. In the middle of the night, the Lord of Sidon ventured into the cemetery long after the mourners left. Eerie and serene, a yellowish moon provided light in the darkness of the tombs as he dug up the body. He pushed back the lid of the sarcophagus. Her luminous eyes peered into his. Lord Sidon made love to the corpse and violated her body.

A voice from the grave quietly said, *Lord of Sidon, hasten to leave here, but return in nine months to find your son.*

The Lord of Sidon dutifully returned to the scene of his passion as commanded the echo. As he removed the lid, the acrid, sticky-sweet odor of death poured out of the sarcophagus. Instead of a boy, the Lord of Sidon found the skeletal remains of The Great Lady. In a nest of maggots, cradled between his mother's crossed legs, lay the gnawed skull of a dead fetus.

The order created the white skull and crossbones as a symbol sewn onto canvas of black sails. This emblem became the heralded nautical flag of the Knights Templar with the largest fleet of ships in the world. Their sworn statement was: *This is a ship of Knights Templar. To attack us is surely to defeat and kill you.*

A rogue group of Templars departed the secret society after Pope Clement V ordered their mass execution. The Brethren adopted their own code of order on the high seas not dictated by a pope or a nation-state. Thereafter, the skull of a fetus and the crossbones of its mother continued to be the symbol of the Templar Knights, death, and piracy.

Within the week, five loyal crew members of Blackbeard rowed quietly up the Hampton River pressing against the shoreline as it narrowed into a small bay. Only the oars being pulled back / the water could be heard. It was an eerie silence. An absent sun provided darkness on a cold early morning.

"There 'e is," pointed the old master gunner. "The bastards placed 'is head on the pole."

The master gunner was the eldest on the *Queen Anne's Revenge*. He was an Englishman with large, strong hands and spotted burn marks that ran up and down his arms. He was a crew member with Blackbeard from the early days of Benjamin Hornigold. A tattoo of a cross was inked poorly onto his left forearm, and a dagger was inked on his right upper arm. Most days, he carried a grin of rotten and missing teeth, but this morning he scowled at seeing his friend and captain atop a pole.

"No one say a word till I have ye head," said the old gunner.

"Let me get it," said a rigger. "I can do it quicker."

The rigger shimmied up the pole as if he had climbed the ropes of a mast a hundred times before. "Someone, throw the bag up to me," he whispered.

The sailing master heaved a canvas bag made from a worn out sail. The rigger placed the skull in the old, dirty canvas bag and slid back down.

"We need to find a silver smith," said the sailing master. The rigger and gunner nodded in the silence of cold air. They could see the breath of the sailing master as he spoke.

Cloaked by the darkness of early hours, the five searched the area of Hampton Roads until they spotted a low orange glow through the cracks of a rickety, tobacco barn. A silhouette of a tall man drew the crewmen in for a closer look. The gunner knocked on the door. The tall Englishman with long red hair and muscular forearms opened the door. Molds of candle stick holders and cups littered the table.

"Might ye be a silversmith?" asked the gunner.

"Yes, I can be. How may I be of help?" stuttered the silversmith.

The master gunner pulled Blackbeard's skull out of the rope tied, canvas bag and held the gruesome trophy aloft in the light of a fire. The silver smith pulled his iron poker from the still-glowing embers and stared at the long black hair of a once formidable pirate.

"I'll be needin' ye to coat silver on this here skull. And please place a silver handle with a rim where 'is jaw would have been."

The silversmith held a serious stare with his cold blue eyes. "I've never done this before," stammered the silversmith. "It's very disturbing to see. Who is this?"

The master gunner stated, "Never you mind, young man. The rim is to read as is written here." The old gunner placed a crumpled scrap of paper on the table. It read, 'DETH TO SPOTSWOODE.'

"Now, we pay handsome," said the gunner. "I want the best, understand, mate?"

The silversmith noticed the gunner had scars of burn marks on his arms and face.

"I can assure you, my trade will be applied well."

The sailing master tossed an escudo onto the table. The gold coin spun around and around while the other four looked on. It came to a stop on the backside. A raised shield was struck onto the obverse side.

"I'll be wantin' the cup by Sunday."

"Hey, who is this for?" asked the silversmith.

As the old gunner scowled again, exposing his rotten teeth, the silversmith felt his skin prickle. "You ask too many questions. Think wise and keep this deal under yer hat."

The rigger placed the canvas sack on the table next to the gold coin. Each man slowly exited the barn door.

"May I ask, again, who this is for?" asked the silversmith sheepishly.

The rigger looked back. "Look at the tattoo of the cross on me arms and the shield on the coin."

The elder gunner opened his tattered shirt to show a tattoo of skull and crossbones on his upper right chest.

The sailing master, wearing a white mantel shirt, showed tattoos of daggers and a red cross on his arms. "Who do you think we are?"

The silver smith searched his memory for symbols and signs wrought in silver from Old England.

"Are you Knights?"

"We're the Brethren," replied the gunner. "But ye need to place your tongue behind your teeth and clap your lips."

At the mention of Brethren, the silversmith knew not to tell a soul or else he would be hanging from atop the pole. "I swear, my lips will not quiver and sealed forever."

By the following Sunday morning, the silversmith completed his task and anticipated the return of the Brethren. He glowed with pride in his artwork and waited patiently.

A quiet, uneventful Sunday slipped by. It was now midnight. A bright, full moon was overhead. Its light slipped through the cracks of the barn and lit up the silver plated skull on the oak table.

The young silversmith waited and waited until darkness fell. He hung his head in deep disappointment and walked slowly out of the barn. None of the brethren returned.

Part 6

Benjamin Hornigold

and

Governor Woodes Rogers of Nassau

ALLEN BALOGH

Chapter Twenty
The Mentor is Overthrown

Hornigold was en route to his new life. While sailing through the Florida Straits, along the bank of the Bahamas, he had a brief encounter with an armed merchant ship. The governor of South Carolina had sent it looking for pirates. They picked on the wrong pirate. Hornigold raised the flag, pursued, and attacked them instead. Out of fear, the captain intentionally ran his ship aground at Cat Cay. After that encounter, it was a peaceful sail all the way to Nassau. A life of retirement with his Norwegian love was on the horizon. Or was it?

A new set of problems had arisen for Hornigold, ones that he never faced before in his life. Hornigold was by himself in his quarters contemplating his next move. The quartermaster, John Martin, knocked on the wooden door.

"May I enter, Captain?"

"Of course."

The small room felt warm and cozy compared to the windy and cold air outside on the deck. Hornigold was sitting at his table, licking his fingers from some roasted boar.

"Have a seat. I'll get you a cup for some rum. Drink wi' me."

John Martin was a trusted confidant for years. His word was the gospel, and many crew members respected him for his courage and seamanship.

"You look troubled. What's on your mind?" asked Hornigold.

Martin stood instead of sitting at the captain's request. He was clean shaven, impeccably dressed, and spoke perfect

'Queen's English.' Each word was spoken slowly and distinctively.

"Captain, the crew and I have been discussing a serious issue for a while."

"And what might that be?"

"You refuse to attack any English flag ships."

Hornigold stood up, took a swig of rum, and wiped the excess from his chin.

"Of course not. I will only attack enemy ships of England. Everyone knows that."

"A lot of cargo and booty sailed by us, time and again, Captain. It's tough to take, sir, sitting idly by and watching. We, on board, have lost . . . a lot, because of you."

Hornigold was perturbed. His annoyance turned to anger, and he threw his cup of rum against the wall.

"I cannot and will not attack an English ship. I owe my allegiance to the king and queen, going back to my privateering days."

"We don't see it that way."

"Then what does the crew think?" hollered Hornigold.

"We believe it's your defense. If you're ever captured and tried, that's your excuse. You can say the ships were never from England."

"That's foolishness. Regardless of the reason, I will never attack an English ship."

"In our eyes, Captain, booty is booty, regardless of flag."

Martin gulped his cup of rum until it was empty. He looked Hornigold in the eye.

"Last night, we took a vote."

"And what type of vote was taken?"

"Sir, it was a vote by the majority of the crew," stated Martin in a forceful, deliberate manner. "All of the men gathered last night. They voted that you to relinquish your captaincy."

"What?" exclaimed Hornigold. "That's absurd, Martin."

"I removed the Articles of Agreement from the quarters. I wanted you and I to read them together."

Martin removed the document from the inside of his jacket and held it in front of Hornigold's face.

"I don't need to read them. Hell, I wrote them. Don't preach to me, damn you."

The air inside the room turned from cold to tense. Hornigold's blood was starting to boil.

"It's the very first one on the Agreement, Captain. '*All men have an equal vote.*'"

"And I am still your captain, deserving of your respect."

"Captain, the crew voted you off the ship. You are no longer in control."

"Is this a mutiny?"

"By no means, Captain, there is no open rebellion against you. We just need to plunder regardless of flag. You were never willing to do that."

Stunned, Hornigold hung his head in silence, at a loss of words. He felt betrayed by the very men whom he had taught. His emotions reeled from silence to outrage.

Uncharacteristically, Hornigold became violent. He grabbed Martin by the throat and pinned him against the door. Martin's head bounced off a coat hook.

"Damn you. It was you that instigated this against me, wasn't it?"

Barely able to speak, Martin squeaked out, "Stop this; it's you . . . not us."

A struggled ensued, and both men fell to the floor. Martin fell on top, made a fist, and pulled his arm back.

"Captain, I do not want this any more than you."

Hornigold's heart was pounding. Out of breath, he tried to regain his senses.

"Hasten the pace of this silent rebellion then."

"Leave with honor, Captain."

"I cannot make amends for what I have done."

Both men helped each other off the floor. It was over.

"Now what?" asked Hornigold.

"I want to remember you as a man of wisdom and courage."

Each looked the other in the eye.

"Captain, take the smaller sloop back to New Providence. And take whatever provisions that you choose. Out of respect, some of the crew members decided to stay with you."

Martin walked out of the cabin and closed the door quietly. Hornigold heard a brief, faint conversation outside his door. The words *he's out* placed a pit in his stomach. Then the heels of quartermaster's boots could be heard as he walked away, eventually disappearing into thin air.

Hornigold sat down in his chair and placed his head in his hands.

I should let this go without a fight. I wanted out anyway, but on my terms. I should have not kept my plans to myself. The crew would have known I was going to call it quits. Now I am a deposed captain . . . damn it, an insult.

It was a cold November night off the Bahamian banks in 1717. The wind whipped out of the north and created heavy seas. Hornigold felt the coldness of the air coming through the cracks of his door. But the cold heart of his crew was too much.

His friends and mates no longer wanted him. Even Captain Benjamin Hornigold was held to the standard of the Articles of Agreement. He was no exception.

Martin returned to the crews' quarters. He stood on the steps leading into the main hold. It was silent. In his articulate manner, Martin gave a short speech.

"Men . . . many pirate ships are the epitome of democracy. We vote on positions, based on experience and knowledge. The captain is no different. Any captain can be deposed for poor performance. He chose not to attack English flag ships. As a group, we decide where to sail, who should be captain, and how any booty should be divided up. Do I hear affirmation?"

In unison, the crew hollered out, "Aye-aye."

Chapter Twenty-One
The New Governor of Nassau

King George I met with his council to discuss piratical offenses. But the meeting was not going well. Queen Anne had passed away. He was an unpopular king, being met with opposition by the Catholics and supporters of James Stuart, called Jacobites. The king was born in Germany and could not even speak English. He married his cousin, Sophia, then divorced and imprisoned her for thirty years for "fookin" a Swedish count, Philip von Koningsmarck. King George had him killed and thrown into the Leine River, some stones used as leg weights. And his mistress, Melusine von der Schulenburg, was a bitch. She flaunted her rise in society after having two kids with the king. England was at war, off and on, with Spain and France. Things were not going all that well in England.

Chans, an English barrister, was concerned about the future of England's coffers. On behalf of the council, he requested an immediate meeting the king. Because Chans was a man of power, the request was granted immediately. He sat at the head of the table of council in a cold, damp room.

"We need to take control of the West Indies, damn it. Does anyone know of a loyal and strong seaman?" asked Chans.

All the council members looked around the table. Many shrugged and looked at each other for an answer.

A councilman's courier was eavesdropping. "Please excuse my indulgence, for I know of a man . . . Woodes Rodgers. He comes from an English family of wealth. And he is a seaman and a successful privateer himself. He is perfect for you."

"Maybe you should be sitting at the table instead of your councilman that you represent," said Chans.

The council members laughed but uneasily. No one knew how to combat the pirates and their wanton disregard of life and property.

"How do you know of him?" asked Chans.

"He is a neighbor."

Chans sat back. He looked at the king to elicit a response.

"And what say ye, King George?"

King George nodded in the affirmative.

"Summon Woodes Rogers before the council as soon as possible," he told the courier.

It was that quick and simple. The councilman's aide left to find his neighbor. The next day, Woodes Rogers appeared before the king and his council.

"Mr. Rogers, I am a barrister for the king. We are prepared to offer you a great deal for your skill and knowledge," said Chans.

Chans, a legal scholar, was a brilliant addition to the council. He was a man of honesty and character. All matters of the king and queen went before him.

"What exactly did you summon me to do?" asked Rogers.

"You have extensive experience sailing on the seas. We are told that your privateering days were prosperous."

"Yes, I know those who sail it . . . and?"

Chans pulled his spectacles off his forehead to read his notes before making another comment.

"The king has authorized me to contract with you. We want you to track down every pirate that has done harm to England."

"That's a mighty tall order for one man," scoffed Rogers.

"We will give you whatever is needed—ships, provisions, and soldiers."

"And what is my reward?"

"For a capture, you receive one hundred pounds for every pirate captain, fifty pounds for senior pirate officers, and twenty pounds for crew. Any holdouts, track them down without mercy and hang them."

"You lay a lot upon me. What would give me the authority to do such?"

"I will draw up a proclamation called *The King's Pardon*, signed by King George. It will pardon all pirates of their crimes if they surrender before September 5, 1718, and take an oath not to return to their former enterprise."

Rogers looked at Chans in disbelief.

"Their option is either to surrender or be hanged? Good grief, what is my legal authority to do so?" asked Rogers.

"You will be commissioned captain-general and governor-in-chief. That will be your legal authority."

"Governor of what?"

"Governor of Nassau, New Providence, and all the Bahama islands."

"This is highly profitable and rewarding, barrister, but extremely dangerous. You're asking me to put my life in jeopardy."

"There is no time to waste. We need an answer now. And what say ye?"

"Sir, my I have a moment of private time?"

"Of course, but not long, we have other important business to attend to as well." Chans refilled his mug with another English ale.

Rogers walked out of the chambers into the hallway. He placed his forehead against the stone wall. *What a predicament. I can make more money than ever and become the powerful governor of Nassau at the same time. But how do I compensate for the risk? I know of these men; they are barbarians.*

Rogers returned to the chambers. Chans was busy writing legal briefs on a long, wooden table filled with flowers and different types of English brew and mugs.

"Mr. Barrister, I have made a decision."

"You may call me Chans, Mr. Rogers. And again, what say ye?"

"I ask for the complete backing of the king and his council, at least a hundred soldiers, provisions for six months, and an escort with man-of-war from the British Naval Fleet."

"I assure you that your requests will be granted. Leave immediately for the docks at the Thames River. I will have a British Naval commander meet you there."

"One more thing barrister," Rogers interjected, "I need a thousand religious pamphlets with spiritual teachings."

"Of course, if you think that will assist." Chans placed his hand over his mouth to cover a chuckle. Chans was quite skeptical of pamphlets turning sinners into saints.

"Then, I say yea," declared Rogers.

As Rogers walked out of the chambers, an elder council man nudged Chans in the elbow. "Do you trust him?"

"Trust him? Hell, I don't' know . . . I just met him."

"He has a reputation for being an honest man."

Chans looked bewildered and scratched the side of his cheekbone.

"That's what bothers me. Can he remain an honest man?"

The elder statesman stopped and looked Chans in the eye.

"The lifestyle of a pirate is like a cactus wanting a hug: free will, plundering, whores, and beautiful islands in the Florida Straits. But it hurts to touch."

"I know . . . your wants become needs."

"Maybe you and I should volunteer to accompany Woodes Rogers to New Providence."

Chans smiled from ear to ear. "Now that's an interesting thought. Two old men sailing to the Bahamas to rid the area of whores and hang pirates. I don't think the misses or the king would approve. But I like the idea."

The elder statesman slapped Chans on the back. "Oh . . . to be young again."

"I would be a privateer, not a politician," stated Chans.

"And maybe I would be a pirate."

"Let that dream go, lad."

Before he knew it, Woodes Rodgers was about to become the new governor of Nassau, a pirate haven. In April 1718, Rogers sailed from the Thames River in England aboard *Delici*a. He was accompanied by three warships of the Royal Navy and a force sufficient to eliminate piracy in the West Indies.

Chans sent an advanced notice to the colonies of the king's proclamation. Governor Bennet of New York sent personal couriers to Nassau with fliers to be posted at all taverns. The couriers were hired to stay behind and read it for those who could not.

Hornigold sailed into Nassau Harbor with a single sloop and a small crew, hardly the fleet of envy and fear that he commanded a mere month before. His mind was still dizzy from what occurred during the prior couple of days.

It was still cold and breezy. A starlit night prompted some deep thought. Standing on the deck of his sloop, overlooking Nassau harbor, it was a time of reflection.

Only three short years ago, I start out in Port Royal. I'm the king of Jamaica; I take on a young lad by the name of Thatch, move to Nassau, create an empire of five vessels, hundreds of men, and wealth. I lose it all. And Woodes Rogers is about to become governor of Nassau. This is too much.

Maybe I should not have announced my plans. That certainly gave God a reason to laugh.

Hornigold could not believe his turn of fate. It was beyond comprehension.

Can't even find my Norwegian beauty. He looked at the moon for an answer. *Hopefully she is looking as well, wondering where I am.*

A new life was about to begin. One that no one, absolutely no one, could have foreseen.

Benjamin Hornigold was back in Nassau. His fellow pirates were at a favorite open-air tavern discussing politics and King George's proclamation. Hornigold turned around and observed several couriers posting fliers at local merchant shops. As they made their way toward the tavern, many onlookers were curious. Hornigold got up from his seat and walked over to read the flier.

It's finally here and just as I heard. We're being asked not to return to piracy in exchange for our freedom without prosecution. And we get to keep our plunder. Amazing.

"Captain Jennings, come here. It's finally here; gather up everyone. I will read the king's proclamation to all who would like to hear."

Jennings swayed when he walked as if still on a ship at sea. His face was lined with wrinkles from too much sun. His hair was pigtailed and bleached. He was a smart pirate, cautious not to take sides. However, his deadly evil eyes and a dagger inside his leather belt belied his calm demeanor.

"Hold on," said Jennings, "let me get Leigh Ashworth, Richard Noland, and Jean Bondavais. They need to hear this. Captain, you know none of us intended to become pirates. All of us were sailors that had no work, trying to make a living. We never took anyone's life."

Hornigold placed his hands on his hips and looked perplexed. "What happened off the coast of La Florida?"

"That was my one and only plunder. 'Twas the Spanish Armada Fleet that went down in the 1715 hurricane. A hundred or so Spanish soldiers were killed. But that was Charles Vane and his crew. They went on shore. Most of the Spanish army ran when they saw him. Those that stayed behind to protect the treasure were tortured and killed. I was there but had no part in the murders. You know how Vane is . . . he's crazy."

"If it was Vane, then what prompted you to get involved?"

"I was in Nassau. There was good rumor about the 1715 Treasure Fleet going down midway up the coast of Florida. Vane thought it be a good idea to check it out. We took my sloop to La Florida, an area the Spanish called Palma de Ayes. To my surprise, we plundered 350,000 pieces of eight. I did not kill anyone. That was Vane."

"Well, you need to encourage others here to turn their back on piracy once and for all. This proclamation will never happen again. Everyone needs to take advantage of it. How could you not?"

Within minutes, hundreds of pirates gathered around the shops and taverns. Hornigold walked halfway up the stairs at a nearby brothel. He looked out over the pirates as if *he* were the governor. Hornigold held a captive audience as he read every word on the flyer. Like Biblical disciples, they listened intently to every syllable that flowed from his mouth. His voice had the power of a Pontius Pilate.

"The king's pardon will cause Nassau to be split down the middle. The more sensible of you will embrace this proclamation. And the more notorious bilge heads will be against it."

Pirates looked to Benjamin Hornigold for his advice and leadership. Hornigold saw the offer of a pardon as a means to help him recover from this indignity and regain his position as one of the leading figures in New Providence.

"Listen, mates, it would be wise to welcome Woodes Rogers. Someone raise the Union Jack on top of Ft. Nassau. Put it near Thatch's watchtower for all to see. It will send a message to the British Naval fleet of our submission to the crown, once and for all."

The pirates looked at one another. They were tired and ready to trade their hardships on the high seas for a normal life on the island or a return to England. As Hornigold spoke, more and more pirates gathered around him inside his favorite tavern, Sparky's.

"Everyone, let's celebrate the day. Drink rum, eat the best of turtle and boar, and get fooked. It's all on me." Hornigold declared. "Where's Bruce, the lobster slayer?"

"He's at the harbor gathering tails for all of us to feast on," said the bartender

Jennings, Ashworth, Noland, and Bondavais raised their tankards of rum above their heads in a toast.

"Here's to our newfound freedom," yelled Nolan. "Let's take advantage of the pardon, it may never happen again."

Richard Nolan was a respected pirate. He was a trusted quartermaster for the famous Black Sam Bellamy.

Nolan continued, "I, too, will be taking the pardon. And here is to you, Captain Benjamin Hornigold, for you have been wronged as well. You are a great man and leader, Godspeed to our new sovereignty."

A quick sea squall rolled into the harbor. Locals were trying to seek cover from the heavy downpour. The midday heat and rain created unbearable humidity. There was a commotion in the narrow alleyway of the merchant shops. Several outraged pirates trampled in the muck toward a canvas-covered, open-air tavern. They bullied and pushed their way through the crowd.

It was the deep-rooted pirates: Edward England, Paulsgrave Williams, Edmund Condent, Calico Jack Rackham, and their undisputed leader, the insane Charles Vane. They were known as Jacobites or Pro Stuarts because of sympathetic politics with the uprising against King George.

Charles Vane was out front of the madmen, waving his sword in the air. Vane's spontaneous viciousness caused his own crew to pull him away from a victim. Vane once partially hung a seaman from the yardarm and burned his eyes out with matchsticks.

"I will kill everyone who succumbs to the king of England," threatened Vane. "All of you pirates, why do you take the side of King George? You are all crazy."

Vane spotted Hornigold near the canvas-topped tavern. His sword was still brandished. In a menacing manner, Vane approached Hornigold. The patrons moved out of their way, expecting a sword fight. Hornigold placed his hand on the bandolier of pistols.

"Hornigold, have you lost your senses? There is no other governor in Nassau except me," said Vane.

"Vane, you're the one that's crazy. It's over. You're only inviting a full-scale invasion from the British Royal Navy. It would destroy us and New Providence."

"This king, who does he think he is, telling us in the Caribbean what we can and cannot do? I am the governor of New Providence."

"Self-proclaimed. Maybe you should take the lead of your former captain Henry Jennings. He had the right mind. It's over, unless you care to be hung."

"Jennings is not worthy to be called a privateer or pirate. He's a lass."

"We had here a rare opportunity, Vane. A beautiful island, merchants, a vibrant business trade, yet, we pissed it away. All of us should be on the end of a rope."

Vane looked at Wells, a well-known fisherman, lobster hunter, and turtle slayer. Wells was a local and separated himself from the pirates in general. He was an honest man and a privateer's best friend.

"Wells, tear down that Union Jack," ordered Vane.

"Sir, with all due respect, I am not a pirate. The Union Jack represents all of the United Kingdom, not just Nassau. The red, white, and blue crosses are the sign of three saints. I am a Godly man."

"Nevertheless, I want it removed immediately. Someone take my flag and place it atop the hill."

A crew member grabbed the black flag with the death's head on it and ran up the rocky ledge for all to see.

"This is my promise to you, Hornigold. I will take the heart of the first Brit officer to set foot on New Providence."

Vane and his crew stomped away and disappeared through the crowd toward the harbor.

The new governor of the Bahamas, Woodes Rogers, was spotted by two of Vane's men approaching New Providence in the evening hours of July 26, 1718. From prior experience, Rogers knew some pirates would be watching for him. So he delayed his landing until the morning hours.

Unbeknownst to Rogers, Vane and his men waited secretly off Nassau Harbor. He wanted to ambush Woodes Rogers in a dramatic way, so he ordered his crew to outfit a captured French sloop as a fire ship. The moon was low over the horizon and little light reflected off the water. It was setting up perfectly.

"I need a crew of one hundred men to row out of the harbor, quietly," ordered Vane. "We will use our French prize. Put as much gunpowder and flammable materials on it as possible."

Within minutes, the vessel was doused with flammable liquids. Vane picked up his crew with his sloop. Five men stayed behind to raise the sails, cut the cable from the mooring, and set it on fire.

"Let it drift quietly toward the enemy," hollered Vane. "Then abandon ship. I will pick you up."

The strategy was working—no moonlight, a strong summer breeze, the element of a surprise attack.

"Now, let's wake those bastards up. I want double shots aimed at the man-o'-war."

Set on fire, the French sloop drifted ominously toward the British Naval Fleet. The sky burst with red and orange hues as the ammunition exploded yards away from Rogers's *Delicia*.

"Men, fire away at will," commanded Vane.

The booming thunder and flashes of the double shots rained on the ships, forcing Rogers's fleet to split into two sections.

Hornigold and Jennings watched onshore from the tavern. Wide eyed with astonishment, they could not believe the balls and insanity of Vane.

The naval vessels were driven out of the west end of Nassau Harbor, giving Vane and his men an escape route out of the harbor's narrow east entrance. Vane's sloop, the *Ranger*, was sleek and fast.

"Men, stay on the northwest quadrant. We are headed to the Americas."

Vane and his quartermaster, Calico Jack, looked back at the burning French sloop and smiled. He slipped through the cracks, in a spectacular disappearance into the night toward the Carolinas to meet up with his old friend, Blackbeard.

"What till Blackbeard gets wind of this," said Vane to Calico Jack. "I cannot wait to tell Blackbeard what's going on. Hornigold was deposed, takes the side of King George, takes a pardon, then aligns himself with the new governor. What's next?"

After clearing away the annoying mess and reorganizing, Rogers and several others boarded smaller boats and rowed to shore the next morning.

"Jennings, they are about to land," hollered Hornigold. "Notify the guard and place them into two lines. Stretch both lines from the harbor all the way to the fort, on top of the hill."

"Most are already in place. We've been waiting since last night," replied Jennings.

Woodes Rogers stopped rowing to let the small boat drift to shore and stick in the sand. He and his entourage exited the side of the boat. They finally arrived in Nassau. It was a typical Caribbean day: bright sun, beautiful white-powder sand, and a light breeze off the sea.

Rogers, a trim and fit man, was dressed in high fashion, sporting a midthigh-length blue-velvet jacket and a tight-fitting linen shirt. His woolen stockings matched his beige pants. His wig was new and bright white. A bandolier of weapons was strategically placed across his chest.

Hornigold was the first to meet them with an honor guard. This prearranged guard made quite a first impression on Woodes Rogers.

"Fire," ordered Hornigold.

Still armed, the pirates fired shots over the head of Rogers as he passed. He and his entourage stopped to meet and greet. His hands were large and scarred from tying canvas and ropes. A missing left index finger was readily apparent.

Rogers looked around and was stuck by the number of pirates who gathered at harbor. Beggars and thieves looked on as the new governor of the Bahamas arrived.

"Who will be the first to be pardoned?" asked Rogers.

"I would like to have that honor."

"And your name?"

"Captain Benjamin Hornigold, Norfolk, England."

Hornigold had his Sunday best on. He stood tall, wearing a long blue coat nearly touching the ground. It was trimmed in beige with folded cuffs up to his elbows. Leather belts and harnesses strapped across his chest, covering a beige satin shirt. His pants were striped and his buckled leather boots stopped at his knees.

"I have heard of you. Your reputation precedes itself."

"And I, you. But from the privateering days, maybe."

"Are you responsible for this greeting?"

"Yes, for the most part. As you can see, there are many others waiting for a pardon as well."

Rogers looked to his aid. "Bring out the parchment for all to sign."

His aide laid the king's pardon on a rickety wooden table.

"Sign here, Hornigold. Do you swear and honor that you will never return to piracy?"

"I do and I will."

"As in the rights and privileges given to me by the king, you are hereby pardoned of all piracy acts. Enjoy your freedom, Captain Hornigold."

The guards fired off multiple shots into the air.

There were about three hundred pirates in this unusual guard and more than a thousand on the island. Edward Thatch was not one of them. Why? Since Thatch and Rogers were both from Bristol, England, would Rogers recognize him as other than Captain Thatch? Would Blackbeard's true identity be unveiled and bring dishonor to his mother and family?

"Captain Hornigold, there is a stipulation in your pardon."

"And what may that be?"

"You will be commissioned to hunt down the other pirates."

"Me . . .why me? Look around; there are hundreds of pirates here. Most hate Vane."

"Hornigold, I have a list of the pirates to be captured. But things changed this past twenty-four hours; I want Vane first. Track him down and bring him to me," demanded Rogers.

Rogers placed his hand on Hornigold's shoulder as he looked him in the eye.

"That's your first assignment. Please do not fail me or the Crown."

"And what are the consequences if I can't find Vane?"

"Judgment will be determined by the Council. I would guess . . . hanging. You're a pirate, Hornigold."

"But I have never boarded an English flagship. That should be considered."

"Quit with the nonsense; find him. And do it expeditiously."

"And I want Stede Bonnet and Edward Thatch, too. Do you understand?"

"Aaaaaaa . . . that's a different story, Governor." Hornigold was shocked. Once again, his mind was in disarray, unable to think clearly.

"You know them better than anyone. Are you now denying the terms of the pardon?"

"No, sir, I'm not."

"Then what's with the quibbling?"

"I have no idea where they are."

Word spread quickly throughout the Bahamas that Hornigold would give his life for the Crown. He was becoming more notorious than ever.

Hornigold walked into his favorite tavern for a rum. He saw one of his favorite whores by herself. She waved her index finger at him. He approached and embraced her. She, in turn, placed her body close to his.

"Captain, we are split. Half of us believe in you and the half of the island find you a traitor. I just want you to know that I am on your side."

Hornigold leaned over and kissed her check. "Thank you, I need all the support I can muster."

"Be careful. I hear a lot. Your life is in danger. Do not trust anyone except me."

Governor Woodes Rogers set up his base in a tent until he could find permanent quarters. As promised upon arrival, he sent off his first letter to the Board of Trade in London. It was dated September 1718.

I met with little opposition in coming in, but found a French ship.(that was taken by the pirates of 22 guns) burning in the harbour, which we were told was set on fire to drive out H.M.S. the Rose who got in too eagerly the evening before me, and cut here[her] cables and run out in the night for fear of being burnt, by one Charles Vane who command'd the pirates and at ours and H.M.S. the Milford's near approach the next morning they finding it impossible to escape us, he with about 90 men fled away in a sloop wearing the black flag, and fir'd guns of defiance when they perceiv'd their sloop out sayl'd the two that I sent to chase them hence. On the 27th I landed and took possession of the fort, where I read H.M. Commission in the presence of my officers, soldiers and about 300 of the people found here, who received me under armes and readily surrendered, shewing then many tokens of joy for the reintroduction of Governmt. I sent officers ashoar at first coming in, but by means of our ship and H.M. ship the Milford running aground I delayed my landing till this day.

Rogers wrote a second letter to the Board of Trade in September of 1719. He needed a rational explanation for his primary target being Vane. More important, the father of the Brethren of the Republic was on now on the hunt. The letter illustrated that Woodes Rogers was in command and making progress in a very short period of time.

to every minute [we expected] to hear of Vaine . . . for on 1st Sepr. three men that came in a boat from Vaine who was then on the coast of Cuba confess'd they promised to meet him again about this time there; And the very day after Capt. Whitney sailed, I had an express sent me that three vessels supposed to be Vaine and his prizes were at Green Turtle Key near Abaco and since I had no strenght to do better, I got a sloop fitted under the command of Capt. Hornygold.

Captain Benjamin Hornigold was fast becoming the favorite of Governor Woodes Rogers.

Chapter Twenty-Two
The Hunted Becomes the Hunter

Benjamin Hornigold, the pirate hunter? Oh hell! Are you kidding?

Was God laughing one more time at Benjamin Hornigold's plan for a serene retirement?

The spiderweb of deceit and betrayal was about to begin. Hornigold had no problem tracking down Vane. Edward Thatch was a different story.

Hornigold sat along Nassau Harbor with his hand on his forehead. He picked away at an old wound on his inner forearm until it bled.

I taught this man, everything. How in the world can I convince Rogers that I will deliver when in my heart, I can't? I need to get Vane first; then I can capture the more pesky pirates. That should satisfy the Crown.

Hornigold was still feeling the effects of losing everything except his wealth. The weight of his loss with self-esteem was heavy.

I lost my crew, my standing, my Norwegian beauty. This might be the one and only break. I regain my reputation in Nassau and on the high seas. But this time, I'm on the other side. And I would love to bring the insane Vane to his demise.

Rogers and his aides took an evening walk to survey the layout of Nassau. He saw Hornigold at the dock by himself. He walked over, tapped him on the shoulder, and stunned the captain.

"Why are you here by yourself?"

"A lot to think about, Rogers. That's a mighty task that you assign to me, near impossible."

"I know the feeling. Just a few months ago, I told the same to King George and his barrister. Likewise, they gave me a tall order to take on, near impossible, that was to capture you and your cohorts."

"What's an old privateer to do?" Hornigold smiled.

"Quite frankly, I'm glad you joined us. This is reminiscent of the old days. But much more dangerous to me personally."

Rogers and Hornigold immediately took a liking to each other. Two veterans on the seas who had seen everything imaginable. Both men even had the same characteristics: handsome, tan, lined faces; hair drawn back into a ponytail; and thoughtful before they spoke. Their lives were etched into their faces. And a daunting task lay ahead of them.

"I was ready, believe me, even before I was deposed of my ship. It takes a toll on the body and mind."

"Hornigold, we're done for the evening. Let's get a rum and talk. Show us your favorite taverns."

"It's within walking distance. Lotsa whores if you're interested."

"No, not at this time. I may hand out some spiritual readings to them, though."

"You got to be joking, mate." Hornigold burst out laughing. "Not these whores. They are as hard as the limestone rock that you stand on."

"Not joking . . . this is part of my plan to civilize the island of New Providence. Maybe the miscreants need the fear of God in their soul."

"Not these residents. They never caught a break and worship the devil's ways. You have to admit, it's a lot more fun."

Rogers shook his head with a slight smile.

As the two and the others walked off the crooked dock, Rogers placed his forearm on Hornigold's shoulder. Like school chums, the two walked and laughed on their way to the tavern. There was a lot of reminiscing about their privateering days.

"You have a nice home. It beats the overcast, cold, rainy days in England. It's depressing; maybe that's why I took to the seas as a privateer," reflected Rogers.

There was a hush as soon as both men walked into the canvas-covered pub. Patrons, pirates, and whores stopped talking.

Hornigold leaned on the pine-soaked bar and looked around to see who was in the tavern.

"Maybe we should have a seat outside instead and talk in private. There are too many open ears," said Rogers.

"Absolutely. Everyone is watching me like a hawk," whispered Hornigold. "Let's get a rum and go back outside."

"Barkeep, two Jamaican rums and some bits of fish," ordered Rogers. "I leave a few English shillings for you. And if you hear any talk of Vane, it increases to pieces of eight."

"He's a mute, Governor. Vane stabbed him in the throat."

Rogers's mouth was agape. "I vow to capture and hang that animal."

The two walked out and sat on the edge of a limestone ledge. A strong breeze was off Nassau Harbor. It was a dimly lit night with a low moon on the horizon. Stars were nonexistent with a low, black storm cloud approaching in the distance. The cracks of lightning and thunder became louder. The kerosene fire lamps were flickering in the background from the merchant shops. The scene was setting up for what was about to happen.

"Hornigold, I toast to you in helping me catch the last of the thieves. You wisely took the king's pardon. Vane decided not to. He is a crazy man who walks into danger."

"And I toast to you, that the king will be pleased with your efforts. You must know Vane will never give in or take the pardon. He represents the last of pirate torture and treachery. The last time I saw 'im, he cut his own mate's throat and left him for dead."

"I understand that. That's why I chose you to capture him. Bring him back to me."

"That's near impossible."

"You're the best; find him. I will give you whatever you need, just like the Crown did for me."

"And how do you suppose I do that? I have no idea where he went."

"I'm sure he let some talk to the others in rebellion here."

"He knows every trap possible."

"I want him brought back to Nassau. His capture will show the ill-willed pirates that English authority is not to be scoffed at."

"That's a well-intentioned strategy."

"I have instructed that a platform be built by the dock. The other pirates will see his eyes pop out of his head when I hang him. I will make it torturous like he does to his victims."

"How's that?"

"He personally put my life in jeopardy with his fire ship. A slow death should suffice—let his neck be sideways, and burn from his own sweat around the noose. I will delay the platform door. Then kick it hard, so his neck snaps and his legs flail in the air. Then rescue him and do it again."

"You will probably hear public cheers. Public hangings work; watching him die twice is even better. He is a fool and a maniac, a very dangerous man to himself and his crew."

"If nothing else, it will show them that rebellion against the Crown will not pay off," boasted Rogers.

"It looks like a small storm is about to come onshore. It's time to retire for the night."

"We can talk more in the morning."

"I may get me a lass for the hilltop tonight and watch the storms from afar. Blackbeard has a nice spot there. I use it when I'm here. Jamaican rum, a soft bed, and a West Indies buxom beauty to play with . . . doesn't get much better."

"One more thing, Hornigold . . . Blackbeard, do you know this man's real name?"

"Edward. But I'm not sure about his last name, either Teach or Thatch. I've heard both."

"I know this name, I think." Rogers squinted, his eyebrows creased. "Maybe an old schoolmate?"

"He is from Bristol, England, and can read and write. His weakness is rum, though. He lets his guard down when he is drunk."

"Hornigold . . . there is a huge reward for you if you capture Blackbeard."

"You put too much on me, Rogers. Vane is one thing; Blackbeard is another. I taught this man. He is always on the move. Without doubt, he is the best. His ship, *Queen Anne's Revenge,* equates to a man-o'-war—in many cases even better.

Hornigold readjusted his black leather tricorn as the wind began to gust. He stared through Rogers with an air of authority.

"Besides, I already have all the wealth a man needs," said Hornigold.

"It's not in the freedom of a king's pardon or the mix of jewels and gold."

"Then. . . what possibly could it be?"

"I know where your Norwegian beauty is."

Chapter Twenty-Three
Game On

In September 1718, Hornigold set out to capture Captain Charles Vane. Governor Johnson of South Carolina was also on the hunt. Who would get to him first?

Hornigold set sail toward the northern chain of the Bahamian Islands, the Abacos, Cat Cay—nothing. He crisscrossed through the Straits of Florida, then south to Cuba. And again, nothing.

Three weeks passed. Woodes Rogers had not heard from Hornigold. He became suspicious. In his daily meetings, the same question was posed to his council.

"Has anyone seen or heard from Benjamin Hornigold?" Rogers demanded to know.

The council looked at one other for a response. No one offered a reply.

Rogers leaned back in his chair. "Answer me, damn it! Has anyone heard anything about Hornigold?"

"No, we have not, sir," answered one of the lieutenants.

A British Naval commander stood up and approached the table Rogers was sitting at. He placed his fists on the table and looked Rogers in the eye. "We think he is up to no good, Governor. Just say when, we will sail to find the bloody bastard."

"That may well be the next move. We can no longer afford to sit and wait."

The absence of Hornigold, Vane, and Thatch deeply disturbed Rogers. His strategy to rid all pirates in Nassau was going awry. Rogers began to think of revenge for Hornigold's betrayal.

That bloody son-of-a-bitch. He double-crossed me. I trusted a privateer who turned pirate. He probably hooked up with Vane and Thatch. If the three of them join forces, all hell will break loose and the pirates retake Nassau. The king will have my head on a platter, for Christ's sake.

Rogers was outraged and pounded his fist on the table. His fair-skinned face turned beet red and the jugular veins popped out. "I want to know immediately of any information about Vane or Hornigold. Get off your asses and get some answers, damn it."

"Sir, we need a plan," said the lieutenant.

Rogers upended a table nearby, spilling a tankard of rum over some documents from the Board of Trade. He became even more furious.

"Infiltrate the pirates who are against the Crown. Let me know of any rumor or telltale sign. Bribe them with pieces of eight if need be. That's the plan."

The council left the tent and dispersed into the crowd of merchants, looking for answers.

A look of scorn and wrath was on the new governor's face.

Unbeknownst to Rogers and his advisors, Hornigold was simply unsuccessful in finding Vane. Hornigold went over and over possible escape routes out of New Providence.

Vane headed northwest toward the Americas when he left Nassau. But he likes misdirection. He must have done a turnabout and sailed out to the Gulf of Mexico toward Honduras. I need to head back and arrest the ones in and around the Bahamas.

Hornigold began his journey back to Nassau and spotted a pirate ship off the Bahamian banks near Cat Cay. It was Nickolas Woodall, a small-time thief, who captained the *Woolfe*. The ship was boarded and confiscated with ease. Hornigold's crew escorted the *Woolfe* back to Nassau for Woodes Rogers's inspection.

"Woodall, I know you trade stolen goods with Vane often. It's best that you tell me his whereabouts," said Hornigold. "If not, I must take you to Nassau, where you become a prisoner of the Crown. It's your choice, mate."

Woodall looked out over his ship and said, "Do what you need to do, Captain. I have no idea where Vane went to."

"Gunner, place this man in leg irons." Hornigold said little else. A navigator took control of the *Woolfe* and sailed the sloop back to Nassau. Hornigold immediately met with Rogers with pride of bringing back a sloop full of pirates on the *Woolfe*.

"Hornigold, I am much relieved. It was discussed that your pardon was an excuse to return to piracy under disguise. You could have been hung," said Rogers.

"Remember? I was deposed because I would not attack any British ships. How could you question my word and deeds?"

"Well, we had not heard from you and became suspect."

"All of my time was spent searching for Vane. He is elusive. I need to go back for him, probably into the Gulf of Mexico. It's going to take some time, Governor."

"Tell me about this pirate that you captured."

"Governor, this man is Woodall, who deals in stolen goods with Vane in Eleuthera. He had a lot of property of others on the *Woolfe*. You may want to board his ship and confiscate whatever you need."

"Great job, Hornigold."

"You need to hang him if he continues to disavow Vane's location. A bit of gibbeting always seemed to work, Governor."

"Leaving dying criminals on public display deters the others for sure. I will turn him over to our militia for proper scrutiny. I will let you know of any results."

Woodall was standing nearby listening to the conversation. His face grimaced as the handcuffs and leg irons cut into his wrists and ankles.

Hornigold grabbed Woodall by the throat until his face turned red. "Do not believe a word this man says. A noose around his neck will convince him to tell the truth."

"Lieutenant, take this man away and give him a swift beating. Then ready him for a hanging," ordered Rogers.

Woodall was dragged through the sand by the British naval officers. Chains were suspended over the projected arm of the scaffold. Woodall imagined himself hung and left suspended after execution.

"In the name of the queen, spare me. I do not know where Vane went."

His statement was completely ignored by Rogers and Hornigold.

Rogers heartily shook Hornigold's hand. Rogers was relieved that the triumvirate of Hornigold, Vane, and Thatch no longer was a threat to his command.

"Just so you know, I am not pleased until I find Vane, Governor."

"I like the attitude, Hornigold."

"And I may throw in Stede Bonnet as well. I can't stand that lying bastard. A wimp of a man who abandoned his kids to become a pirate. Something is wrong with that."

"Just keep naming and catching them. No one on the island has the expertise that you do. I wish you well."

"I will do my best. The king will be proud of your efforts."

"Well, I am pleased with your efforts. I even wrote the English Council about you."

In his many letters to the English Council of Trade and Plantations, in October of 1718, Rogers wrote:

but to my great satisfaction he return'd in about three weeks having lain most of that time concealed and viewing of Vaine the Pirate in order to surprise him or some of men that they expected would be near them in their boats, but tho they failed in this Capt. Hornygold brought wth. Him a sloop of this place, that got leave from me to go out a turtling but had been trading wth. Vaine who had then wth. Him two ships and a brigantine, his sloop that he escaped hence in being run away with by another set of new pirates, the two ships he took coming out of Carolina one of 400 and the other of 200 tons loaded wth. Rice, pitch and tarr and skins bound for London the Neptune Capt. King being the largest he sunk and the Emperour Capt. Arnold Gowers he left without doing her any damage except taking away their provisions. I have secured the mercht. That traded wth. Vaine and having not yet a power to make an example of them here he remains in irons to be sent home to England by the next ship.

Capt. Hornygold having proved honest, and disobliged his old friends by seazing this vessel it devides the people here and makes me stronger then[than] I expected.

Rogers and Hornigold walked along the pier at the harbor. Each man was dependent on the other for their own success. A renewed sense of trust was developing.

"Governor, Vane is a stupid man. Three years ago, he and Jennings raided the Spanish camp in Florida. They stole a half a million pesos off the Spanish soldiers and lost it in a scheme by Black Sam."

"I heard about the Spanish fleet when I was in London. I feel more for the passengers than I do Vane or Black Sam. The will all get what they deserve in the end."

"The captains, Echeverz and Ubilla should have been privateers or pirates." Hornigold removed his tricorn. "Maybe, I should have stayed in England."

"Well, I have a new problem, Hornigold. The pirate John Auger was pardoned. We gave him a vessel for cargo. He disappeared and out pirating again with it. I need for you to find him."

"I know exactly where to find him."

Within the week, Hornigold returned with Auger and his crew. Interestingly enough, William Cunningham—formerly a gunner for Blackbeard—was on board. After more interrogation, none of the men would discuss Vane or Blackbeard, even when threatened with execution.

On October 10, 1718, a court order was issued against the pirates. They were the first to be arrested and hung. The judgment simply stated:

To be hanged by the neck till you shall be dead, dead, dead.

A new set of gallows were built near the harbor. The crossbeam was hard oak and nailed to two upright structures for double hangings. The merchants and residents started to congregate as the prisoners were dragged through the sand.

"Hang him high, so we can see," yelled a merchant.

More and more people gathered in front of the gallows. An English hangman waited until a large crowd had assembled, so all could see that the new governor meant business.

"I've not seen a hanging since my days in Port Royal," stated a mulatto fisherman.

Twelve pirates were publicly hung that day. A question was posed to each, asking for any last-minute requests.

"Do you have a last request?" asked the hangman.

"May I have a glass of wine?" replied Auger.

"Someone fetch this dead-man walking some wine."

A local delivered a wicker cask of red wine within moments. Auger held his gloved hand high in the air and toasted to the hangman.

"With wishes for the good success of the Bahamian Islands and the new governor."

Within seconds, Auger's neck snapped. His chin rested peacefully on his chest.

The next to be hung was Blackbeard's gunner, William Cunningham.

"Do you have any last words before being hung?"

Cunningham declined to say anything and spat on the ground in protest of the corruptness of the British Crown.

There were two more unusual requests by the two other gunners.

"I had always promised not to die with my shoes on," said the first gunner.

He removed his shoes and threw them over the wooden plank. The trap door was released with such force, his tongue protruded from his mouth.

"And I always had wanted to die drunk," said the second gunner.

"Someone get this man a bottle of rum," ordered the hangman.

The gunner was allowed to drink as much as rum as he could possibly consume. The trap door opened but he remained alive. He regurgitated the rum as the noose did not cut off his airway. Vomit flew out of his mouth onto the wooden deck. Subsequently, he choked to death on his own spirit.

All twelve men were left hanging in public for that week. Seagulls flying off the harbor sat on their shoulders, pecking their way into the ears and eyes of each man. This was a clear signal sent by Governor Rogers that he could be just as ruthless.

Rogers wrote another letter to the Board of Trade in London in December 1718. It stated:

I am glad of this new proof that Capt'n Hornigold has given to the world to wipe off the infamous name he has hither been known by Though he has admitted most people spoke well of his generosity.

For the next eighteen months Hornigold brought back many pirates, just not the more notorious. He knew of their hideouts in the outer islands: the Abacos in the northern Bahamian chain (Green Turtle Key and Marsh Harbor), Eleuthera Islands to the west, and Cat Cay to the northeast.

The outer islands were a perfect place to hide. Deep blue waters were safe sailing, but the shoals surrounding the islands created problems. The glass-like appearance of turquoise water was accompanied with white powder soft sand. The lookouts in the crow's nests watched carefully to avoid running aground in the inviting shallow water.

But Charles Vane was nowhere in sight.

Hornigold never captured the most notorious pirates, only those locally known. Did he play and dupe Rogers? Was selective pirate hunting in the works?

Governor Rogers reconvened his council to discuss strategies to turn around Nassau. So far, so good. But, it was time to search for Vane again. Hornigold was summoned before Rogers.

"Hornigold, time to depart. I desperately need you to capture Vane. I appreciate your efforts very much thus far. However, Vane and Blackbeard are still out there."

"Give me a day or two to prepare the ship with provisions. We'll set sail toward Honduras. This may take several weeks, Governor. Vane is crafty. It must be his hideout until the Royal Navy departs back to London."

It was a stormy summer in 1719, and tropical winds hit the Caribbean with vengeance. Hornigold felt pressured by Rogers to seek out Vane. He sailed into rolling seas against his better judgment.

"Bo'sun, make sure you inspect all the rigging and sails. We have a long way to go."

"Aye, Captain, I will triple-check."

The boatswain adjusted the rigging for proper angles and weight. He climbed down the heavy crossbars onto the deck. He smiled and looked at Hornigold in the eye.

"Ya know, Captain, I always thought it was interesting the color you chose for the sails was black."

"Mind your business. Set course for the Gulf of Mexico. We will follow the coastline down to Honduras," ordered Hornigold.

Rain showers began about three hours out of port as the ship sailed through the Straits of Florida. They were about to enter the massive Gulf of Mexico. A halo briefly appeared over the island of Cuba.

Hornigold smiled. *Must be my Norwegian beauty smilin' back at me.*

By midmorning, the winds became stronger out of the east. It made for good sailing. However, Hornigold did not like the look of the cloud formations. Within hours, the seas rolled and ominous black clouds followed them.

That fookin' Vane is going to be the cause of my death yet.

"Mates, it's too late to turn around," hollered Hornigold. "The sun will be blotted out soon; light the lamps and man your posts."

Dense, heavy fog soon settled in. The ship began to sway, port to starboard, out of control.

"Who is steering this? For you are doing a piss-poor job, mate. You're going to kill us all. Keep it on course," hollered Hornigold.

"I can't, Captain."

"Where in the hell did you learn to sail?" barked Hornigold.

"It's not me, Captain. Something broke away. I could feel the bottom of the ship shuddering."

Suddenly, the crew was pitched forward. The ship slammed into a ledge of coral rock. It was a massive fringe reef buffering the coast of Cuba.

"Bo'sun, drop the anchor," commanded Hornigold. "Bo'sun... Bo'sun, where are you?"

Unknown to Hornigold, several crew members, including the boatswain, had been swept overboard into the water. Their ragged shirts and pants were caught on branch coral, making it nearly impossible for them to surface.

The Bo'sun surfaced momentarily. "Help! Help me, Captain," he cried, before a twenty-foot wave took him under again. He was the first to visit Davey Jones's Locker.

At low tide, the ship ran aground at the worst possible time. The sky was pitch-black. Rain pelted the crew's faces like sharp darts, and the seas grew out of control.

"Tie you yourselves down. The worst is yet to come," hollered Hornigold.

Hornigold's commands fell on deaf ears as the ferocious wind started to howl. The crew scrambled for safety in the hold of the ship. The storm turned into a vicious hurricane.

"I can't breathe. The air and driving rain is suffocating me," the navigator said with a grimace.

"Get below deck; go to the highest point of the hold," yelled Hornigold. "We can ride it out."

The ship was caught on a dense boulder and its bottom was ripped out. The lines to the rigging and masts began to snap. The canvas sails were torn to shreds by the high winds. Wave after wave of salt water crashed over the ship as it began to sink.

"Abandon ship!" shouted Hornigold.

No one heard a word.

Thirty miles southwest of Nassau, a British naval commander was on patrol looking for outlaws. He spotted a canoe floating aimlessly with five men in it. They were dehydrated and barely alive. Their lips were cracked, blistered, and bleeding from the hot sun. He placed them on his vessel and took them back to Nassau. The on-board surgeon applied beeswax and fresh water to their parched lips.

In a barely audible voice, a young runaway from Bristol repeated, "Everyone drowned . . . help."

The naval commander held his hand as if the runaway was his own son. He bowed his head and prayed.

"Navigator, full sails ahead, dead reckon back to New Providence immediately," said the commander.

The trade winds favored sailing at a fast pace. The ship was in Nassau Harbor by midday.

"Gunner, get some men and help the surgeon. I need to see Governor Rogers right away," the commander said sharply.

"Anything else, sir?"

"Prepare a small boat to go onshore."

The commander and five others rowed into Nassau Harbor. He jumped off the boat near a fishermen's dock and ran up a ledge toward Rogers's headquarters. He respectfully opened a netted door and leaned inside.

"Governor . . . sir, my I have a word?"

"Of course. Have a seat."

"Thank you, but I'd rather stand for this."

"Whatever your choosing."

"Governor, we picked up five seamen in a canoe. They're from Hornigold's sloop. The surgeon had to cut off the leg of one. It was severely broken—twisted backward and the bone pierced the skin. The mate lost a lot of blood."

"Are you sure they're Hornigold's men?"

"Positive, Governor. A young crew member was able to talk to me on the way back."

"And?"

"Captain Benjamin Hornigold perished at sea."

Rogers stared off over the harbor as if to see Hornigold sailing in by himself.

"What happened?"

"The hurricane that brushed New Providence last week hit full force in the Florida Straits. The ship hit a reef and sank. Hornigold went down with the ship, sir."

Rogers bit the inside of his lip and bowed his head. Two heartfelt prayers were said: one for his lost friend, and one for his next move.

Chapter Twenty-Four
The Whim of a King

With Benjamin Hornigold dead, who would be willing and able to capture the worst pirates? Another twist was about to take place in Nassau.

A couple of months after Hornigold disappeared at sea, a large man-of-war arrived on the shores of Nassau. Another top royal naval commander was on board and officially dressed to the hilt, with a new white wig, a red coat with gold laced buttons, and beige pants to the knees. The white stockings were worn tightly around his legs down to his black buttoned shoes. A scabbard was attached to his belt on the inside of his coat.

"This is the most beautiful water I have ever seen. No wonder the pirates chose New Providence as their safe haven," sighed the commander to his lieutenant.

The Royal Navy commander left London with a court order; the instructions were very explicit. He and his twenty-man escort walked down the main street of Nassau. All of the patrons, whores, and merchants sneered as they walked by.

The royal commander stopped and approached a buxom, vivacious redhead and said, "Can you tell me, please, where I can find the good governor of Nassau?"

The redhead was the madam of the most popular brothel in Nassau. "Get off our island and take Rogers with you," she replied curtly. "We don't want or welcome your kind here. We are free to do as we please. We don't need the Crown to tell us how to act and what to do." She spat near his shoes. "May your mother become my employee in her old age," said the madam indignantly.

A pro-Rogers pirate approached the commander. "Yes, I know. He and his council meet every day at this time on the west side of the harbor," said the pirate. "I'm walking that way; I can show you." The pirate was bald with a pot belly. A couple of rotten teeth showed when he spoke. Weathered wrinkles on his face turned to deep lines of sea experience when he smiled. A scar ran down his cheek from an empty eye socket. "Come with me," said the miscreant.

The commander and his officers walked briskly behind him along a natural wall of pinkish coral rock.

"All these merchant shops, I made out of old sails," offered the elder sea dog with pride. "The governor's tent is nearest the water. The governor picked the best site to overlook everything."

The officers brandished their swords.

"What a greeting the British Navy has—very impressive. Is the governor getting a promotion?" asked the old pirate.

"You may leave now, thank you. Lieutenant, give this man a sixpence or two for his help," said the commander with a nod.

Several officers gathered around the commander.

"I only want two guards. The rest of you remain behind but in close quarters as I speak to the governor alone."

The governor was by himself. He was astonished at the sight of a commander walking into the open-air tent. He stood out of respect for the Crown.

"May I speak to Governor Woodes Rogers, please?"

"I am he. How may I be of help?"

"Sir, I come to inform you of some terrible news."

"Oh my goodness, did something happen to my loved ones—my wife?"

"No, it's nothing like that."

"Then, what is your purpose?"

"We have received orders from the Crown to place you under arrest for violation of His Majesty's laws."

"That's crazy. Who put you up to this . . . Chans, the legal scholar?"

"No, he was on your side."

"I have a warrant for your arrest, sir. It's from an English court, not a person."

"For what?"

"The warrant states: for indebtedness to creditors. And you have not paid your taxes to the Crown. I must place you under arrest, sir."

"What? That is outrageous." Rogers stammered, looking for words. "But, but, I . . . I *represent* the Crown."

"Guards, take this man into custody and place him in the hold of the ship," the commander ordered.

Rogers was shocked speechless—stung as if a venomous snake had bitten him in the throat.

Woodes Rogers, the captain general and governor-in-chief of New Providence, was shackled like a common thief-pirate. The British officers escorted Rogers through the streets of Nassau.

Rogers, deeply humiliated, asked, "Where are we sailing to, Commander?"

"Back to London, for imprisonment."

Part 7

Calico Jack Rackham and Charles Vane

1715 Fleet Reflection

ALLEN BALOGH

Chapter Twenty-Five
Rackham and Vane

Life off the sea was abundant to meet the wants and needs of rogue men in Port Royal and Nassau. Gold, silver, and rum flowed like cascading waterfalls in Ocho Rios. The local merchants reveled in the pirate's wealth.

The island was eventually abandoned by many of its settlers. Nassau was taken over by lawless pirates, a thousand in number. They governed by their own informal code of conduct, creating havoc. There was outcry heard all the way to London. The residents complained the pirate government was destroying their island and demanded the Crown remove them.

A minister who arrived to meet spiritual needs immediately left on the same ship. He declared to a few local Sunday churchgoers, "since the majority of its population consists of pirates, cutthroats, whores, and some of the vilest persons in the whole of the world, I felt my permanence here was of no use."

Governor Woodes Rogers was given three insurmountable duties by the Crown when he arrived at Nassau, Bahamas, on July 1718. His plan was to rebuild Nassau's fortifications, gather intelligence about Spain's quest to retake the island from English hands, and hang the most vicious pirates. The first two plans were easy compared to tracking down the elusive, cold-blooded pirates. Dismantling the Republic of Pirates was not going to be an easy task.

Rogers met with all those who would listen to him at the harbor in Nassau. A crowd quickly gathered when the governor stood on top of the rocks that formed the breakwater inside the harbor.

"I offer royal pardons to all of you. It's your last chance for freedom." He wiped his forehead with a gentleman's hanky. Rogers was not used to the sweltering heat and humidity of a midafternoon summer in the Bahamas.

Rogers extended his hands, sweaty palms up, as if to give an offering. "If not, you will be hung, every last one of you."

"We promise not to go against the Crown for here on out. You have our word," cried an elderly gent. "I was a privateer once, an honorable profession, working for the good king and queen of England."

Rogers turned and stared at the entrance to Nassau. He saw thick masts rocking back and forth at the docks. At least fifty sloops and ships were moored in the deep water harbor.

"I expect each and every captain docked here to cooperate. If not, then it will be a hot day for a hanging for all of you."

An impish, slovenly sailor stepped forward and commented, "I trust that Your Excellency enjoyed a restful night. Our evening breezes are quite unlike those in London."

"It's none of your concern to comment on my night."

"Sir, with all due respect, most of us will take the pardon. But, the more ruthless, like Vane, Thatch, and Rackham have left the island."

"Before long, I will have my best track them down like the scoundrels they are."

"Sir, may I speak with you in private?"

"And your name is?"

"James Bonny."

"And where are ye from?'

"I sailed here with the wife, from South Carolina, but I was born in England."

Escorted by two guards, Rogers and Bonny walked along the harbor. The intruder perturbed the elegantly dressed guards. Sweat beaded on their foreheads from the heat and their required dress, long blue naval coats with white shirts tucked into their wool pants.

"Governor, can I speak with you in private?" Bonny was persistent and annoying. "Hey, hey, I have valuable information. You should listen to me."

Rogers pointed his finger at the guards and waved his hand toward the docks. "Stay close by, but give us some privacy."

"All right, Mr. Bonny, you have my undivided attention. Now what?"

"I would like to be paid for what I know. It's valuable, I assure you."

"If it's worthy and verifiable, we can negotiate payment. If not, you will hang with the rest of them."

A gibbet was being erected at the low-water mark of the harbor. The miscreants were threatened with public execution. Even the vilest rogue was deterred from committing more crimes against the Crown. Bonny was no exception.

Bonny continued with his pestering. "But how much, Governor? Would the payment be in . . . rum, food, doubloons?"

Bonny's petty bargaining agitated Rogers.

"Good God, you're nothing more than a thief. Quit your squabbling." Rogers pulled back his long, black coat and reached for his pistol. "Enough of your words."

"No need for that, Governor. I know where some of the pirates are. You will be quite happy with me."

"And which pirates might those be?"

"Charles Vane and Jack Rackham," said James Bonny.

Rogers's eyebrows raised and curled inward. "Tell me more."

"Vane wants you dead."

Rogers bit his lip. "Oh, he does, does he?" Rogers took a step closer and looked down at him. "Where is he now?"

"He's at Green Turtle Cay, near Abaco. It's a two-day sail from here. He is with the others who left when they heard your vessels were off shore."

Rogers turned to the guard. "I want you and another sentinel to summon Benjamin Hornigold. Now."

Within the hour, Hornigold and Rogers met at Hornigold's favorite open-air tavern. It was perfect for watching ships approaching and leaving from both sides of the harbor.

The governor pulled out a chair from the table. He sat facing the harbor's east entrance. The crystal-clear waters and the deep-blue sky enticed the governor to sit back and relax.

"Hornigold, I like your choice of pubs. You get to scan the entire horizon from your perch, from sunset to sunrise."

"And I like your style, Governor."

Hornigold rested his elbow on the table and placed his other hand on Rogers's shoulder. Their new friendship and respect was solidified.

"Benjamin, you wisely took the king's pardon. Vane chose not to." The governor leaned in and whispered, "Vane must pay the consequence of death."

Hornigold leaned back in his chair. "He's a stupid, brutal madman."

"I need for you to find him."

"Governor, you're dealing with a barbarian. He beat a merchant man with his bare hands because he was defiant." Hornigold placed his thick hands on Rogers's shoulder. "He squeezed a cord around another man's neck till his eyeballs popped out."

"I've seen his likes before."

"How about this, Governor? Vane hogtied a disobedient crew member. The man was a mute and unable to communicate. He stuck oakum in his mouth to suffocate him. To add to the poor man's suffering, he lit the oakum on fire."

"Hornigold, I promise you, he will be hanged as a murderer. The bastard will rot in the sun."

"If I were you, Governor, I'd be sleepin' with me eyes open."

"I'll worry about that. Just capture Vane and bring him to me. You will be paid handsomely."

"I'll take John Cockram with me. He is a pirate not to be questioned. He and Vane have a score to settle. It will make things interesting."

Rogers and Hornigold, onetime enemies, shook hands like brothers.

"We'll leave by the time the next tide rolls in."

Hornigold, Cockram, and their crews left Nassau at sunrise, sailing to the Abacos, the outer islands of the Bahamas. As they sailed out of the harbor, another sloop passed them by. It was the local courier delivering mail and news.

The courier ran up the jagged, coquina rocks to Woodes Rogers, who stood at the harbor's edge near the gibbet.

"Sir, I knew you would want to read this right away. It's a threatening message from Charles Vane."

Rogers' sweaty fingers opened the letter. It read:

Your Excellency, may please to understand that we are willing to accept his Majesty's most gracious pardon but it must be on the following terms, viz:

We will not dispose of all our goods now in our possession. Likewise, to act as we see fit, with every Thing belonging to us. We shall continue to lead the life of freedom under the Skies, to come and go at our whim. You, on the other hand, have no right to occupy our island, New Providence. You must leave. If your Excellency shall please to comply with this, we shall, with all readiness, accept of his Majesty's Act of Grace. If not, we are obliged to stand on our own defense.

Your Humble Servants,

Charles Vane and Company

"Governor, Vane told me to tell you that Edward Thatch would be with him as well, to retake the island. Your authority and life is in question, for sure."

Rogers scratched his forehead and slipped the salty paper into his belt.

On November 23, 1718, Vane and his ninety-man crew on the *Ranger* encountered a large French vessel.

"Is that a frigate?" asked Vane.

The navigator peered through his spyglass and replied, "Hell no, it's a man-o'-war flying a French flag."

"Let me see that."

Vane stood at the helm and took a closer look. To his surprise, the man-o'-war was heeled over and cutting a clear path toward the *Ranger*. "The French bastard is pursuing us. It's too much for us to handle."

The navigator thought otherwise. "Captain, we don't run. We are in favor of pursuing, not running."

"No, it's an unwise decision. It's twice the size of the *Ranger*. Vane looked around to see if any other ships were on the horizon. "Let's break off now and make a run for it."

The quartermaster, Jack Rackham, spoke the loudest. "We contest your decision, Vane." The veins were popping in Rackham's neck. "That vessel will have plenty of riches on board. We will have a much larger vessel at our disposal."

Vane clenched his fist at Rackham. "I'll hear none of it."

"Cryin' out loud, Captain. Why the decision to run?" hollered Rackham. "They're French, for Christ's sake."

"We'll be in their firing range soon."

"Captain, the French squeal like fair maidens. Let me cut their throats, you'll see."

"You're quartermaster, Rackham. I'm captain. I will make those decisions, not you."

"Vane, you're a miserable person. As captain, you're required to fight, not flee."

"I'll do as I please, Rackham."

"You attack small fishing boats and merchant vessels—that's it."

Vane pulled his cutlass out of its scabbard. "You better think twice before opposing me."

Rackham had overwhelming support to stay and fight. Vane stared at the navigator and ordered, "Do as I say or you will be the first to die with a cutlass up your arse."

As the faster *Ranger* fled toward the horizon, the most vicious men on the sea exchanged embarrassed glances with one another and muttered angrily.

"Vane's a coward," Rackham yelled. "We need a vote to remove him. Do I hear yea?"

The decision was quick and without incident. The near unanimous "Yea" thundered along the deck rails. Hands were raised and fists were closed to support Rackham.

Rackham approached Vane. "The men just gave you a vote of no confidence. You were declared to be a coward." Rackham placed his right hand on his pistol. "You will be marooned within the hour."

Speechless, Vane froze in his steps. "Me—marooned? And who is the new captain?"

"The men voted for me."

"You, Jack Rackham, have little experience." Vane laughed.

"I had enough experience for you to place me as your quartermaster."

"That was a mistake."

"Regardless, you will be marooned on the next island."

Jack Rackham was now a name to be reckoned with in the Caribbean. He earned the nickname "Calico Jack" for his taste in clothes made of outlandish, multicolored Indian Calico cloth.

Jack Rackham's big boost was his gutsiness in contradicting the wildly unpredictable Vane, especially at a time when Vane was uncharacteristically careful. Sailors, especially pirates, thought cowardice was a personal invitation to mutiny, if not death.

"Men, as my first order . . . let's sail onto the Greater Antilles and into the Jamaican Channel." The crew cheered in delight. "Let's go plunder—English, Spanish, French, I don't give a rat's ass."

In December 1718, Rackham arrived on the northern shore of Jamaica. He pulled out his spyglass to study the harbor at Port Royal.

"We're in luck, mates. There's a large cargo ship leaving the port."

It was the *Kingston*, loaded in rich cargo with an estimated worth of £20,000. An incredible amount of the value rested in gold watches, hidden in the hull. Gold was rare in Europe, and the London watchmakers and merchants demanded gold for pocket watches, pendants, and wrist watches. The French and Germans took notice as well.

"Navigator, set full sail; let's give chase," ordered Rackham. A loud cheer was heard from his small crew. "Finally, a ship of worthy cargo to be attacked," hollered the gunner.

The *Kingston* was still within sight of Port Royal. The local merchants watched in shock and anger as the plunder took place.

"We cannot let that pirate escape with our property," exclaimed the local jewelry maker. "All men of courage, we must gather up and hire hunters to give chase."

It was a Caribbean December. The seas were choppy, and cold wind blew harshly against the faces of the crew. The sun was sinking behind the horizon and the winds were dying out.

Rackham had the advantage of outrunning the bounty hunters until the hunters caught up with the *Ranger* in February 1719. The *Ranger* was anchored at Isla de Pinos, Cuba. The lookouts found most of Rackham's crew on shore, drinking and hungover. Many were in temporary tents made of old sails, snoozing away. The pirate hunters swarmed ashore, firing muskets as most of the crew ran to hide in the woods.

The pirate hunters not only retrieved the *Kingston* but also took the crewless *Ranger* back to Port Royal without Rackham's crew. With the exception of a few gold watches, the merchant's property was still intact.

Rackham and his crew were left behind at Isla de Pinos. "Damn it to hell. Now what?" Rackham asked his navigator. "I don't know and couldn't care less. I must drink to our health, if anything."

Both men watched as their sloop disappeared into the horizon. An argument among the crew ensued over what to do next.

The navigator raised his tankard of rum. "Put it to a vote, Captain."

The remaining crew agreed to head back to New Providence. It was a long sail back to Nassau in the two small piraguas. They were cramped, shoulder to shoulder, and the crew was fortunate to escape with their lives.

"I'm still the captain. There is no use in fooling ourselves. We have little; maybe it's time to sail back to Nassau. Hell, Rogers may even give us a pardon."

Rackham and his crew arrived in mid-May 1719. He made a trek around the island on foot looking for Governor Woodes Rogers. Finally, Rackham spotted Rogers at a local brothel. He was handing out religious pamphlets.

"Governor, may I see you alone?"

"And who are you?"

"I'm Captain Rackham."

Rogers was speechless. His jaw locked, unable to utter a word.

"Governor, I come to you to ask for compassion and a pardon, not only for me but for my men as well."

"Are you Calico Jack Rackham?"

"Yes, I am."

"Why would I do something so preposterous? I should place you under lock and key."

"For what?"

"Piracy. Your value has increased this past year."

"We're done with pirating, Governor. Honestly, it was Vane who forced us to plunder. Either we obeyed to his orders or be killed. As you may have heard, Vane is a madman."

"I have heard such. What do you have to offer?"

"We will cease and obey."

Rogers leaned back on a railing and pondered his decision. His eyes focused on the pamphlets in his hand. "You must guarantee in writing that you will submit to the Crown's authority before I will even consider your request."

"I'll do whatever is needed."

Rogers handed a pamphlet to Rackham. "And place religion in your heart instead of piracy."

"I'm a believer." Rackham smiled, sensing his mission was accomplished.

"I need your signature on the pardon."

"I can't write, Governor." Rackham held his head down, in shame. "May I place an *X* wherever you want?"

"Mind you, one step out of line, and you will hang from the gallows, like the others."

Rackham drew an *X* over the top of the governor's signature, a harbinger of things to come.

Calico Jack Rackham was now free to roam Nassau. However, as the money ran out, the crew abandoned him and shipped out on other pirate or merchant ships. Rackham lived in Nassau alone for a couple of months, hawking golden watches, colored stockings, and calico clothing.

Within the week, Rackham met the two Nassau mermaids whose lives were about to completely overshadow his. The legendary aquatic creatures with the upper body of a curvy female and a tale of a fish foretold disaster. Or, they could be beneficent, bestowing boons or falling in love with humans. Rackham was about to find out.

Part 8

Anne Bonny & Mary Read

1715 Fleet Full Circle

ALLEN BALOGH

Chapter Twenty-Six
Female Pirates Dominant the Scene

Anne smacked James Bonny across the face with an open hand. "You disgust me. Yer cowardice makes me ill to my stomach." James flinched in fear of being hit again as his upper lip started to bleed.

"Was it you that turned in Vane and Rackham to Governor Rogers?" Anne demanded an answer. "I asked a question, James."

James cowered and said nothing.

"Yer the only one that knew Vane and Calico Jack were in the Abacos, you bastard." Anne spit on his shoddy, black boots and walked away. "I've had it with ya, James."

Anne spent the remaining afternoon drinking at the local taverns in Nassau. She loved to seduce rogues to make James angry. On more than one occasion, Anne was caught sleeping in a hammock with those in need of pleasurable affection.

"Any of ya lads up for some fun?" asked Anne.

"You have the beauty of a mermaid," an aging sailor said quietly. "This is for you, lass." A toast of rum was ordered for Anne.

All eyes turned to the front of the tavern. One of the leaders of the Republic of Pirates made his presence known. Calico Jack swaggered in and stood underneath the jasmine overhanging the entrance. He was dressed in a silk shirt with calico pants. His hair was light brown streaked golden by the sun, tied back with a ribbon.

Calico Jack scanned the canvas overhangs to see who might buy his goods. He dangled a gold watch to entice those sitting at the bar.

"And who might buy this beautiful locket of time?"

A sensuous "mermaid" sat on a wooden barrel. She gazed at Rackham. He held his hand to his forehead to block the sun glaring through the canvas openings.

Anne stood up. She was tall. Her long, auburn hair flowed down her back when she removed her hat. "I'll buy it." Her piercing blue eyes stared through Rackham. He stared back.

Rackham smiled. "Sold, but I prefer payment in the arms of passion, not silver."

"We can do that."

Desire set in, and each became irresistible to the other.

Rackham and Anne sat together at the bar, playing with each other's thighs. A tankard of rum was ordered from the barkeep.

"Rackham, you have made a name for ya-self in Nassau. And it's all good. I always wanted to meet ya."

"I have seen you, but with another."

Rackham and Anne spent the rest of the day together, walking in and out of the local shops. They walked hand in hand to his outpost on top of Nassau hill. Rackham made dinner for Anne: boiled green turtle soup, bits of pineapple on top of cuts of snapper. A bottle of wine, plundered from a French ship, sat on top of a rock.

"Rackham, you're too much: handsome, daring, and a masterful cook."

Rackham placed his finger on her lips. "Shhh, isn't this beautiful, Annie?" The two lovers sat on the rocks with their arms resting on their knees. "It's the best lookout in all of New Providence. Thatch showed it to me."

"I can see why."

"Have you heard? Thatch is now known as Blackbeard."

"I've heard that. The name fits him."

Throughout the week, one was never seen without the other. The dashing Calico Jack did not want to share his mermaid, especially with someone of the likes of James Bonny.

"Annie, let's take a walk to Nassau Harbor. It's a night to share."

The moon was shining off the sea. Rackham lit a small fire. They discussed their future. Stars twinkled, off and on, like the hearts of lovers. Jack placed his hand on Anne's thigh.

"Good grief, Anne. What were you thinking? James is a li'l twerp with big ears."

Anne removed Jack's hand. "Shut up. You don't know my story."

"Annie, I'm going to ask your husband to seek annulment of your marriage. The governor has the authority to do so."

"Good gosh, he is a snitch for the governor."

"If he refuses, then I will offer him a good sum of money."

"Jack, I am not a marriage or divorce that can be purchased or sold like an animal."

"Well, I want to be with you forever."

"James asked that I go with him to see Governor Rogers tomorrow. I think he is up to no good, but I can handle myself."

The remainder of the evening and throughout the night, Anne and Jack lay in a large hammock, kissing, caressing, and watching the heavens.

It was a warm morning. The sun arose behind the horizon. Seagulls squawked and awoke the two whose arms held each other.

"Jack, I need to leave."

"Where to?"

"The governor's quarters, back in town."

"Should I go with you?"

"No, this is better done by me-self. I'll be back by midafternoon."

Anne kissed Rackham on his cheek and put her clothes back on. She walked down the jagged rocks onto a path leading to the harbor. She stopped by an open-air tavern for a quick shot of rum. *I'm not looking forward to this at all. I wonder what the miscreant is up to.*

Anne stepped over a couple of drunkards as she left the tavern and continued walking along the water's edge. Several garrison soldiers patrolled the harbor, watching for any pirates entering Nassau.

The governor's quarters was within view. James was waiting at the entrance with his hands on his hips.

"About time, Anne."

"What are you up to, James? What kind of scheme do you have going now?"

A matted, mongrel dog laid in front of the tent, guarding his newfound owner, the governor of New Providence. James pulled back the canvas opening.

"Pardon, sir. May we have a word?"

Governor Rogers sat at a table, drinking rich, robust Jamaican coffee, writing out pardons for many of the local rogues. Each morning, he arose with the sun.

"Ahhh, James." Rogers stood up and approached Anne. He pushed his chest out to show off his proper English dress of a seasoned military man. A beige tunic with matching stockings and a blue doublet was too much for the heat of the Caribbean.

"Governor, I would like to introduce you to my wife, Anne."

"Anne, as you know, I am Governor Woodes Rogers."

"Yes, I know. What I don't know is . . . why am I here?"

"I know of your affair with Jack Rackham." Rogers bit his lip. "I met him recently, a man of flair."

"And how do you know that?"

James interrupted, "The governor has the authority, Anne, to grant an annulment that I heard you wanted. Everyone at One Eye's tavern told me about it. Go ahead and ask."

Both stood in front of the governor.

"Governor, I am in love with another man. I seek your authority for a divorce."

"I'm on the side of James, not you."

"Then . . . why did James bring me here?"

"Mrs. Bonny, I am considering charges of adultery."

Anne was stunned. "What?"

"The punishment will be a whipping for your loose behavior."

"What did I do that was so wrong to deserve death?" Anne's blood began to rush to her head.

"That's not all. Jack Rackham will be the one to lash you till your death."

Anne turned to her husband. Without hesitation, Anne grabbed the pistol out of James's belt. With the butt, she turned and cold-cocked him in his jaw. "You bastard."

Anne whipped James with his own pistol. He fell to the ground. The back of his head struck a jagged edge of coquina rock, knocking him out. Anne pointed the pistol back at Governor Rogers.

Rogers knew his life was on the line the day he accepted the position from the Crown. However, marital disputes were not in the agreement with the Crown.

Anne stared wildly into his eyes. "Fook you, Governor," said Anne angrily. "It's my turn."

Rogers lowered his hand toward his belt, fidgeting to find his pistol.

"Are you really that big a fool, Governor? Go ahead; there will be two of you dead, before that lying bastard awakens."

Governor Woodes Rogers was alone, looking down the barrel of a large, steel flintlock pistol.

"It would be my pleasure to torture you, in the way you planned to torture me. Instead, I'd rather kill you."

"Mrs. Bonny, you're about to—"

"Mrs. Bonny? Now, I'm Mrs. Bonny? Seal yer lips, Governor. You're squawking like a seagull caught in the harbor. You sound like my husband, James."

Growing livid over the betrayal of her husband and the governor, she remembered a time in her childhood. Her father's breaking of the father-daughter contract raised its ugly head. The urge to torture and kill these men who betrayed her raced through every part of her trembling body.

I hate these men. Why should I spare them, when they disavowed me?

"Is this the way you would treat yer wife? For I'm sure she is back in London fookin' the king's court."

Governor Rogers peered through the tent opening, hoping a sentinel was nearby.

"You're all hypocrites, every last one. Get on yer knees, Governor."

Woodes Rogers faced death many times in battle. Now, he faced it at the hands of a sociopathic young girl. Rogers's deep tanned faced turned pale. His eyes began to swell.

"Please don't kill me. I have children back in England. Please, please don't."

Anne slowly backed out of the door. She cocked the pistol.

On that night of August 22, 1720, Rackham, Bonny, and a handful of disgruntled ex-pirates stole a twelve-gun Bahamian sloop, the *William*. The vessel belonged to Jack Ham. The pirates sailed out of Nassau in the middle of the night.

Jack Rackham happily returned to his old life of piracy. However, he had no idea about the make up of two of his new crew. The mermaids—with perfect breasts, shapely hips, and soft lips—would look you over, slice your throat, and watch you bleed to death. A sympathetic heart was not one of their attributes.

Most of his crew came from brothels, gaming houses, and open air bars. More often than not, their lives were at stake from duels, cheating at cards, and disease.

Anne never felt as free as she did under a full moon night and glistening constellations.

Freedom from all the hypocrisy of English propriety, freedom to sail the endless seas. I love life at sea.

When the sun rose, a guard saw Woodes Rogers in his tent, writing on his personal wooden table brought from England. It was a proclamation:

Jack Rackuman, Ann Bonney and their said Company are hereby proclaimed Pirates and Enemies of the Crown of Great Britain, and are to be treated and Deem'd by all His Majesty's subjects. Their punishment shall be death by hanging.

The same bright sunlight broke through the billowing sails of the *William*. It was a warm and humid morning. The aqua-blue waters were calm, not a wave to be broken. Calico Jack stretched as he awoke from a cat nap. Anne lay beside him in the captain's quarters.

"Annie, wake up."

Anne answered, covering her eyes from the blinding sunlight. "Jack, what's wrong?"

"Annie, you must change clothes."

"What? . . . Right now?"

"Yes. You must dress as a man . . . before someone sees you."

"Why?"

"It's the oath. You know that. It's in all Articles of Agreement; no women can be on board. The punishment is death."

"I knew that. My mind is still back in the governor's tent. I should have shot that bastard between the eyes."

"Why didn't you?"

"I couldn't, Jack." Anne paused. "He looked too much like my father. And as much as I despised him, I still couldn't pull the trigger."

"Forget that, for now. There's a bag in the corner; pick what you want." Rackham pointed in the direction of the door. "Annie, make sure it fits loosely."

Anne rifled through the bag to choose from Rackham's pants and shirt. She preferred the Indian Calico print but chose a torn tunic and short pants. After dressing, Anne walked outside and breathed in the morning air. She looked onto the deck below and saw the crew trimming the sails to get full speed and sail on to the outer islands of the Bahamas.

Well after midnight, the *William* arrived at Great Harbor Cay. Anne noticed a young rogue at the bow checking the water depth ahead. With a small crew on board, his duty was to notify the navigator of any shallow water. The *William* was about to anchor for the night.

Anne approached the young scamp. She whispered in his ear, "I saw you back at the tavern."

"And I saw you as well." The young man's face flushed. "Your disguise as a sailor fits you well. I would never take you for a girl."

"You noticed?"

"Yes, but don't worry. I said nothing to no one."

"Yer face is flawless. Yer very handsome."

The shy young man looked away. *Oh no, what do I do? Should I tell her who I am? If I do, my life will be in jeopardy.*

"I need to finish my duties. As you can see, most of the men are passed out, or below the deck sleeping," said the young man.

"Finish what you must. I'll be back," said Anne.

Great Harbor Cay was an alluring piece of the world. The *William* anchored under a starry Caribbean night. A high moon illuminated the island. The water was motionless. Pixie dust could have fallen from the skies.

Anne tapped him on his shoulder. "It's just you and me now." As he turned around, they stood hip to hip.

"Ahhhhh, I . . . I," the young man stammered.

Anne placed her hands on his waist. "I must say that I was very attracted to you back in Nassau. Yer eyes struck me as being innocent. I wanted you then," said Anne softly. "What is yer name?"

"Mark Read."

Anne ran her fingers down his legs.

"Look, I do not want the wrath of Captain Jack Rackham."

Anne tried to seduce the handsome new recruit. A slight breeze opened her partially unbuttoned shirt. Her breasts were exposed slightly, enough to entice anyone.

"Do you want to touch me?"

Staring at the buxom Anne, an evening wave created a slight rocking of the ship. Anne's breasts rolled with the waves. Her enticement was met with some hesitancy by her new beau.

"Jack Rackham will have my head if I touch you."

Anne became reassuring in her words. "Look at me; don't worry about him." She placed his hands on her breasts.

Nervousness set in for both, an unlikely occurrence for two rogues at sea.

"I am not who you think I am. I am not the young man that you want to make love to."

Anne was perturbed at the cat-and-mouse game. "Then, who are you?"

"Doesn't matter; you won't believe me."

Anne's adrenaline rushed. "Are you one of Governor Rogers's informants? Don't tell me that!"

"Good Lord, no, you need to know that I am a young girl."

"What? Prove it."

The young rogue hid behind the wide mast, out of sight of the others. Her back was arched against the spar. Anne was startled not only because of who he was, but what she saw. An open shirt revealed a beautiful pair of breasts.

"You've uncovered my secret."

Anne gasped. "Good Lord, you are a girl?"

"Do you like what you see, as well?"

"Yes, very much so; yer skin is beautiful."

Mary removed her floppy hat. Her dark-brown hair fell onto her shoulders as she removed a piece of tied twine. Her brown puppy eyes looked up.

Anne opened her linen shirt and bared her breasts as well. "Isn't this crazy?" Anne laughed. "We're both girls dressed like men."

"Tis true, but no one knows," replied Mary. "If we're found out, it's death for sure."

"What's yer real name then?"

"It's Mary Read."

"Wait till Rackham finds out; he'll flip like a shark in a feeding frenzy."

"Oh, please no . . . don't tell."

Anne hesitated. "Mary, you have my word. I will not say anything to Rackham." Their new passion and desire for one another overrode any trust between Anne and Rackham.

Both women hugged at the helm in consolation of each other's plight. The hug turned to a meaningful embrace. Anne kissed Mary on the lips and waited for a reaction. Mary smiled back and flicked her tongue. Both kissed softly and fondled the freshness of someone new and different.

Chapter Twenty-Seven
A Confession Like No Other Before

Anne and Mary stayed at the helm throughout the night, enjoying the extraordinary beauty of Great Harbor Cay in the moonlight. Light laps of water splashed against the sides of the *William* as it anchored in an isolated enclave. Fingers intertwined, they watched the high moon reflect its light off the white sand shallows. The Abacos and Berry Islands of the Bahamas were simply paradise, meant for lovers.

Anne stooped to dip a ladle into a wooden canister of fresh water.

"Here. You first, Mary."

Mary swirled the water around in her mouth and spit it out.

"My lips were parched from the late afternoon sun. Thank you."

Mary turned to look at her new friend's body profile against the glinting waters. An unobscured view clearly outlined Anne's high cheek bones and voluptuousness in the moonlight.

"Where are you from, Anne?"

"I was born in Kinsale, Ireland." Anne spoke softly. "But I moved to Charles Town a couple years ago and then to New Providence."

"Why?" Mary became perplexed. "Why from Ireland and then all the way to the colony of South Carolina and end up in Nassau?"

"I have a bit of a story, Mary. My father was an attorney. His name was William Cormac. He had standing in Kinsale."

Both women looked over the rail onto the deck below. A bright moon lit up the carcass of a dead rat and slovenly men laying drunk on the urine-stained wooden deck.

"If you were born of wealth and means, why are you here, on a ship loaded with filth?"

"Father had an affair with our maid." Anne began to fiddle with her hair. "I was born out of wedlock. When father's wife found out, she promptly left us."

"So, your real mum is the maid?"

"Yes, me mum's name was Mary Brennan."

Anne sensed she could trust Mary with her story. "William grew fond of me, though, so I'm told. He arranged for the maid to live with us all the time. It was quite a scandal in the small town of Kinsale."

"Oh, I'm sure." Mary Read placed her hand over her mouth to suppress a giggle.

"Father lied to everyone and dressed me as a boy. He told everyone that I was a relative who was entrusted to his care."

"Oh, Anne, I do feel for you."

Anne grimaced. "Well, eventually, the town found out. Me mum told on us. Everyone in town knew that I was a girl of ill repute."

"Goodness, Anne."

"You're right, though. Father was humiliated by me. He never, ever called me his daughter or his li'l girl. It hurt so much growin' up with naught a tender touch from him."

Mary bowed her head, demure and meek, feeling the pain of Anne's memory.

Anne paused to gather her thoughts. "We moved to Charles Town, in South Carolina, so he would not have to face our neighbors any longer."

"How old were you?"

"About thirteen. Things changed a lot. We lived on a rice plantation. Father sent me to the best schools, learning music, dancing, and reading. I dressed in petticoats, rouged up me cheeks, wore the best of perfumes."

Mary eyed her friend with new respect, but a touch of jealousy crept in her voice. "You're lucky; I can read a little, though."

"But Father would not hug me or kiss me, even on holidays."

"Neither would mine, Anne."

Anne gazed across the bow in deep thought and lost in memories. "Things went awry, Mary. The neighbors must have found out. They called me the little red-headed bitch."

"And?"

"Then me mum, the maid, died."

"Gracious, Anne. Your father was still pretending his lover was a maid? Who did the chores?"

Anne smirked. "I helped for a little while. I churned butter and made soap; sometimes I sewed. But father said that I was above that. He spent a lot of money on my schooling." Anne's face blushed and became flustered. She started to pull her hair. "Mary, I have something to confess."

Mary held Anne's hand and stroked the back of it. "Go ahead; you can tell me anything."

"I once killed someone."

Mary stepped back.

"Really? Who was it?"

"It was the servant girl. Father started liking her more than me."

"So what happened?"

"I stabbed her in the belly with a kitchen knife. It felt good piercing her stomach, feeling the mushiness of her innards and watching her groan in pain. When she fell onto her knees, I kicked her in the head. She died, right there and then."

"Did your father find out?"

"I knew that I'd brought further disgrace to him. So I told Father she quit. I buried her out back of the house."

"Didn't your father suspect you of anything?"

"Oh, he suspected me all right. All his pestering with his never-ending questions got to be too much, so I ran away." Anne drifted off into private thoughts. *Everyone I ever loved, was so embarrassed of me.* "Then I got into more trouble, Mary. A sailor in Charles Town tried to rape me. He was a large, fat man with bushy eyebrows and beard. He stank to high heaven. As he climbed on top of me, I bludgeoned him nearly to death with a piece of iron."

"Oh my, Anne, you have been through a lot for such a young age. I see why you didn't stay in South Carolina."

Anne was clearly confused and upset. "Father said that he loved me dearly. But if that's true, why did he hide me? Why didn't he show me any affection?"

Mary held Anne's hand in comfort.

"To get back at Father, I fooked everyone in Charles Town: fishermen, drunks, the minister. I couldn't care less. I wanted to hurt him, let him know how it felt."

"Different reasons though, Anne. Your father was confused as well. There must have been resentment. Not for you, but toward his town. He hated the people of Kinsale and Charles Town, not you. Maybe he held guilt in his heart and not shame."

Anne pulled on her tunic and adjusted her short pants worn by Rackham.

"Jesus, now Calico Jack wants me to dress as a boy as well. It brings back a lot of bad memories of when I was a tyke in Ireland."

"Our lives growing up were such a mess, Anne."

Tears welled in Anne's eyes, but they then turned vicious. "No, Mary, he wanted to hide me from the beginning. He was embarrassed of me."

Mary kissed Anne on the forehead. "It doesn't matter anymore. Let's take a break and enjoy the evening."

Anne leaned against the wooden railing and looked over the bow. "I'm done. I told him about the mindless servant girl that I killed and the sailor." Anne looked down to hide her shame.

"Brave of you, Anne. What did he say to that?"

"He didn't utter a word. He just stared at me."

A lasting lull in sharing memories with Mary broke the concentration of Anne. Her grieving was temporary and short lived.

Mary continued, "How did you end up in Nassau?"

"Father disowned me. I hooked up with a penniless sailor. Told me I was a good-for-nothin', li'l tramp. We eloped and sailed to the Florida Strait and eventually to New Providence."

"What's his name?"

"James Bonny, a fool. He works for Governor Rogers as a snitch. I have an inkling to tell Jack, so he can fookin' kill 'im."

Mary felt the night breeze loosen her hair at the edges of her cap as she linked her arm through Anne's. "Oh my gosh, Anne. We have so much in common as little girls."

"You know, Anne? I was illegitimate too. And I had to dress as a boy."

"Really?" Anne turned toward Mary, at last, leaving her own memories to delve into those of someone else.

"You think you had a story to tell? I had to dress as my dead half-brother. How horrible is that?"

"Oh my gosh!"

"I was born in Plymouth, England, the same year as you, Anne. Me mum gave birth to a boy; then her husband died at sea right after. But he was a sickly baby and died. Me mum took up with another man. She got pregnant. The result was me."

"So why did you have to dress as a boy all the time?"

"My maternal grandmother took pity on me mum. She offered money to help with my half-brother, until he was grown."

Anne stroked Mary's hair, hoping to offer some comfort. Her fingertips glided across Mary's high cheek bones.

"Mum dressed me up as him so she would not lose any money. Grandmother did not know he died."

"That is so strange and wicked."

Mary nodded. "Sometimes, Mum rented me to a French woman as a footboy to make more money. Then I served in the Finnish army for a while."

"The army, really?"

"I served on a British man-of-war, carrying bags of gunpowder. I disguised myself as a male. Then, I enlisted in a foot regiment."

"Your looks are so deceiving. You fooled me back at One Eye's."

Mary ginned. "It's all in the bearing, lass." The girls laughed at each other. "Now this part is a bit awkward, Anne. I fell in love with my bunk mate. Eventually, I told him that I was a girl. We fell in love but he then died . . . just like me mum's husband. Caught a fever and was gone, just like that."

"Oh, Mary, I'm so sorry for yer loss. But, keep going. How did *you* end up in Nassau?"

"I needed to escape, so I hopped on the next ship out of Ireland to the West Indies."

"Oh, good decision," Anne remarked. "It's so beautiful in the Caribbean compared to the cold and fog of Great Britain. Who would ever want to go back to England or Ireland?"

Mary scratched the back of her neck. A lingering mosquito from the nearby island buzzed round her collar.

"Anne, I, too, have a confession."

"And?"

"I, too, killed someone, with a knife, just like you."

There was pause before Anne asked, "How did it feel?"

"At first my stomach dropped. Then I had this overwhelming feeling of satisfaction."

Sweat beaded on Mary's forehead. She raised her hand and propelled it forward to imitate her killing.

"Was it deserving?"

"He was the bully on the ship to the West Indies. He picked on my new love, constantly. I took issue and our captain forced us to duel."

"How did you manage to kill 'im?"

"As he raised his cutlass to slice me, I opened my shirt. All he saw were my breasts. He hesitated."

Anne grinned. "I can see why, Mary. I hesitated as well. You're beautiful."

"When he dropped the cutlass to his side, I plunged the dagger into his heart as deep as I could. I could hear him gasping for air. He was big and fat. He fell to his knees and then onto his chest."

Anne placed her hand under Mary's chin. "We're both illegitimate and offspring of debauchery. We've dressed as boys to hide our identity. We've killed in retribution."

"I know, believe me, there is no other explanation."

Mary smiled, "Oh my, Anne, you speak like a snobby aristocrat, not a common wench."

As Calico Jack walked down the narrow steps of the hold, he heard giggling. A candle was lit near the bed. There was Anne, in the embrace of another, making love to the young rogue.

Instinctively, his blood ran hot. Rackham pulled out his knife. "Fookin' bastard. How dare you? I'll slice your gourd from ear to ear."

"Stop," hollered Anne, looking up from the young man she had been caressing. "It's not what you think."

Rackham, paralyzed in fear of losing his lover, was momentarily lost in thought and confused.

"Go ahead, show him," said Anne.

The young man opened the linen shirt. Rackham saw that the rogue was a well-endowed woman.

Rackham stared the two women in disbelief. "Good God! What the hell . . ."

"Leave us be, Jack. Leave now; we can talk about this later."

Sheepishly, Jack turned around in his drunken stupor and stumbled back up the steps onto the deck. He was envious of his new crew hand.

Anne placed her arms around Mary and embraced her, hip to hip.

"Mary, I care for you a lot. I have no trace of apprehension. It feels so natural to touch you."

The candle continued to flicker in the dark of the hold.

Anne gazed into Mary's eyes. "Yer eyes, they flicker like the stars."

Mary hesitated. "Anne, do you think stars are holes in the sky to get into heaven?"

"Oh, I never heard that before. Maybe."

Anne stroked Mary's cheeks with the back of her hand. She kissed Mary on the lips, gently.

Mary started to wiggle from the body heat they felt between them. A sheen of sweat dampened their loose-fitting shirts. The hugs became sensual embraces. Anne began to breathe heavily. "Oh, Mary, I've become so fond of you."

Anne placed her hand on top of Mary's and guided it inside and down her baggy pants. Mary slid her fingers slowly onto her soft skin, caressing and playing. The intensity became too much.

Anne drew in a deep breath and whispered, "Mary, I need you to stop."

"Why?" Mary's insistent fingers continued to caress and play.

"I'm pregnant."

Mary removed her fingers and placed them on her lips. "Shhhh, I have a confession as well, like none other." Mary hesitated, "I'm pregnant too."

Chapter Twenty-Eight
The Capture

Bonny and Read were inextricably bound to each other. They shared a reputation as "fierce hellcats" for their violent tempers and ferocious fighting. In times of battle, no one on board was as ruthless and bloodthirsty as these two "mermaids." Anne's temperament for violence was one of chilling ease.

"You're taller than me, Anne," Mary observed. "Stand closer in and intimidate the lesser men."

"I look down at them and spit in their faces. That's what I do."

Mary nodded in approval. "Yes, you have more height than me, but I have the experience of battle. I consider myself well suited whether it maritime labor or piracy." Mary Read reached into her canvas bag. "Take this cutlass and axe, hitch them to each side of your hips."

Anne pulled back a brace of pistols wrapped around her loose tunic top. She chose leather straps to fasten the new weapons to her red sash.

"It's best to have as many armaments at your disposal as possible." Mary smiled. "You look robust, fierce, and gorgeous."

Anne smiled back. "And bandolier across yer chest with matching flintlocks is very manly and sensuous."

"I have more. You just can't see them."

"Mary, I was thinking last night, as I fell asleep. It all goes back to our childhood. You took on duties out of economic necessity. And I turned my back on economic advantage, my father's fortune. I set aside wealth for freedom."

"You're talking that aristocratic, nobility stuff again. Talk like us or you will give yourself away, regardless if you dress like a man or not."

"Jack said the same thing to me. I learned to cuss at every turn, picked it up easily at One Eye's tavern."

"Oh, and what I wouldn't give for a draught at One Eye's now."

In September 1718, Rackham and his crew boarded seven fishing boats and two sloops near Harbor Island, in the Bahamas. Mary led the raid against a schooner, shouting at the crew as her men climbed aboard, cursing as they gathered their plunder. Unsure of their intentions, Rackham, Bonny, and Read held their captives for two days before releasing them.

During battles, Anne and Mary fought side by side, wearing billowing jackets and long trousers and handkerchiefs wrapped around their heads. The mermaids challenged the sailors' adage that a woman's presence on shipboard invites bad luck.

"Ya know, Annie, the crew respects you two, for your ruthlessness," said Rackham.

"We fight as well if not better than most of the crew. It's about time you noticed," said Anne.

Rackham shook his head. "You wield pistols in both hands and Read flies around with a machete threatening to cut anyone in her way. It's quite frightening, really."

"Let's move on, Jack." Anne pointed her finger into Rackham's chest. "Let's plunder a ship of worthy cargo, not one of sugar or turtles."

Bonny and Read may have been in a somewhat precarious situation, two women on board a pirate ship, but pity the fool who tried to take advantage of them.

Rackham worked his way west along the northern coast of Jamaica. His fate was about to be in another person's hands.

"Who is that on the horizon?" asked Rackham. "It's a ship that I've never seen before."

"I don't know," replied the cannon master. "What would you like to do?"

"Well, fire on him. We'll find out quickly." Unwisely, Rackham fired on Jean Bondavais, a Bahamian pirate. On this particular occasion, Bondavais, uncharacteristically chose not to pursue but instead retreated. He reported the sighting to his friend and pirate hunter, Jonathan Barnet. Bondavais had more important things to do than waste time with Rackham. He terrorized the Spanish shipping lanes for major cargo shipments, not small-time bandits.

Rackham's nemesis was lying in wait for him at the pass of Montego Bay off Point Negril Pointe, Jamaica. Rackham and his crew celebrated their recent victories in their typical hard-drinking styles.

Near midnight on October 20, 1720, a British Navy sloop, the man-o'-war *Albion*, captained by Jonathan Barnet surprised them. He sailed during the evening hours from the Windward Passage, between Cuba and Hispaniola. He correctly surmised Rackham's predictable movements. Anne and Rackham were on deck when they noticed a mysterious sloop glide alongside them.

"Identify yourself," yelled Barnet from his ship.

Rackham, half drunk, said to Anne, "Damn, she's hard abeam. How did that happen?"

"Everyone's drunk."

"Respond, what say ye?"

"I'm Calico Jack from Cuba."

"You're a liar," responded Barnet. "Surrender, Jack Rackham. Or you will not like the consequence."

Rackham and another crew member replied by firing a swivel gun. Barnet promptly retaliated with a broadside and musket counterattack.

"Fire a broadside and a hail of small arms! Aim for the boom and deck," ordered Barnet.

The noise was deafening, and smoky residue filled the air as a barrage of firearms disabled Rackham's ship. One of the heavier rounds severed the *William*'s boom and mast. Crackling and splintering, they crashed to the deck, pinning men below the solid wood supports.

Unable to maneuver the disabled sloop, Rackham sent his men on deck to cower in the hold.

While Rackham and the drunken pirates cowered below decks, Read and Bonny remained on the decks, fighting with their cutlasses. They verbally called out their crew and berated the men for their spinelessness.

"Come up, you cowards, and fight like men." Mary turned her rage on them. "If there's a man among ye, ye'll come up and fight like the man ye are to be!" When not a single comrade responded, Mary Read fired several shots down into the hold, killing one of them and wounding several others.

Barnet's men stormed over the rails and onto the deck of the *William*. Outnumbered and overpowered, Rackham signaled surrender and called for quarter. Overwhelmed, the women were captured as well.

Captain Barnet strutted across the wooden planks to face the subdued Rackham. "Yer time's up, Rackham. It's back to Spanish Town for you, and a date with th' judge. Better break out yer prettiest calico fer that."

Two days later, Rackham and his crew were escorted into militia headquarters at Spanish Town. Trudging into their jail cells, the pirates caught a glimpse of a man peering through the bars. It was impossible to make out the features against the brightness of the sun.

As they walked through the jail, a man peered through the sunlight coming in the widow.

"Rackham, you're responsible for this mess. If I get the chance, I'll squish you under my boot like the cockroach that you are."

Rackham snapped his head around and froze in his footsteps. He recognized the voice and the cackling psychotic laugh of the insane Charles Vane.

Chapter Twenty-Nine
The Trial and Conviction in Spanish Town

Strong tremors and a tsunami destroyed Port Royal, the unofficial capital of Jamaica. The massive earthquake struck in 1692, placing it forty feet under water. The government moved to the small city of Villa de la Vega, on the west side of the Rio Cobre, a river that resembled a cobra snake. Subsequently, the English ravaged the city in heavy fighting with the Spanish. They had to rebuild what they destroyed. Villa de la Vega became known as Spanish Town to new settlers.

The English had a difficult time adjusting to the climate and the tropical diseases of their newly acquired island. The Taino Indians and Maroons fled to the mountains during the Spanish occupation. English settlers found themselves under attack from the hillsides. The Maroons, escaped slaves, came into Spanish Town at night to loot, burned adjacent villages, and slaughtered the English settlers.

Spanish Town was overcrowded and its narrow streets were littered with garbage. The streets were an endless flow of merchants, some legitimate, but mostly taverns and brothels. Prostitutes with missing teeth and infected boils on their skin were the norm, not the exception. With all the chaos, Jamaica remained a hub of trade and commerce. The sugar industry rose to new heights. Rum, the by-product of sugar, was called "kill devil." And the cold, clean water running down the Jamaican mountains perfected the creation.

A red-and-white cross hung at the intersection of Red Church Street and White Church Street, a clandestine nod to the secretive Knights Templar. And an oval circle, inside the city, served to hold meetings for the new English citizens. The inmates of the main prison of Jamaica had a limited view of the circle from their jail cells.

All heads turned toward the bridge over the Rio Cobre. A judge arrived in his horse-driven carriage, crossing over the bridge onto the cobblestone street of Spanish Town. From the rampant rumors throughout the jail, the inmates knew someone was about to hang. The townspeople watched as the judge crossed himself in the name of the Lord after passing a painting of St. Catherine at the entrance of the city. The inmates imitated his gesture.

A slave grabbed the horse's heavy leather collar as it reared its head. Another slave held out his arm to assist the opulent judge from the open-air carriage. The Admiralty Court of Justice was waiting for him.

The judge held court on a breezy November morning. The heat and humidity of the tropics was nonexistent. A light wind out of the north turned into a morning breeze encapsulating the city.

"It's a beautiful day for a hanging, Your Excellency," stated the jail keeper.

"It is indeed."

The judge was dressed in a long, black coat and a white collared shirt. He looked to the jail keeper and asked, "Who is first on the docket this morning?"

"Your Excellency, we have one of the most famous pirates on trial this morning. His name is Jack Rackham." The jail keeper smiled as if he and the royalty were best friends.

"Yes, I heard at dinner last night. Rackham's claim of being from Cuba was just a clever ruse, but not much of a secret to those of us in authority. The man must be an idiot."

"And with him are two girls, an Anne Bonny and Mary Read."

"Are there any witnesses to their piracy?"

"Yes, we have several."

"Retrieve the pirates and the women. Make sure they are in shackles. I want the witnesses to stand before them."

Rackham, Bonny, and Read shuffled from their cells in leg irons guarded heavily by the military sentry. They smelled from a week without bathing. Rackham held his head low in subservience to His Excellency. In stark contrast, Bonny and Read were livid, spitting and spewing vulgarities.

Rackham whispered to Anne, "I didn't see Vane in his cell. I wonder if he escaped."

"What in the hell is wrong with you, Jack? We're about to be hung. Jeysus Christo."

"May I have the first witness?" The judge paused to read the statement scrawled on a piece of paper. "And your name?"

"My name is Dorothy Thomas." She stepped forward and bowed. Hesitancy showed on her face as she covered her mouth. Her eyes were wide-eyed in fear of testifying against the vicious defendants.

"And what do you have to say?"

"I was captured by Rackham and his crew in Harbor Town. They held me prisoner for a time."

"Do you recognize your offenders?"

"These two wenches in front of me, as well as that pirate dressed in colored cloth." Dorothy Thomas glanced at the three, all with shackles on their wrists and ankles, and quickly looked away.

"Tell me the circumstances of your encounter with them, Miss Thomas."

"First, you need to know that the wenches wanted to murder me, so I could not testify against them someday. The male pirate insisted not."

"Look at the bubblies on that red-haired wench," shouted a sailor. "Like to put my face between 'em and clean me cheeks." There were shouts and laughter from the crowd.

The judge half stood, pointed, and admonished the sailor. "Guard, remove that drunk. If anyone else disrupts this hearing, the jail keeper will pay you a visit."

But the sailor's remark caught the judge's attention. He stared at Anne, who, being well endowed, wore a low-cut blouse to show off her cleavage. Anne stared back and winked.

The judge composed himself. "Order, please! Do not disturb this woman's testimony. Continue, Miss Thomas."

"I'm a simple fisherwoman, Your Honor. The two wenches boarded my sloop and stole everything I had, including the turtle meat."

"Any properties that distinguish them from others?"

I've cut open the underbelly of a shark once. It flopped over my vessel with its blood and guts spewing out." The fisherwoman smiled showing some missing and rotted teeth. "That's what they look like, the scourge of the earth, I say."

"I meant physical traits; hair, eyes, height and weight."

"They did not look like what you see, Your Excellency. They wore men's clothes and handkerchiefs tied about their heads."

"Any weapons?"

"The red-haired wench had a machete and pistol in her hands, threatening to kill me. The other wench cursed at me constantly. She had a cutlass above me head."

"How long were you held captive?"

"I was a prisoner for two days."

"Do you have anything else to testify to?"

"Sometimes the wenches dressed like men, other times like women. If it wasn't for the largeness of their breasts, I may not know them as women."

The Judge looked at Anne, then at Mary and stated, "Neither of you fooled anyone."

"They are the worst of women and should be disposed of . . . hung," Dorothy whined.

"You're excused. Next witness, please."

Jack Besnick and Peter Cornelius stepped forward to testify together.

Besnick spoke first. "Likewise, Your Honor. Both women boarded out sloops as well. We are merchantmen. Our livelihood depends on our cargo of dyes and pigs. We were held captive and our lives were threatened."

"And you, Mr. Cornelius?"

"Your Honor, they boarded other sloops with cargo as well. The wench with the red hair was more hostile. The other was too drunk and very profligate," recalled Cornelius. "Both were very active on board and willing to do anything. Ms. Bonny was more hostile toward us. She swore more than the thieves in her crew."

Mary hollered, "He's a liar. I wasn't drunk." Snickers and jeers ran through the crowd.

Hosea Tisdell was the last to testify. He identified Rackham as the man who attacked him.

Jonathan Barnet stood off to the sides watching the proceedings.

"Your Excellency, may I interrupt?"

"Yes, you may, but for the record, present your name and positon."

Barnet stepped forward directly in front of the Judge and bowed for a prolonged time to show his respect. Barnet was in full dress; a long blue coat, white collared ruffled shirt, and tan pants tucked into his polished black boots. His uniform was tailored to match his physique. A bright silver sabre hung from his right hip.

"I am Captain Jonathan Barnet, a pirate hunter," he stated with authority and pride.

"Do you wish to testify?"

"I am on the list."

"Go ahead."

"Your Honor, I'm the captain of British Navy sloop the *Albion*, a man-o'-war. I captured these rogues."

"I know of you. Continue, Captain."

"Your Honor, they boarded seven cargo vessels over the past couple months."

"What did you see?"

"The two women were the only ones who put up a fight. They fought like men, using pistols, cutlasses, and axes."

"Where was the rest of the crew?"

"They hid in the hold. Ms. Read was irate. She screamed, 'Come out you cowards; fight like men.' When they refused, she fired into the hold and killed a couple men and wounded several more."

"Do any of the deponents have anything to say?"
No one spoke.

On November 18, 1720, the Vice Admiral Court sentenced Rackham. Governor Lawes of Jamaica proclaimed the sentence.

"Jack Rackham, you are found guilty. You shall receive the usual sentence. Ye shall hang by the neck until you are dead, dead, dead. May the Lord have mercy on your soul."

Rackham turned his head toward the crowd and smiled to show his valor and worthiness as a pirate.

Calico Jack Rackham and his mermaids were escorted back to their jail cells, shackled. As they trudged past several cells, Rackham and Vane made eye contact.

"Vane, you deserve this more than me. Why haven't you been hung yet?"

Vane stared Rackham in the eyes. "The court is making me suffer without dying. I rot day to day. Look at the open sores on me arms and legs. The rats in the jail can't wait for me to fall asleep."

Rackham echoed a Vane psychotic laugh. "How does it feel to be tortured like those unsuspecting people that you tortured? At least I can keep me pride and respect and hang as a pirate."

"Keep moving," said the jailer.

Rackham, Bonny, and Read all were placed in separate cells. Within the hour, Rackham banged on the iron bars with a cup.

"Jail keeper, may I have a word with you?" pleaded Rackham.

The jail keeper placed the keys to their cells onto a wooden crate. "What do you want?"

Rackham spoke softly. "I feel trapped. My life is about to end. I would like to see my love before being hung." Rackham cupped his hands as if to pray. "Sir, may I see me Annie, one more time?"

"I see no harm as long as you remain in leg irons. Place your hands in front so I can cuff your wrists."

The burly jail keeper took Rackham by the arm to Anne's cell. Both men stood facing her. Rackham stood as close to the iron bars as possible.

"Annie, I want you to know that I love you."

Anne gave him a scornful look. Her daunting steel-blue eyes pierced him with anger. "I'm sorry to see you there, but had you fought like a man, you need not be hang'd like a dog."

Rackham looked into her eyes for the last time, hung his head, and walked away. "Good bye, Annie."

Anne bit her lower lip. "Good bye, Jack."

Rackham shuffled back to his cell. He raised the back of his right hand to wipe away a lone teardrop sliding down his cheek.

On the morning of November 18, 1720, Rackham was escorted to the gallows. A strong wind blew off of Port Royal harbor. The morning turned chilly with a wintery burst of cold northern air.

Leg shackled and handcuffed, Rackham climbed up the steps of the wooden platform to the hangman's noose. He peered out over Port Royal Harbor.

That's what I'm going to miss the most, besides my Annie; the mystery and beauty of the sea.

The executioner stood aside of him and placed the noose over his head. Without fanfare, the executioner hollered, "Pull!" The floor fell out from underneath Rackham. There was a moment of silence. His head jerked sideways, his tongue protruded, and his eyes bulged out of his sockets. His purple face was disfigured as his chin met his chest. His body convulsed uncontrollably and his legs kicked wildly in the cold air.

Eventually, Rackham's body went limp. Urine and excrement left his body and seeped down his calico pants onto the wooden deck.

"He's dead," declared the executioner.

The governor flipped a gold coin to the executioner, one of the many in Rackham's personal stash. "Take his body down and take him to the island at the harbor. I want all to see him as they enter Port Royal."

Rackham's body was removed from the noose and moved to the entrance of the harbor. His body was placed at the gibbet as a warning to others. He was left hanging, suspended in chains.

Ten days later, on November 28, Anne and Mary also stood trial at the Admiralty Court of Villa de la Vega, Jamaica.

"Bring the next rogues into place," the judge said.

Anne and Mary were shackled in irons with their hands behind their backs.

"You have been charged with piracy. And how do you plead?"

"Not guilty of all charges," responded Anne.

"Likewise, wi' me," said Mary.

"You, Mary Read and Anne Bonny, alias Bonn, are to go from hence to the place from whence you came, and from thence to the place of execution; where you shall be individually hanged by the neck till you are dead. And may God in his infinite mercy be merciful to both your souls. Do you have anything to say before you hang?"

"Mi-lord," came the reply, "we plead our bellies."

"What does that mean?"

"We are both quick with child, Yer Excellency." Anne caressed her stomach. "By English law, the court cannot take the life of an unborn child by executing the mother."

"Once your statements are verified, your life will be spared of the noose and gallows until time you give birth. But we must verify that you are quick with child."

"Look for yourself," said Mary as she pulled up her skirt.

"Put it down; it's much too early in the morning for that."

Mary laughed at the judge's modesty.

The judge looked up from his table. "I set in place additional inquiry that indeed you women are pregnant and gave respite if that is the case."

Anne Bonny stared into the eyes of the judge.

"Before you are taken away, do either of you have anything to say for yourselves?"

Mary Read was fuming. Her repressed anger flew in the face of the court. "You cowardly rogues on shore use the law as an instrument of oppression. You vilify us, you scoundrels, when there is only this difference. You rob from the poor under the cover of laws, forsooth, and we plunder the rich under the protection of our own courage."

Anne spit on the ground to acknowledge her contempt for the court as well.

"Take these wenches away," ordered the judge. "I prefer not to hear or be vilified by a wench of the seas."

Five months into her pregnancy, Mary became deathly ill. Anne looked through the adjoining cell. Mary was in terrific abdominal pain and vomiting.

"My baby. I'm going to lose the baby."

"Mary, what's wrong?" Anne's fingers reached through the bars, straining toward her friend. "Yer skin, it's turned yellow and yer soakin' wet with fever."

Within the minute, Mary Read doubled over and fell onto the hay-covered floor, dead.

With her death, Mary Read's quest for freedom came to an end. She was given a respectable burial at St. Catherine's church in Jamaica on April 28, 1721.

Anne Bonny disappeared soon after with her unborn child. No one knows for sure what became of her and her child. However, the *Oxford Dictionary of National Biography* notes evidence provided by Anne Bonny's descendants suggests that her father secured her release from jail and brought her back to Charleston, South Carolina. She supposedly gave birth to Rackham's child. Then, on December 21, 1721, she married Joseph Burleigh and eventually bore him ten children. Her life of piracy well behind her, she died a respectable woman at the age of eighty on April 22, 1782.

Jack Rackham is famous for permitting female pirates on board his ships during a time when many sailors viewed women as not only sex objects of fantasy and adoration but also as sources of bad luck or, worse, sources of conflict, a breach in the male order of seagoing solidarity. Rackham was strictly a small-time operator, never getting close to the level of infamy of someone like Edward Thatch or Sam Bellamy.

As a pirate, Read didn't leave much of a mark. Nevertheless, Read and Bonny have captured the public imagination as being the only two well-documented female pirates of the Golden Age of Piracy. In an age and society where the freedom of women was greatly restricted, Read and Bonny lived a life at sea as full members of a pirate crew. As subsequent generations increasingly romanticized piracy and the likes of Rackham, Bonny and Read, their stature grew larger than their lives.

As for Charles Vane, he remained in prison for several months after Rackham was hung. On March 29, 1721, he was hung at Gallows Point in Port Royal, Jamaica. Governor Lawes had his corpse cut down and carried to Gun Cay Island, displaying as a warning at the harbor's entrance for all mariners.

Vane was hung in Spanish Town, separate from Rackham, but their corpses swung within sight of each other across the harbor of Port Royal. Had he been alive, Vane could have seen Rackham's rotted body hanging in chains from the gibbet, left with only a shredded Indian Calico shirt waving in the wind.

Vane's last thought: *So let my heart be frozen to keep away the rot.*

With the death of Vane, Rackham, and his two mermaids, the last link of the chain disappeared, a chain of events that had begun five years earlier during the hurricane off the coast of Florida. The Golden Age of Piracy in the Caribbean was over.

ALLEN BALOGH

Epilogue

The research was the catalyst for *Black Sails 1715*. My son said, "Dad, write it like you tell it." Being buried in articles, manifests, books, and try to reasonably figure out who did what to whom, started 30 years earlier than the novel. Snorkeling the waters off the edges of Nassau harbor, the Pirate Republic, added to the inspiration. And if I were standing on the beach on July 29th, 1715, I would have seen the Spanish Fleet sailing back to Spain from the beach in my home in Jupiter, Florida. It's all fascinating, really. Scholars search in long-forgotten Spanish and French archives and the treasure salvers look beneath the shifting sands of the ocean floor.

In the mid 1970's, the inherent dangers of diving were taught to me by a PADI instructor, off the coast of the Palm Beaches. The effects of nitrogen narcosis scared the heck out of me. The other was experience in diving or the lack thereof, I should say. Different species of sharks, tails waving back and forth, propelled themselves at any speed they wished. The notorious bull shark was not uncommon to see. They use the 'bump and bite" technique and eat whatever is readily available; fins, masks and an occasional Florida license plate. They are the garbage men of the sea. A bull shark sighting, meant out of the water for me, pronto. I was the "chicken of the sea." Even the calmer nurse sharks lying motionless on the bottom elevated my use of oxygen.

However, it was Bernard Romans's recount of history that caught my eye in 1985. Bernard Romans, a cartographer, charted the east coast of Florida in 1774. From a passage of his *1715 History of Florida*, he indicated the location of the 1715 Spanish Armada.

He stated, "*Opposite this River, perished the Admiral, commanding the Plate Fleet 1715, the rest of the Fleet 14 in number between this and ye Bleech Yard.*" *And just below was a notation, 'el palmar.' This Lagoon stretches parallel to the sea, until the latitude 27:20, where it has an out-watering, or mouth.*"

This statement was equivalent to a rum headache. The Sebastian Inlet was not indicated on Romans' map but the Sebastian Creek was. And the inlet to the south was in Jensen Beach/Stuart which was man-made, not natural. Peck's Lake, near Hobe Sound, was the original, natural inlet, several miles south of the Stuart Inlet.

The Romans' map clearly stated, "Santa Lucia." The river in Jensen Beach/Stuart is called the St. Lucie River and we've always known Rio in Jensen Beach as "Ye Bleech Yards," where sailors bleached out their salt-soaked sails. Or was it both, one ship to the north and the other to the south. Was the natural mouth out-watering at Hobe Sound? Or maybe, Romans was slightly incorrect in citing the latitude of 27:20 in 1774. Was the southernmost ship of the 1751 Fleet in our backyard?

The Architvo General de Indias in Seville, Spain, is a repository of historical Spanish American documents. In the Archives is a document by a surviving captain of the 1715 hurricane. It was submitted to the governor of the Spanish settlement in St. Augustine, Florida.

Captain Sebastian Mendez, pilot of the *Nuestra Senora del Carmen*, alias La Holandesa, under control of Don Antonio de Echeverz, commander of the *Galleos* stated: *Departed Havana* *on the 24th of July (1715) and he was lost on Wednesday, the 31st, at two o'clock in the morning, because of a hurricane. . . had never seen anything like it for violence, and his ship and all the others were lost, some before and some after Palmar de Ays, at 28* 1-' (north latitude), in an area 12 leagues (27 miles) north to south.*

Those two clues stood out in stark contrast to most research. The southernmost ship had to be "lying at the rocks" off Hutchinson Island. We had access to aircraft and flew the coastline from Palm Beach to Cape Kennedy. At an altitude of one thousand feet, an extended stretch of 'rocks' was clearly seen at Blowing Rocks in Hobe Sound, then a separation, and another set of extended rocks at Hutchinson Island in Stuart. A recent nor'easter storm had exposed the shore line acting as a bulldozer, pushing the sand toward the dune lines to give us a clear picture.

My two colleagues and I searched that summer, when time allowed, in the crystal, clear-blue waters off Hutchinson Island. Incidentally, a mere half a degree off would put us roughly thirty miles in the direction and into the leases of the great treasure hunters of our time: Kip Wagner, Art McKee, Bob Marx, Carl Fismer, Bob "Frogfoot" Weller, and Mel Fisher—not a good idea for amateurs, such as ourselves.

Eleven or more ships sunk between Hutchinson Island and Sebastian Inlet in the hurricane of 1715. Lost at sea were approximately a thousand crew members and passengers and $14 million in registered treasure. It was common back then, for the treasure hunters to be armed with guns and assault rifles on their work boats. Modern-day pirates, charter boat captains and local fishermen docked in Sebastian, Ft. Pierce and Port Salerno were on the heels, snooping, and watching the Real Eight Company & Treasure Salvors Inc. in their search for gold, silver, and jewelry along the Treasure Coast.

According to Sir Robert Marx, author and treasure hunter, "Salvage efforts on the wrecks began immediately and by the end of December, the officials in charge of the operation reported they had already recovered all the king's treasure and the major part of that belonging to private individuals, totaling 5,200,000 pesos. The following spring they recovered an additional small amount, so that by July the Spaniards called a halt to their salvage efforts. When the Spaniards stopped their salvage work, a total of 1,244,900 pesos of registered treasure remained lost. Add an estimated nineteen percent contraband, and we believe 2,200,000 pesos remain. Using a conservative sale price of $250 per coin, we feel over $550 million of treasure remains to be recovered."

In the summer of 2011, I traveled to the Berry Islands and New Providence Island, the known sites of the Pirates of the Republic. The fort still sets atop Nassau hill, where Blackbeard had his trysts. The water at Nassau harbor where Henry Jennings and Charles Vane docked their ships, was turquoise blue. And the main street in Nassau is called Woodes Rogers Walk. Stingrays were abundant in the outer edges of the island at Blackbeard's Cay.

In November, 2011, a revisit to the encampment in Vero Beach was in order. The fresh water hole still exists on the back side of the dune line where the treasure was protected by the Spanish soldiers. It didn't' take much imagination to visualize Jennings and Vane arriving, looting and scaring the 'bejesus' out of the Spanish soldiers guarding the chests of treasure at the dune.

Later that November day, a few miles south, just north of the Ft. Pierce Inlet, was the site of the 350-ton *Urca de Lima*. It's very eerie to stand at the waterline, knowing that on July 31, 1715, hundreds of bodies washed on the beach at my footsteps while three thousand emeralds were scattered on the ocean floor. The *Urca* lay between two reefs, laying less than two hundred yards offshore, in fifteen feet of water.

In June 2015, a diving family from Sanford, Florida, hit for $1.2 million in gold at Douglas Beach, just south of Ft. Pierce Inlet. In 1985, we were twenty miles south of the sunken galleon—pretty close for amateurs.

On July 30, 2015, to commemorate the three-hundred-year anniversary of the sinking of the fleet, the 1715 Fleet Society sponsored a week long seminar in Sebastian and Vero Beach. Luminary guests and experts descended onto the beaches for tours and round tables discussions. On the last night, we sat in the banquet room of Hiram's Resort, chit-chatting, comparing notes, and sipping on our rums. Off to the side of the room, stood Brent Brisben and a couple of his divers, waiting patiently and respectfully, for the last speaker to finish for the evening.

Finally, addressing the entire room, Brent shouted, "Today was the day!"—the infamous Mel Fisher mantra of success. Brent had hit for an estimated $4.2 million in gold coins in waist high water, less than a couple hundred feet off the beach. More incredibly, nine Royals, coins made specifically for King Philip IV, were among the find. There was silence at first, everyone stunned at the announcement. A then a loud cheer erupted as everyone stood and cheered, as if we were the ones who found the gold.

There are 36,524.21 days in a century. The odds of Brent and his crew discovering the gold coins three hundred years later on the very month of the hurricane is 109,572.65 to 1. That's magic.

The following day, several of us went to the beach to observe and feel the sensation. I took a couple of photos at the Sandy Pointe wreck with a former CIA officer to show his students at a northern university. Likewise, he did the same for me for my students in Palm Beach.

As I drove home from the 1715 Fleet commemorative, I stopped at the Spanish encampment in Vero Beach and then walked on Wabasso Beach, the area best known for 'hot' spots.

The legs of the lobster were tightening around my arm again. Like Kip Wagner, Art McKee, Robert Marx, and Mel Fisher in the early 1960's, I looked over the ocean as well and wondered.

Where in the hell are the rest of the galleons.

Author's Notes #1
Q & A with Experts December 2015

Dr. Timothy Walton, Retired CIA officer, Professor of Intelligence Analysis, James Madison University, Author, The Spanish Treasure Fleets (1994)

Q1: The exploitation of mineral wealth in South America and Mexico transformed the world financial markets. Why was the triangular trade the catalyst in spurring the Age of Piracy.

Piracy--then and now--is a result of three main factors: (1) rich and vulnerable cargoes, (2) geography that focuses shipping into easy-to-predict pathways, and (3) shortage of stronger,countermeasures.

The triangular trade patterns of the early 18th century (rum, sugar, tobacco, slaves, and the continuing Spanish treasure fleets, among other things) meant that the Atlantic and Caribbean were the busiest maritime trade routes in the world. To keep costs down (and thus maximize profits) shippers did not spend a lot of money on cannons, or other forms of protection on board their ships.

Patterns of wind and ocean currents, along with the fact that there were only a few key ports, meant that ships generally traveled on routes that were pretty easy to calculate. Find a strategic spot, and wait; and pretty soon a worthwhile target ship would come along.

Until the British Royal Navy took on the mission of anti-piracy, there was not a force with the resources and determination to track down and destroy pirates.

Notice that exactly the same factors gave rise to a more recent problem of piracy off the coast of Somalia.

Dr. John de Bry, Director of the Center for Historical Archaeology, French and Spanish language paleographer, historical and maritime archaeologist.

Q2: The exploitation of mineral wealth in South America and Mexico transformed the world financial markets. Why was the triangular trade the catalyst in spurring the Age of Piracy.

The triangular trade refers to the slave trade where ships left the Atlantic coast of Western Europe, including England, sailed to the west coast of Africa to pick up slaves and gold, ten sailed to the Americas to sell the slaves and barter gold for exotic New World products, although they usually kept the majority of the gold which was usually in the form of gold powder and broken Akan jewelry. After selling their human cargo and upon sailing back to their port-of-call those ships usually carried a significant amount of money. While the African slaves had a monetary value, pirates, as a rule of thumb, did not get involved in the slave trade and in fact often freed such captives, the gold and species, however, were what usually attracted the pirates as well as the ships themselves, usually well-built and well-armed.

Q3: What types of technology propelled underwater archaeology into the 21st century.

The advent of SCUBA equipment and diving in the 1950s was the catalyst for the development of underwater archaeology, but modern technology, particularly in the electronic area, propelled it to the level it is at today. Introduction of highly sensitive and reliable equipment such as magnetometers, side-scan sonars, sub-bottom profilers, and the Global Positioning System (GPS), combined with the ability to dive longer and deeper made it possible for underwater archaeology to progress by leaps and bounds. DNA analysis, which can also be used on submerge objects, has added a new dimension to the discipline.

Author's Notes #2
The Aftermath of Blackbeard's Crew

Thirteen members of Blackbeard's crew— James Blake, James Brooks, Black Caesar, Joseph Carnes, Stephen Daniel, Stephen Gates, John Greensail, Richard Martin, John Phillips, Joseph Robbins, James Salter, Edward Stiles, and Richard White—met their fate and hung in Williamsburg in March 1719, at present day Capitol Landing Road.

Killed in Blackbeard's last battle at Ocracoke Inlet were James Archer, John Brooks, Joseph Curtis, Joseph Gibbens, Garrat Husk, John Jackson, Nathaniel Miller, Thomas Morton, and Phillip (gunner).

Acquitted in Williamsburg were Robert Owens (carpenter), Matthew Tryer, Lieutenant Richards (second in command of the *Queen Anne's Revenge*). He was not with Blackbeard on the day of the battle. Samuel Odell survived seventy slash wounds. Israel Hands was captured, tried, and convicted in March 1719, but he was pardoned. He returned to London and became a beggar in the streets.

Edward Thatch, also known as Edward Teach, (Blackbeard) was beheaded at Ocracoke Island, North Carolina, on November 22, 1718.

The Fate of the Other Prominent Characters

Anne Bonny was convicted on November 28, 1720. There's no record of her being hung and her location is unknown; possibly her father paid for her release and she returned to Charles Town, South Carolina.

Stede Bonnet was captured at Cape Fear, North Carolina, and hung in Charleston, South Carolina, on December 1, 1718.

Sam Bellamy, the wealthiest pirate in history, drowned in a hurricane off the coast of Cape Cod, April 26, 1717.

Black Caesar was hung in Williamsburg, Virginia, March 1719.

Benjamin Hornigold either drowned in a tropical storm or was killed in a battle, spring 1719.

Henry Jennings lived longer than any pirate and enjoyed retirement in Bermuda; he passed of old age in 1745.

Lazue was hung in Charles Town, South Carolina, c 1705.

Calico Jack Rackham was hung in Port Royal, Jamaica, on November 18, 1720.

Mary Read was convicted on November 28, 1720, died from fever in prison on April 28, 1721.

Governor Woodes Rogers was sent back to England to debtor's prison, returned to Nassau to resume his duties by order of King George II, and died within the year of the plague, on July 15, 1732.

Charles Vane was hung in Port Royal, Jamaica, on November 18, 1720.

Paulsgrave Williams was last seen off the coast of Africa, serving as a quartermaster with the French pirate Olivier La Buse in April 1720.

Author's Notes #3
Top-Earning Pirates

Since the beginning of ancient times, early civilizations equated gold with gods and rulers. The oldest book ever written, *Genesis,* records that "the river Pison flows out of Eden, and "the land of Havilah, where there is gold and the gold of that land is good." King Solomon brought shiploads of gold from the land of Ophir. In both the *Iliad and Odyssey,* Homer states gold as being the glory of the immortals and a sign of wealth among ordinary humans. The code of Menes, the first Egyptian royal dynasty, separated the value; one part of gold is equal to two and one half parts of silver. Gold was fashioned into plates, vases, cups and idols, such as the celebrated "Golden Calf" of the Hebrews who followed Moses into the Sinai. In the Americas, the Incas referred to gold as the 'tears of the Sun." We find this type of thinking about gold throughout ancient and modern civilizations.

Piracy on the high seas was no different. The amount of gold available could be thought as the equivalent to the gold reserves in Kentucky. Millions of dollars were pillaged during the Golden Age of Piracy. Privateers and pirates used modern-day economics terms; good positioning, aggressive, and global trade. An increase in spending on the island increased income and consumption, greater than the initial amount spent by the pirates. Slaves, sugar, rum, turtles, prostitution, silver and gold, were the consistent multiplier effects in Nassau and Port Royal. Commerce was at an all-time high in the West Indies. In other words, the Dow Jones Average spiked and was at an all-time high.

Interestingly, *Forbes* magazine composed a listing of the wealthiest pirates in modern dollars. The highest-earning pirate ever was Samuel "Black Sam" Bellamy. He made his millions along the New England coast. "Black Sam" plundered an estimated $120 million during the course of his short career. His biggest windfall came in February 1717, when he captured a slave ship. The *Whydah* reportedly carried more than four and a half tons of gold and silver. The Prince of Pirates made the *Whydah* his flagship. He gave his previous vessel, the *Sultan,* to the defeated crew of the *Whydah.* Nice guy.

Sir Francis Drake was a sixteenth-century privateer, slaver, and pirate of the Elizabethan era. He saved England from the Spanish Armada and became a favorite of Queen Elizabeth I of England. King Philip II of Spain detested Drake (El Draque) so much that he offered twenty thousand ducats ($6.5 million) for his head. King Philip saved a ton of money when Drake died in 1596 from dysentery after an unsuccessful attack on Puerto Rico. His lifetime earnings were $115 million.

Who in the heck is Thomas Tew? He placed third on the *Forbes* list. Tew was a seventeenth-century privateer turned pirate who hailed from Rhode Island. He stayed under the radar in the Americas by sailing his seventy-foot sloop, the *Amity*, to the source of slavery, West Africa. En route, he plundered a ship full of gold en route from India to the Ottoman Empire. He died in 1695 in the Red Sea in another battle with an Indian trading ship. While he may have cheated the gallows, Captain Tew was disemboweled by a canon shot. Tew's earnings totaled $102 million.

So, where did all this money go? Much of the silver and gold is lying on the bottom of the oceans, deposited there by tropical storms and hurricanes, such as the one that claimed

Black Sam's *Whydah* and the majestic 1715 Fleet. It is interesting to note that a pirate captain received only twice the amount of a regular crew member's share, divided equally, of any given plunder. Not much was left for the captain. The more respected captains acted as benevolent CEOs, splitting shares for loyalty, rank, or injury. A crew member who lost a limb was reimbursed between £1,000 to £2,000 per limb.

The cost of running a business on the high seas was expensive: broken masts, ripped sails, rotted hulls, deck repairs, the expense of provisions, weapons, and ammunition. And, of course, wenches and prostitutes. Prostitutes drained a lot of the free-flowing money. The rogues would spend a couple thousand pieces of eight for one night. Other prostitutes may charge up to five hundred pieces of eight just for a peek. Rum and wine was an obligatory salutation.

If the captain was greedy and hoarded a take, the crew deposed, marooned, or killed him. If any of the crew concealed part of the booty, death was imminent, likewise with the captain. The corpse was kicked overboard into the sea, without a second thought.

The shareholders were still in control, not the chairman of the board. No wonder Blackbeard preferred intimidation or Black Sam acted as the nonviolent pirate, a sort of Robin Hood. If there were no injuries or deaths on board, there was more money to split. Maybe impatient and reckless investment bankers could take note of cheating their investors out of profits, fearing retribution or death at the hands of irate shareholders.

Then the government intervened for their share of the loot. The state of South Carolina absconded with Stede Bonnet's take of some $4 million. Plus there is an untold amount that many government officials, such as Lord Hamilton of Jamaica, personally extorted or stole.

Soon, nothing is left. All the money is gone.

The rest, we just don't know. That's why we have underwater archaeologists, such as the highly respected diver/maritime scholar, Dr. John de Bry, who toils through the archives, sifting through and translating old, worm-infested documents. Prior to editing, I spoke with Dr. De Bry, via e-mail correspondence. He just returned from his ninth trip to Cuba since 2001, working with his Cuban colleagues and archaeologists.

The War of Spanish Succession left many privateers unemployed. The privateers had good reason to work in a democratic society of a pirate captain. To these men, the concept of having a substantial impact upon their working conditions, and even upon the direction of the ship's operations was deeply satisfying.

Many of them had previously served under the harsh conditions on merchant or warships. The slightest breach of discipline could bring about a bloody whipping. A man could be hung for disobeying an officer. The food was atrocious and the pay meager. To switch to pirating was an easy option for them.

The fact of the matter is this: pirate life was short; random murders, tropical diseases, and venereal disease nearly wiped out entire crews. Most pirates died at sea of illness—or else at the gallows.

Forbes Magazine, 20 Highest-Earning Pirates

Pirate	Wealth (2008 dollars)
Samuel "Black Sam" Bellamy	$120 million
Sir Francis Drake	$115 million
Thomas Tew	$103 million
John Bowen	$40 million
Bartholomew "Black Bart" Roberts	$32 million
Jean Fleury	$31.5 million
Thomas White	$16 million
John Halsey	$13 million
Harry Morgan	$13 million
Edward "Blackbeard" Teach	$12.5 million
Samuel Burgess	$9.5 million
Edward England	$8 million
Francois le Clerc	$7.5 million
Howell Davis	$4.5 million
Stede Bonnet	$4.5 million
Richard Worley	$3.5 million
Charles Vane	$2.3 million
Edward Low	$1.8 million
John Rackham	$1.5 million
James Martel	$1.5 million

Author's Notes #4
History of the Urca de Lima

The *Santissima Trinidad y Nuestra Senora de la Concepcion,* also known as the *Urca de Lima,* was the supply ship or refuerzo of General Ubilla. The ship was named after the owner Don Miguel de Lima. It was built by the Dutch, rated at 350 tons, and carried 20 canons.

This ship was well salvaged after the hurricane because it stayed afloat for a while. *Urca* broke up near the shore and the top decks were still exposed. The refuerzo was burnt to the waterline to avoid detection.

The wreck site, located north of the Ft. Pierce Inlet, is called the Wedge Wreck. Pie cut wedges of silver and a conglomerate of 25 gold coins were recovered in 1963. It is also fair to say, that even though the manifests were detailed, a lot of contraband and cargo was hidden by the crew members for their own purposes. Jewelry and gems were in abundance.

However, the John Brandon Report disputes the State of Florida's location of the Urca de LIma. Mr. Brandon's report has compelling arguments to the contrary. Excerpts of the report have been extracted for review.

ALLEN BALOGH

The John Brandon Report
A Letter to the State of Florida Division or Historical
Resources, dated September 22, 2015
(Excerpts)

Information Concerning the Loss and Possible/Probable Location of the Santissima Trinidad y Nuestra Senora de la Concepcion Alias the Urca de Lima, A Registry Vessel of the 1715 Spanish Plate Fleet

By John Brandon
Historical Shipwreck Salvor

Any discussion concerning the identity of any of the 1715 Plate Fleet shipwrecks as to their registry names as contained in the Spanish archival documentation and their actual locations along the middle east coast of Florida, now known as the Treasure Coast due to the sinking and then the modern rediscovery of the 1715 fleet, must start with this fundamental premise and historical fact. That none of the known 1715 fleet wreck sites can be positively identified in an academic fashion.

That is to say, that there exists no positive and provable correlation between any of the archival/historical data and the on-site archaeological data that would provide for a conclusive and verifiable positive identity of any of the known 1715 fleet wreck sites to be arrived at. This would include the 1715 fleet wreck site known commonly as the Wedge Wreck. However, regardless of what the archival and historical research indicates, the Florida Division of Historical Resources (DHR) and the Bureau of Archaeological Research (BAR) has insisted on conclusively identifying the Wedge Wreck as the Santissima Trinidad y Nuestra Senora de la Concepcion also known as the Urca de Lima and has named a shipwreck preserve located at the site of the Wedge Wreck, some 2.5 miles north of the Ft. Pierce Inlet, the Urca de Lima Underwater Archaeological Preserve. At this point in time, only circumstantial evidence exists as to the identities of the 1715 fleet wreck sites and there is still much debate between the historical shipwreck salvors as to which of the known 1715 fleet wreck sites represents which of the 1715 fleet registry vessels, including the site of the Wedge Wreck.

Unlike DHR/BAR, at least in this particular instance, the majority of the salvors tend to rely on archaeological and archival/historical facts in the identity of a given shipwreck site. This is why to this day the known 1715 fleet wreck sites are identified by the salvors on the state data recording sheets by their modern place names, such as Corrigan's Wreck (8IR19/S25), Douglas Beach Wreck (8SL17/S26), Rio Mar Wreck (8IR/S23), etc. and even the Wedge Wreck (8SL24). Not their suspected 1715 fleet registry vessel names, which are only speculations currently.

As to specifically the loss and location of the Urca de Lima there exists a body of archival and historical information that tends to strongly indicate that the 1715 fleet wreck site now called the Urca de Lima by DHR/BAR might well prove not to be the Urca de Lima at all. It should be noted that when dealing with centuries old archival documentation there can be much interpretation as to what the original information meant and how it is now interpreted and understood today. But again, the archival and historical information available concerning the location of the Urca de Lima seems not to support DHR's/BAR's conclusions of the Wedge Wreck as being the wreck site of the Urca de Lima.

First, as information for general reference, the Urca de Lima was a Dutch built ship which was refitted for the cross Atlantic trade routes. She was of 305 tons and carried 20 iron cannon. All of the ships comprising both the New Spain and Tierra Firma contingents of the 1715 Spanish Plate Fleet, including the Capitanas and Almirantas of the 1715 fleet, were privately owned vessels, as was the Urca de Lima. The Urca de Lima was owned by Miguel de Lima y Melo. Her Captain was Juan Antonio Laviosa, her pilot was Manuel Chavez and her Chaplain was J. Fabrega. She was a registry vessel of the 1715 Spanish Plate Fleet sailing in convoy with that fleet as part of the New Spain contingent commanded by General Don

Juan Esteban de Ubilla. (Ubilla was also the overall commander of the entire combined 1715 Plate Fleet) She carried a general cargo of merchandise, goods and New World agricultural products similar in nature to the lading of the rest of the 1715 fleet vessels, along with 252,171 pesos of registered treasure belonging to private sector persons. No registered treasures for the king was consigned or registered to the Urca de Lima.

On the night of July 30, 1715 the fleet was struck by the primary circulation of an intense hurricane. All the 1715 fleet ships including the Urca de Lima, except one, were lost along the Florida Middle East coast by dawn of July 31, 1715 in an area called by the Spanish "Palmar de Ayz". Translated as palm grove or land of the Ais Indians. (Ais is the more typical spelling used today) This area was also sometimes referred to in the Spanish documents as the "Rio de Ayz". Literally the river of the Ais. The Ais Indians were the native Florida inhabitants who lived along the stretch of the Florida east coast paralleled by what in modern times was called the Indian River and now the Indian River Lagoon. This lagoon spans the Florida coast from Cape Canaveral on the north to St. Lucie Inlet on the south.

According to the archival and historical documents, the Urca de Lima sank before the mouth of an inlet, which might well prove to be the St. Lucie Inlet, based upon the archival and historical information, rather than the old Indian River Inlet. The

Indian River Inlet was a natural inlet which used to be located approximately 2.5 miles north of the present day Ft. Pierce Inlet, but which has closed up since the opening of the permanent Ft. Pierce Inlet in the early 20th century. In the vicinity of the old Indian River Inlet is where the Wedge Wreck rests today.

The Spanish archival documentation provides a number of clues as to the location of the wreck of the Urca de Lima. Two of the most important are Latitude sightings given by Miguel de Lima, owner of the Urca de Lima and by Don Alonso de Armenta de Cassano y Guzman a high ranking Spanish official who sailed aboard the Urca de Lima. These Latitude bearings taken with a quadrant, the navigational instrument the Spanish would have used in 1715, can be subject to variables from one person to another even when taken on solid ground, making for some interpretation of the data today. Though generally the sightings are fairly reliable.

Over All Possible/Probable Conclusions:

In the final analysis and has been noted at the beginning of this report, the absolute positive identity of none of the registry vessels of the 1715 Spanish Plate Fleet can be proven with certainty as would relate to the remains of the known 1715 fleet shipwrecks and their locations today.

The archival and historical research and information coupled with the archaeological data from the individual known 1715 fleet wreck sites as recovered and recorded in modern times by Florida's historical shipwreck salvors, most notably by Kip Wagner and his Real Eight Corporation and Mel Fisher and his Treasure Salvors, Inc. and Cobb Coin Company, Inc., simply does not provide the conclusive evidence needed to allow for definitive identifications of the known 1715 fleet wreck sites to be arrived at.

In the case of the Santissima Trinidad y Nuestra Senora de la Concepcion better known as the Urca de Lima, it is difficult to understand how the Florida Division of Historical Resources and the Florida Bureau of Archaeological Research ever decided to definitively identify the 1715 fleet wreck site known as the Wedge Wreck as the Urca de Lima. The preponderance of archival and historical data, coupled with the limited archaeological information recovered from the site, would seem not to tend to support this conclusion and DHR/BAR had all of the Spanish archival research available to them. Rather, the archival and historical data would seem to indicate that the wreck of the Urca de Lima may be more likely somewhere in the vicinity of the St. Lucie Inlet rather than the old Indian River Inlet.

The Spanish Latitude bearings place the Urca de Lima closer to St. Lucie Inlet rather than the old Indian River Inlet, with one of the bearings going directly through the mouth of the present day St. Lucie Inlet. The other bearing is 15 nautical miles south of the Wedge Wreck but only 5 nautical miles north of St. Lucie Inlet.

The Spanish research clearly states that the Urca de Lima is the farthest of the 1715 fleet wrecks to the south and closest to the Florida Keys and Cuba. However, the 1715 fleet wreck now known as the Douglas Beach Wreck lies five nautical miles to the south of the Wedge Wreck and it is doubtful and very unlikely that the Spanish would not have been aware and known of this 1715 fleet shipwreck's existence to the south. So the Wedge Wreck is not the farthest south of the 1715 fleet shipwrecks.

Recommendations:

First, it is absolutely impossible for anyone, including DHR/BAR staff, to definitively prove in an academic fashion the

1715 fleet registry name of the 1715 fleet shipwreck site known as the

Wedge Wreck as the Santissima Trinidad y Nuestra Senora de la Concepcion better known as the Urca de Lima. Or to prove any other 1715 fleet registry name for this site for that matter. Indeed, the vast majority of the archival, historical and archaeological data, as contained in this report, tends to strongly suggest that the Wedge Wreck may in fact not be the wreck site of the Urca de Lima at all.

Based on this information, the name of the state's preserve area at the Wedge Wreck site should be changed in all of its publications and references and especially in the Preserve brochure to "Wedge Wreck Underwater Archaeological Preserve" to more accurately reflect the known archival, historical and archaeological data we have concerning this site. The Preserve brochure name needs to reflect that the 1715 fleet registry name of this wreck site cannot be conclusively proven.

At the very most, the Preserve brochure could state that the Wedge Wreck could "possibly be" or "may be" the Urca de Lima, although even this may not be advisable to be historically correct, unless some new archival or historical data is located strongly indicating this possibility. To be absolutely archaeologically and historically correct, within the text of the Preserve brochure it should state that, "The Wedge Wreck is an unidentified registry vessel of the 1715 Spanish Plate Fleet whose registry name has yet to be determined based on the archival and historical documents and archaeological data currently available".

Further, and as noted in my letter to Mr. Robert Bendus dated September 22, 2015 which accompanied this report, (See Appendix A), other inaccuracies contained in the state's Preserve brochure for this site need to be corrected as well. Such as the numbers of cannon recovered in modern times, the numbers of silver wedges recovered and especially the erroneous Latitude/Longitude given for the location of the Wedge Wreck should all be corrected, among other points. Archaeologist Mr. David Moore also records in his 1993 Wedge Wreck report many of these same points.

Lastly, the Wedge Wreck has been nominated and placed on the National Register of Historic Places as the Urca de Lima. Placement on the NRHP as the Urca de Lima should have required DHR/BAR to provide essentially irrefutable archival, historical and archaeological proof that the Wedge Wreck is definitively the site of the Urca de Lima. However, no such archival/historical or archaeological proof exists to support that conclusion. To the contrary, most of the archival and historical data indicates that the Wedge Wreck is possibly, if not probably, not the wreck site of the Urca de lima.

The Wedge Wreck listed as the Urca de Lima on the NRHP should be removed under that name.

Manifest of Nuestra Senora de la Concepcion (Urca de Lima)

252,171 pesos in silver coins in 81 chests
13 chests of worked silver
280 serones of cochineal 595 serones and chests of indigo
21 barrels and jugs of liquid amber
257 uncured half hides
6 jugs of balsam 198 bales of Purga de Jalapa (a drug)
75 chests of ceramic drinking vessels
30 chests of chocolate
19 bales of cocoa
22 chests of vanilla
25 tons of Brazilwood
11 bales of sneeze-wort (a type of snuff)
136 chests of gifts
77 serones and chests of uncultivated cochineal
300 uncured hides
3 Chinese folding screens
32 chests of Chinese porcelain
3 ½ tons of sarsaparilla
2 bales of quinine bark
1 chest of sugar
2 copper discs or ingots

Manifest of Nuestra Senora de la Regla

2,687,416 pesos in 684 chests and sacks of gold and silver
728 leather bags of cochineal
1702 leather bags of indigo
139 sheets of copper
682 tanned leather hides
26 chests of earthen vessels
48 chests of vanilla beans
85 chests of gifts
8 earthen jars of balsam and liquid amber
2 chests of writing desks
40 chests of chocolate and dust of oazaca
2 chests of bathing oil
30 sacks of wild cochineal
12 chests of red dye
53 chests of worked silver
14 chests of Chinese porcelain
500 quintales of brazilwood

Author's Notes #5
Articles of Agreement

1. Every Man has an equal Vote; equal title to the fresh Provisions, or strong Liquors.

2. Defrauded of Value of Dollar, in Plate, Jewels or Money, punished by Marooning.

3. If the Robbery was only between one another, slitting the Ears or Nose of him that was Guilty, and set him on shore, and somewhere, uninhabited.

3. No Person shall gamble, at Cards or Dice for Money

4. The Lights and Candles to be put out at eight o'Clock at Night: If any of the Crew, after that Hour, still remained inclin'd for Drinking, they shall do so on the open Deck.

5. To keep their Piece, Pistols, and Cutlass clean, and fit for Service.

6. No Boy or Woman to be allowed amongst them, if disguised, he shall suffer Death.

7. To Desert the Ship, or their Quarters in Battle, was punished with Death or Marooning.

8. No striking one another on Board, Quarrels to be ended on Shore, at Sword and Pistol.

9. If loss of Limb, become Cripple or lose an eye, he shall have 800 pieces of eight.

10. The Captain and the Quarter-master to receive two Shares of a Prize; the Master, Boatswain, and Gunner, one Share and a half, and other Officers, one and a Quarter.

11. The Musicians to have Rest on the Sabbath Day, but the other Six Days and Nights, none, without special Favour.

Author's Notes #6
The Origin of Pirate Flags

The exact origin of the black flag is unknown. However, after putting the pieces of the puzzle together, a plausible theory exists with a connection to the Templar Knights.

The first recorded use of the skull and cross bone flag dates back to the 17th century. The Barbary pirates operated out of Tunis, Tripoli, and Algiers in northern Africa. Their purpose was to capture Christians and sell them to the Ottoman slave trade, and to the Arabic market in northern Africa and the Mideast. I know, rather ironical, isn't it?

The Barbary pirates were known to fly the Muslim black flag to denote their commercial alliance with the Muslim traders. The logical argument could be stated that this was the original Templar-Pirate connection to the black background of the Jolly Roger flag.

Upon the order of Pope Urban II, Christian knights from Western Europe waged religious war in 1095 against the Muslims. This multi-war quest to gain control over the Holy Land, which was sacred to Christians, Jews, and Muslims, was known as the Crusades. Ironically, many Jews fought side by side with Muslim soldiers to defend Jerusalem against the Christian attackers. It was not uncommon for the marauding Crusaders to take on the mission, 'while we are here, let's kill all the Jews as well.' The Templar-Pirate connection was growing stronger in the Mediterranean Sea as the fleet of the Crusaders took refuge at Tyre.

The first of seven Crusades was successful. Armies of Christian soldiers, with the leadership of the Knights of the Templar fleet, took control of Jerusalem. The Crusaders were hell bent on eliminating Muslims and Jews. Despite the animosity generated by the Crusades, the Christians temporarily reclaimed the Holy Land. The Muslims in the region vowed holy war, Jihad, against the Christians.

The Knights Templar staked out their headquarters on the Temple Mount in Jerusalem. The Crusaders called it the Temple of Solomon, and from this location, their name Templar was derived.

King Louis VII of France, at a meeting in Paris with the Pope Urban II, recommended that the Knights wear a white surcoat with a red cross and a white mantle also with a red cross.

A flag was subsequently struck for the fleet of the Crusaders. The black background of the skull and crossbones was the "Jolie Rouge," the French translation of Jolly Roger.

The Elizabethan era English ships flew a flags of the National Registry, with emblems such as the Tutor rose. On the other hand, the Spanish ship's flags were distinguished by Catholic crosses. With the advent of privateering and pirating, the national emblems were replaced with flags representing a code of conduct of the ship and the personality of the individual captain.

Images of the Jolly Roger became the symbol of pirates, representing defiance, destruction and death. Pirate flags were designed to strike fear into the hearts of merchant men and nation-states. So effective was this tactic, that even the youngest child knows that the skull and crossbones represent poison.

A black-and-white flag sent ripples of terror through any ship and its crew, as well as a command to surrender immediately. A red-and-white flag meant unmerciful bloodshedding and no quarter (mercy) would be given otherwise.

The black flags were further embellished by graphic symbols of death: the skull, crossed bones, a skeleton spear, swords, and cutlasses. An empty fist or cutlass in hand meant a swift death was in store for anyone who dared put up a struggle.

All who saw the Jolly Roger knew what it meant. Pirate flags were valuable instruments of psychological warfare on their enemies. They were an important element used in the building the fearsome reputation of the pirate vessels, a skill that Blackbeard excelled in. With his flag, as well as his actions, he threatened, intimidated, and terrorized everyone on the seas.

Pirate Flags & Symbolism

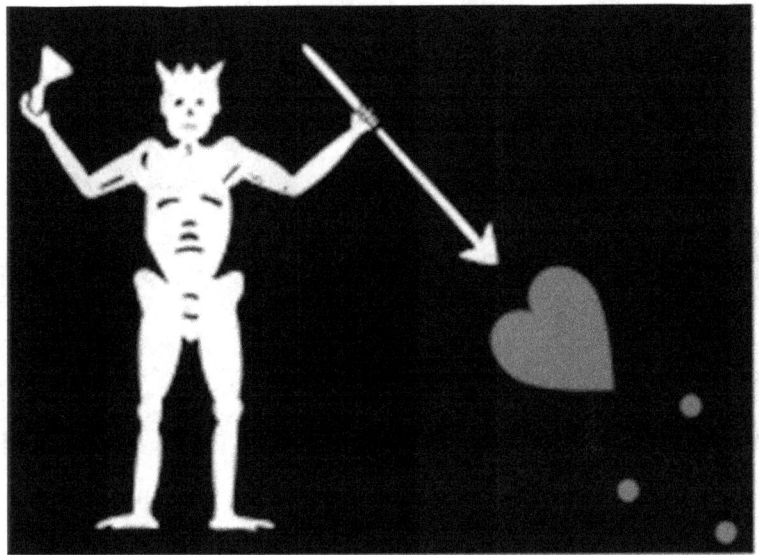

Blackbeard's Flag: a skeleton with horns of the devil, holding a spear in one hand and hourglass. The hourglass meant your time was up. In the other hand was a spear pointing toward a heart dripping three blood spots. A heart pieced with a knife or sword meant merciless death. A spear indicated an even more violent death, while dripping blood symbolized a long, drawn-out, and torturous death.

Black Sam Bellamy's Flag: Simple and to the point, all ships should surrender swiftly.

Calico Jack Rackham's Flag: Surrender or die by the cutlass.

Stede Bonnet's: A white skull above a horizontal bone meaning death by a dagger to the heart.

The Red Pirate Flag of the Elizabethan Era indicating bloodshed and no quarter given.

Flag of the Barbary Pirates of North Africa and the Mideast.

Selected Bibliography

Burgess, Robert F. and Carl J. Clausen. *Florida's Golden Galleons*: *The Search for the 1715 Spanish Treasure Fleet.* Port Salerno: Florida Classics Library, 1982 (9).

Choundas, George, *The Pirate Primer,* Ohio, Writers Digest Books, 2007 (1)

Konstam. Angus. *Blackbeard.* New Jersey, John Wiley & Sons, 2006 (1)

Lee, Robert E. *Blackbeard the Pirate.* North Carolina, John F. Blair, Publisher, 2009 (15)

Rediker, Marcus Dr. *Villains of All Nations.* University of Pittsburgh, 2005

Schonhorn, Manuel. *Daniel DeFoe: A General History of the Pyrates.* New York, Dover Publications, 1999 (20)

Wagner, Kip. *Pieces of Eight: Recovering the Riches of a Lost Spanish Treasure Fleet.* New York: E.P.Dutton & Co, 1966 (8)

Wagner, Kip. *Drowned Galleons Yield Spanish Gold.* National Geographic, Jan Edition, 1965.

Woodard, Colin. *The Republic of the Pirates.* New York: Harcourt Publishing, 2007 (11)

Woolsey, Matt, *Top Earning Pirates,* New Jersey, *Forbes Magazine,* 2008, 9/19/08 Issue

About the Author

Allen Balogh is a retired educator who taught World and U.S. History for over twenty years. In 1985, he began exploring the locations of the southernmost ship of the 1715 Armada Fleet off the coast of Stuart/Hutchinson Island, Florida. He is a lecturer and historian on the Golden Age of Piracy.

For pleasure, Allen plays 1st violin in a symphony-orchestra in Boca Raton, Florida and enjoys lobstering with his buddies in the Florida Keys.

He is a member of the Florida Historic Society, the National Historic Preservation Society, and the 1715 Fleet Society.

Black Sails 1715 is the first of his Black and Gold series. He is currently writing the second in the series, *Black Sails 1715, The Goat with the Glass Eye*.

Allen resides in Palm Beach County.

ALLEN BALOGH

Acknowledgements

Abacoa Writers Guild and Abacoa Starbucks Crew

Especially

Lauren Mosko Bailey, a Kentucky southern belle. You are extraordinary.

I'm so thankful that you chose to accept my manuscript. Lazue, my dear, you're the best.

An Ending Note

A salute of Papa's Pillar 24 Rum to lost loves: Blackbeard and Lazue, Black Sam Bellamy and Maria Hallett, Paulsgrave Williams and Mary, Henry Jennings and Agnes Dickenson, Mary Read and her Flemish soldier, Calico Jack and Anne Bonny, Governor Woodes Rogers and Sarah Whetstone.

Here's to ya, mates.

And Charles Vane? Well, Charles is Charles, no love lost there, for sure.

Printed in the USA
CPSIA information can be obtained
at www.ICGtesting.com
JSHW010736070823
46062JS00002B/30